# Female Remedies

# By Janys Thornton

# Contents

## August 1914 – Vevey Switzerland

Hattie helps Maisie undress. She hangs the green silk kimono and the nightgown on the back of the bathroom door, which she has firmly closed. She tests the heat of the water and briefly turns on the hot tap again before inviting Maisie to get into the roll top bath.

She has heard that you should add mustard to draw out the toxins, but the only mustard available here is Dijon, and not the more potent English variety. She also wonders if brandy will work as well as the gin is supposed to. Is it just to deaden the pain, or did it have other therapeutic properties? It is unheard of for Miss Garrett to have thought to buy the spirits at all, as she is staunchly tee total.

Hattie holds Maisie's hand as she climbs into the bath and lies back, her breast bobbing with the water. All the bruises have now faded. Maisie gently rubs her lower stomach as the cramps start to build. She groans with the pain. She drinks the brandy-laced tea and Hattie tops her cup up with neat spirit. Maisie gulps it down in one and holds up the teacup to be refilled. Hattie can see that the alcohol is beginning to take effect.

"I loved him Hattie, I thought he loved me. But he didn't, did he?" Maisie starts to cry, her pretty face crumples and becomes red and blotchy. Her nose runs and she wipes it away with the back of her hand. Her head is thumping from the combination of the pennyroyal pills and neat brandy.

"I wanted him so badly it hurt," she continues, through her sobs, rubbing her fists into her eyes. "When he spoke, I couldn't take my eyes from his mouth. I used to link my hand through his arm, so I could feel how muscular he was. I used to watch him walk; he moved like a wild animal." Another cramp seizes her, and she groans aloud as she bends forward with the pain. The bath water starts turning pink with blood, getting redder as Maisie's body starts to reject what she carries.

Hattie rubs her friend's back and makes comforting noises, whilst topping up Maisie's cup again with the neat brandy. By now, over half of the bottle is gone.

"Am I a wanton woman? Will I burn in hell for wanting a man so much?" she asks her friend. She's becoming incoherent, and her head is lolling. Hattie looks down at the bloody bath water and gets her friend to stand up. It isn't easy, the bath being slippery, and Maisie is a dead weight. Hattie gets Maisie to lift one leg, then the other, over the rim, all the time telling her it will be okay. She wraps her in one of the new towels that Ena has bought, and

5

drapes the kimono from her shoulders, like a defeated prize fighter.

"Don't say any more about how much you wanted Edward in front of Miss Garrett and Ena," Hattie advises, "They are only helping you because he raped you." But Maisie is too far gone to comprehend what her friend is saying.

A thin trickle of blood runs down the inside of Maisie's leg as the two women shuffle back into the bedroom where the two older women wait.

# Part 1
# The Dockyard

## October 1913

The railway porter helps Maisie out to the front of the station with her trunk, then disappears back to his duties. A keen North-Easterly wind, straight from the Ural Mountains, cuts through her sharper than a soldier's bayonet and whips her skirt round her ankles. The unfamiliar sea salt stings her blue eyes and cracks her full lips. She will need to buy some lip balm to live in this dockyard town, she thinks.

A narrow, severe looking woman, with equally narrow views on life, is waiting outside. Maisie notices her tight bun and even tighter features as the woman steps towards her and asks if she is Miss Kendall.

She introduces herself. "I'm Elsie Garrett, but it will be easier if you call me by my formal name, Miss Garrett, as you would at school."

She calls Maisie "Miss Kendall" throughout their walk to her home, and she rarely ever uses her first name again.

Miss Garrett has borrowed a handcart to transport Maisie's belongings. Maisie looks round to see who has been hired to push the cart to her new landlady's house, but it is apparent that she is expected to do this herself. She tries lifting the trunk, but she isn't strong enough. Just then, a naval officer came out of the station. He is not conventionally handsome, but there is something about him that makes women look again.

"Can I be of assistance?" the young sub-lieutenant asks, making towards Maisie's heavy luggage.

"We can manage," Miss Garret replies, with a hint of vinegar, as she instructs Maisie to take one side of the trunk as she takes the other, and between them they load it onto the handcart.

Maisie gives the officer an apologetic smile as Miss Garret secures the trunk with some cord that she produces from nowhere. Maisie has been brought up to always be polite and is uncomfortable with her new colleague's abrupt ways. The officer touches his cap in acknowledgement, as the two women leave the station. He turns and walks off in the direction of the dockyard, turning back once to catch Maisie's eye, and give her a half smile before he is swallowed up by the crowd.

Miss Garrett speaks as rapidly as she walks, leaving no space for any interruptions.

"Mrs Bills, the housekeeper, has got your room ready. She does all the cleaning and prepares our meals. She will do your laundry too, but you will need to pay her separately for that."

As they clatter along, Maisie tries to engage Miss Garrett in small talk about the weather and her train journey, which she found exciting, travelling for the first time on her own. But Miss Garrett has no time for such niceties.

Maisie tries again. "Victoria Station was so busy. I couldn't work out where to go. Then, a helpful porter explained it's two stations next door to one another, and I needed the South-Eastern and Chatham part for Sheerness. He took my trunk round to the correct platform for me, and I gave him a threepenny bit for his trouble."

"It's his job to help passengers," Miss Garrett says dismissively, causing Maisie to fall silent again.

As they push the cart through the High Street, they pass groups of soldiers and sailors who stand about chatting and smoking, or are going in and out of the shops and pubs. The men openly eye up the young woman and catcall to her things like, "I've got something you can pull on, missy!" "I don't think much of yours mate!" and "Fancy a threesome?"

"Ignore them," Miss Garrett hisses at her as they trundle past.

Maisie is bewildered and discomforted by their comments and looks to the older woman to explain what the servicemen mean. Nobody has ever spoken to her like that before, but Miss Garrett just scorns the men as beneath her. One drunken sailor starts singing a grand love song, whilst standing in their way, but Miss Garrett simply steers the handcart around him. Maisie swallows her embarrassed laughter, knowing instinctively that Miss Garrett will not laugh with her.

The older woman keeps up a brisk pace as she helps Maisie push the handcart home through the grey, cobbled streets. They rattle past grubby girls playing in their wind torn-ribbons and darned elbows; past small boys making complicated transactions with marbles for currency; past scrubbed-up housewives cleaning steps for the rent collector's foot; past proud pipe smoking dockyard workers keeping the Royal Navy at sea. Many greet Miss Garrett by wishing her a "Good morning," and the men doff their caps at her. She responds with curt nods and the occasional clipped "Morning."

Maisie smiles and murmurs, "Morning," to the women and children, and gives a shy nod in return to the working men.

One brave child asks, "Are you the new teacher, Miss?" and Maisie can only quickly say, "Yes," and smile, as Miss Garrett whisks them past.

As they enter the more affluent part of town, Maisie notices how all the streets race towards the promenade in joyous anticipation of another day at the seaside. Only the best houses parade along the prom. These are taller, smarter houses - either guest houses for holiday makers, or bigger houses to accommodate a "well-to-do" family with servants. The houses sit fat and smug as they block the sea view of the skilled dock workers' terraces behind, which run parallel to one another, replicating street on street. These industrial back streets are not what Maisie expected when she applied for the post of "Assistant Mistress" at the Girls Broadway School in Sheerness. After all, Kent is supposed to be the Garden of England.

The teaching post is to be Maisie's first paid employment. Before the death of her father, the Reverend Kendall, she was a part-time, unpaid, assistant teacher at her local school. Women of Maisie's class are not expected to work for a living, but to marry well; having to find a job has been a shock to the young woman. The Kendall family have lived in the rectory and Maisie led a sheltered life in the picturesque Sussex village of Chiddingly. She never mixed with the labouring classes, except to visit the sick with her mother and she certainly would never have ventured into the back streets of the nearby bigger town of Hailsham, on her rare visits there.

Upon her father's death, the family's world has been turns upside down. Maisie and her mother have no income, and the rectory is needed by the new incumbent. The two women agreed that she would look for a full-time teaching assistant's post, where qualifications or attendance at one of the new teacher training colleges is deemed unnecessary, or positively an extravagance.

Maisie scoured the newspapers and responded to advertisements near her mother's new home with her aunt, in West Meon, in Hampshire, but soon, other counties in southern England were also considered. Few schools want an unqualified teacher. She was on the brink of applying for posts further afield when a position at the Sheerness Girls Broadway School was offered to her. Her predecessor had left to get married rather quickly, causing a mid-school year vacancy that needed filling immediately. Speaking French helped her application considerably, even though there is no requirement to teach it to the girls, whose dropped aitches and use of the word "ain't" murder the King's English on a daily basis.

When she wrote to the headmistress, Miss Morrison, to accept the position, Maisie asked if she knew of any accommodation she could rent at a reasonable rate. Fortunately, Miss Garrett, the deputy headmistress, has a spare room, where a number of other teachers have previously lived during their time at the school. Most of them left to get married, but occasionally they move on to more senior teaching posts, or just to escape the beady, judgemental eye of Miss Garrett.

Maisie corresponded with her new landlady to arrange meeting times. Miss Garrett astounded Maisie by providing a complete itinerary from leaving West Meon to Sheerness, including train changes. She even suggested catching the stopping train to Victoria, not the fast train to Waterloo, so Maisie wouldn't have to transport her trunk between stations. Although a more practical route, Maisie is disappointed that she hasn't seen anything of London beyond the station concourse. She has only been to London once before as a child, and the thought of the big city fired her imagination, as she is starved of excitement. The view from the train windows, both arriving and departing from Victoria Station,  provides little of interest, except for a fleeting glimpse of the city further down the Thames.

Miss Garrett wastes no time when they arrive at her home. The trunk is quickly untied, and the two women wrestle it up the stairs and into Maisie's room. "You best unpack, then we can have lunch," Miss Garrett says.

Maisie opens the lid and starts to remove her belongings, as the older woman remains in the doorway. Miss Garrett can't help her nosiness, but tells herself she is on hand to help the girl if she is needed. She watches as Maisie unpacks her books and places them onto the waiting shelves, next to the fireplace. They are all romantic novels - Austen, all the different Bronte sisters, Mrs Radcliffe, Mrs Gaskell. There are a couple of family photos in silver frames that Maisie carefully places on the small table.

Miss Garrett asks, "Is that your mother and father?" eyeing the stern looking pastor and his prim looking wife. Maisie concedes it is, and brushes a stray tear from her cheek. It is only when the trunk is empty and there is no more to see that Miss Garrett leaves Maisie to settle in.

Just before lunch, Miss Garrett gives Maisie a quick tour of the house. It is semi-detached with a small frontage that takes it slightly off the street, as though it wants nothing to do with the terrace houses across the road, rather like its owner. It is only a few years old, and there is an upstairs bathroom with hot running water from an already wheezy gas geyser. There is an enclosed garden at the back with a gate to the alley for discretion, and a big bay window at the front for snobbery.

The smell of beeswax polish and carbolic pervade the house. Everything is well scrubbed and in its place. The sofa and armchairs sport white antimacassars, even though no gentleman is ever invited in, and if one strayed in by accident, he certainly won't be encouraged to rest his head on the back of the sofa.

Maisie feels a strange mix of independence and homesickness. She has never been apart from her mother, and so soon after the death of her father too. But she is excited to be able to come and go as she pleases, to make new friends and enjoy her new freedom.

Mrs Bills prepares a lunch of thinly sliced bread and butter, and even thinner cold boiled ham topped with tangy piccalilli, made by Barnes Best Pickles. It is no wonder the deputy headmistress is as thin as she is.

Miss Garrett looks up from the slice of bread she is scraping with butter and says to Maisie, "After lunch, I will take you into the town centre to show you where the school is and the local amenities." They set off as soon as they finish eating, leaving Mrs Bills to clear away.

Everything is within easy walking distance and again Maisie is overwhelmed by the change from her village life. Even though the town itself is small, it is beyond her previous experience. The town of Hailsham is only five miles away from the village of Chiddingly but her parents just went there when they had business. Those rare visits to the shops were a welcomed diversion for Maisie. But her parents had never given enough time to really browse as she would have liked, even though she had little money of her own to spend.

In the backstreets of the dockyard town, there is every kind of shop you might require: grocers, butchers, greengrocers, fishmongers, ironmongers, and drapers. They all proclaim themselves to be "High-Class" purveyors of quality meats, fish, wools, or exotic fruits, offering goods on tick to their regulars, for settlement on pay day, or the pay day after. Occasionally, the shop is a pawn shop selling the second-hand belongings of those who can't afford to redeem them – granddad's pocket watch, a medal from the Crimea, mum's best coat, her best hat, her wedding ring.

Every so often, there is a coach entrance leading to a yard behind where the tang of horses' sweat seeps out on to the street. These entrances sport grand signs advertising the occupation of the horse and owner; "Gordon Brothers – High-Class Builders," "Grimwade's – High-Class Coal Merchant," or "Dawson's – Respectable High-Class Undertaker." When the horses become too old to work, they are sold to the knacker's yard, who sell the meat for pet food and the bones to the glue works in Queenborough, where the smell of boiled carrion clings to your clothes. There are no High-Class funerals for the horses.

Some boys are playing football in the street with a heavy leather ball that has seen better days. As it bounces dangerously near to Miss Garrett, she exclaims, "If that ball comes near me again, I'll have your guts for garters!" sending the boys off down a back alley for safety.

They walk part way along the promenade so that Miss Garrett can show Maisie the sea. Maisie has only been to the seaside twice before and she can't believe it is now on her doorstep. The wind whips up the waves and makes small clouds scud along past the sun; she thinks it is magical. She is mesmerised by how many naval ships are in the estuary.

"Every day must be like a holiday when you live at the seaside," enthuses Maisie, her eyes sparkling, "So many ships!" But Miss Garrett just sniffs and responds, "That's the dockyard at the end of the sea front," pointing towards the naval base with its high walls, moat, and gates guarded by uniformed armed soldiers. Maisie is nervous about the prospect of living so close to this bastion of manhood. But, at the same time, she remembers how naval officers feature in Jane Austen's novel *Persuasion* and her curiosity is aroused.

Miss Garrett looks at Maisie out of the corner of her eye and thinks her pretty enough. She is still youngish at twenty-six and has a pleasing shape and shiny, light brown hair. She thinks the girl's clothes are more sober than her own. Miss Garrett dresses so as not to encourage any misunderstandings from the opposite sex, so she wears no jewellery, just two pins for the *Church League for Women's Suffrage* and the *National Union of Women Teachers,* and as far as she is concerned, being straight laced is not just an expression. But everything Maisie wears is one shade of grey or another – dove grey blouse, battleship grey skirt, lava grey jacket. If the young woman's mother intends this to be a way to make her daughter invisible to the opposite sex, like some bird camouflaging its chick to avoid predators, she has wasted her time. It will take more than that to stop the prowling, predatory military men, who are always looking for someone to ease their time ashore.

The town boasts two new-fangled picture houses and a theatre. Maisie has never been to a cinema before and lingers to read the posters outside advertising forthcoming entertainments. A travelling picture show occasionally came to Chiddingly village hall, but here all the latest films are on offer every night of the week.

She has to trot to catch Miss Garrett up, as her colleague doesn't wait for her.

"There are a lot more pubs here than at home," Maisie remarks, as they continued their walk past the bright painted pubs with large etched glass windows. The gaudy name signs tell you something of the type of landlord that may occupy the place – *The Copper Kettle*- a tinker; *The Hero of Crimea* - a soldier; *The British Admiral*- surely, a sailor. The pubs smell of beer, gin, and wasted money better spent on children's shoes or a scraping of jam to go on their bread.

"You stay well away from that end of town," Miss Garrett warns, indicating the pubs and shops on the other side of the dock gates which divides the town in two. "It's where the men go for entertainment. Keep away and you will be fine." She doesn't specify which men or what kind of entertainment they find there, as such definitions are beneath her. Maisie gathers that it must be something unsavoury. However, this is not something she has encountered before.

"Surely, they will respect a gentle woman?" Maisie asks, innocently.

"You've read too many romances," comes the blunt response from Miss Garrett. "They are men, with men's' needs. Jane Austen forgot to mention that in her novels."

Maisie looks at her wide-eyed, and wonders what she means.

"Even you are pretty enough to catch their eye," Miss Garrett continues, "So don't ever give any of them an inch, or they will take liberties."

Maisie is not sure she understands what Miss Garrett means by "liberties," but she thinks it must be something unwelcome. Her mother has never given her such a warning, but then, her mother would never leave her alone with a man.

They walk back along the High Street, and Maisie peers into the shop windows trying to catch a glimpse of her reflection. She has never been told she is pretty before, even in the back handed way that Miss Garrett said it. Her father believed vanity is a sin, and, as a result, there were no mirrors in the rectory. For the first time, she notices how the soldiers and sailors try to catch her eye as they stand on the street corners and outside the many pubs. She finds that she enjoys the attention, but the men smell of beer, sweat, tobacco, and masculinity, and radiate an aura of knowingness as they look at her in a way that quite unnerves her.

"Men with tattoos get into fights in pubs," Miss Garrett says, as though it explains everything Maisie needs to know about the servicemen.

Miss Garrett is impervious to the interest of men. At over forty, she has come to terms with her spinsterhood and quite enjoys her independence, but she can see that a young woman like Maisie

Kendall might want to be married and have a family of her own. She will be tempted to go to dances and such like, as all the young girls in town want to marry a naval officer.

The older teacher is financially solvent, so marriage does not interest her as a means of security. She has savings in the Co-op, and even owns her house in Crimea Road, a small legacy allowing her to buy the property a few years ago. By having Maisie and her predecessors as lodgers, it helps pay the bills and gives her a bit of company in the evenings. She has no use for a husband. She finds men, at best, patronising and, at worst, misogynistic. Twenty plus years of trying to live an independent life with a career and being constantly thwarted, side-lined, and ignored makes her short and bitter in her dealings with men. And, to cap it all, they are all just interested in one thing!

When they walk back to Miss Garrett's house, Maisie asks, "Are there always that many men about? There seem to be more of them than women."

Miss Garrett gives a little disapproving sniff. "It's a naval dockyard town. Some ships have scores of crew on board and there are dozens of ships in the dockyard or at the anchorage. But usually, they are not all on shore leave at once, and most stay the other end of town where we didn't go today. It's not a place for a young lady to go. You may meet some of the officers at various functions." She gives another sniff. "But they are no better than the men. If not worse, because at least with the ratings you know they only have one thing on their mind. The officers do their best to come over as decent human beings, but they can't be trusted alone with a woman." And thinking about how Miss Clark needed to get married at very short notice, so creating the vacancy that Miss Kendall is about to fill, she finishes with, "Steer clear of all of them," in a way that doesn't invite further conversation on the matter.

Back in her room, Maisie gazes at herself in the mirror. She remembers how the servicemen looked at her hungrily, and realises she must be cautious. At the same time, she enjoys the feeling of power she got as she walked along the street. She remembers how the porter at Victoria Station smiled at her and she wonders if he thought her pretty too. And then there was the naval officer who offered to help with her trunk. There was a glint in his eye as he touched his cap. No man has ever looked at her like that when she was with her parents. It is very strange, but exciting too.

On Sunday morning, to the sound of the church bells, Miss Garrett invites Maisie to join her

23

at the Congregational church, where she plays the organ for the morning service and enjoys watching the congregation through the mirror set up above the instrument. It enables her to see who is pious, bored, or asleep, whilst remaining unobserved herself. She is also a Sunday school teacher, and a Girl Guide leader. She helped set up a troop in 1911, when Agnes Baden Powell and her more famous brother founded the new organisation. But Maisie declines, saying, "Thank you, but my father would disapprove of me attending a non-conformist chapel. Do you know which Church of England service I might attend? I noticed there is a choice of the Trinity church in town or St Paul's in the dockyard which looks much grander."

Miss Garrett responds with her customary sniff, indicating her disapproval of high church. She firmly believes the members of each local church have the right to decide their own forms of worship, and that they should administer their own affairs without any outside interference. The Congregational church appeals to her no-nonsense, egalitarian views of the world.

"In my opinion, you should stay away from St Paul's. Every week, the navy has church parade through the town. All the sailors are in the gallery, looking down on the women who attend, and you know their minds are not on the Almighty. The officers are there in their smart uniforms, along with the Rear Admiral of the dockyard and his wife and daughters. The men squash into the pews beside you, pressing their legs up against you in an unseemly way. After the service, the Rear Admiral stands beside the chaplain and shakes everyone's hand. The chaplain is also navy, so he doesn't involve himself with the community, unless it's to further the aims of the Admiralty."

"And what is the Trinity church like?" Maisie ventures, realising that Miss Garrett is not likely to give an unbiased opinion.

"It's okay if you like that Anglo-Catholicism nonsense with incense and what-not." She says this with a very dismissive sniff indeed. "If you want to come with me today, I'm sure one of the other teachers can take you along to the C of E next week and introduce you."

Maisie decides to follow this option and not mention it to her mother in her next letter, as she knows her mother believes non-conformists are barely Christians.

After Sunday school, Miss Garrett promises to introduce Maisie to her friend and colleague, Ena Briggs. Ena's full name is Serena, but there is little serenity about the busy little woman, so she seldom uses it. Miss Garrett arranges for them to go to tea at Ena's house in nearby Inkerman Street. It isn't far

25

to walk, but Maisie is soon confused, as all the streets are dissected by the back alleys which crossed and criss-crossed the town. It is through these back-alleys that Miss Garrett leads Maisie, stepping fastidiously over the dog dirt languishing there. Ena's house is somewhere near the middle of the street, and the net curtains shield the female inhabitants from the outside world beyond the front step.

A heavily pregnant black and white cat sits expectantly on the doorstep waiting to be let in with them, and, as soon as the door opens, she skedaddles up the stairs, slipping through Ena's legs to avoid capture and being returned to the street. Ena lets out a small curse and says, "She isn't really our cat, but she keeps coming in. Hattie, my lodger," she adds for the benefit of Maisie, "feeds her scraps and lets her sleep on her bed." Miss Garrett gives a sniff of disapproval together with a look to sour the cat's cream.

Inside Ena's house, every possible space is given over to books. There are books in every room and on every subject - mathematics, geology, chemistry, physics, politics, economics. Ena is fortunate enough to have attended Newnham College, Cambridge, where she read chemistry and learned to ride a bicycle. It is this thirst for knowledge that led to the vast numbers of books on such varied subjects, subjects which Ena will never teach the girls in school. Maisie wonders why she needs so many of them.

Miss Garrett and Ena have been friends for some years. They both joined the Broadway School when it opened in 1901. Ena has previously lived in Portsmouth, before she moved to Sheerness. She was around thirty years old then, and taught the senior girls, whilst Miss Garrett taught the juniors at that time. Now, Miss Garrett is deputy headmistress to Miss Morrison, but Ena is still teaching the same age group of girls, her career not having progressed.

Ena is short and borders on stocky, more muscular than fat, as she keeps fit by riding her bicycle to nip to the various reading groups and sewing circles she belongs to. She keeps her hair under control with the same firm hand used on her students and no disobedience is brooked from either. Behind her spectacles, she has keen eyes that have a hint of kindness in them that their owner tries to suppress. The sharp exterior she presents is just a shell to hide a soft inside, like a razor clam on the beach. She dresses in sensible boots which encase her thick ankles, and a warm green cardigan over her purple-coloured skirt and white blouse. She also wears the same lapel pins as Miss Garrett and, surprisingly, some rather ostentatious earrings and a large brooch at her neck.

"Jewellery is my weakness," Ena always says, and has a bigger collection than anyone would give her credit for, as she only wore it in her home, never out, so only a few people saw just how much she has.

It is rumoured that Ena was once engaged to a naval officer but, for some reason that no one ever mentions, the wedding never happened. Ena is a little too free when it comes to rapping her students' knuckles, which some think might hint at some bitterness and therefore a broken relationship not of her doing. The whole thing remains a mystery to her colleagues and friends, but nobody ever asks her outright what happened.

Maisie is introduced to Miss Harriet Roberts. Hattie (as she likes to be called) is Ena's lodger. She teaches physical education at the school, favouring the new "*Swedish Drill*" with Indian clubs and mechanised, repetitive actions for the girls. Following the 1912 Olympics in Stockholm, Hattie was inspired to organise swimming classes after school for the girls in the dockyard pool. Australian, Fanny Durack, was the first female Olympic swimming champion, winning the women's one hundred metre freestyle event and the British women won the first 4 x 100 metre freestyle relay. Hattie regularly competes in the local summer swimming gala where races for women started in recent years. She mastered the new Australian crawl to ensure she is the winner.

Hattie longs to earn her living just doing sport, but there are no such opportunities for women. Teaching gives her some scope to achieve this. The Broadway School, being a modern establishment, is among the first to take physical education seriously. But it means leaving her comfortable home and family behind in Suffolk, to find lodgings near the school where she works.

Cricket is Hattie's favourite sport– if any of the men will let her join in. She has eight brothers and learnt to give as good as she got from them, and played cricket from an early age. When she moved to Sheerness, she soon made friends with the local schools' cricket crowd who call her "Harry," and invite her to be the twelfth man on the team if they are short. She is often in the first eleven, as the captain will lie to the opposition and say one or other of the team has an injury. Hattie is the better cricketer than most of the team, and the various injuries the captain cites are a ruse to have her in the team and bend the rules. But this wide circle of male friends never seems to lead to any romance for Hattie. They all treat her as their sister and joke with her in quite a different way to how anyone speaks to any of the other young women teachers in their circle.

Like Miss Garrett and Ena, Hattie is an active supporter of women's enfranchisement. She follows the activities of the suffragettes in the papers and bought a red lipstick to wear to a rally in Chatham she attended. She considered joining the *Women's Social and Political Union (WSPU)* after meeting a local woman, Miss Riviere, and her fellow suffragettes, when they were on their summer caravan tour, but she never quite got round to it.

Maisie instantly wants to be more like her new colleague – assured and in control of herself. She takes in Hattie's clothes and observes how her russet skirt is more slim-line and finishes on the ankle, rather than sweeping the floor like her own. The sleeves on her own blouse are also much puffier than Hattie's, as though she is concealing beefy arms beneath. She determines to try to update her own clothes as best she can and will try to borrow some ladies' magazines like *Weldon's Ladies' Journal,* which offers dress patterns for threepence or *Woman's Weekly,* which is cheaper at just a penny.

"Come and tell me all about yourself whilst we wait for tea to be ready," Hattie says, and invites Maisie into Ena's best front parlour where they sit down together on the horsehair sofa.

Maisie can't conceal her curiosity any longer and asks Hattie, "What are the badges you are all wearing?"

Hattie tells her and, as she is doing so, she realises that Maisie seems completely ignorant about the emancipation question, so she explains the aims of the suffrage organisations and what can be done by local women to support the movement.

"My father believed God created woman to be man's helpmeet," Maisie says, "and that a husband always has his wife's best interests at heart, so she doesn't need to vote. I've never thought about the vote before. I won't know who to vote for anyway if I have it."

The three women give her a hard look and she tries not to fidget under their scrutiny. They are going to have to educate her in the ways of the modern world. Miss Garrett gives a bigger sniff than usual to indicate the scale of Maisie's heresy. "Without wishing to contradict your good, departed father," she says, "as single women, we need to look after our own interests and ensure that we are treated fairly and as equals. The *National Union of Women Teachers* is building a case for equal pay to men teachers. We do the same work as them, but are paid less. And because we can't vote, we can't vote out those men who believe we are less than equal."

Maisie sees that she needs to think of wider issues if she is going to live amongst these women and be one of them.

Tea consists of triangular sandwiches of cheese, ham or eggs, crusts on, no waste; and a homemade Victoria sponge, all served on Ena's best Crown Derby tea service. Ena recently started giving the girls cookery classes in a newly fitted out classroom with modern gas cookers, where they learn to make simple dinners and bake cakes. The girls' education doesn't stretch to them learning that for all right-angled triangular sandwiches, the square on the hypotenuse is equal to the sum of the squares on the other two sides, nor that a straight line that passes from one side of a circular cake to the other through the centre is called the diameter – they only learn what size cake tin they need, as the School Board considers mathematics to be wasted on the girls.

The cookery classes are proving a big success and Ena blames her expanding waistline on the cake baking. Having been university educated herself and coming from a middle-class background, cooking is not a skill she learned at home. Her first teaching post was at a girls' grammar school where she taught science. But she changed her career direction when she arrived at the Sheerness Broadway School, and teaches more general subjects. When the new home economics classroom was proposed, she volunteered to teach the subject, applying her scientific brain to recipes as though they are experiments, and finds she is excellent at it.

During tea, Ena launches into a quick run down of what the girls are like in Maisie's class. "You will need to watch Valerie Smith, she answers back; I've sent her to stand in the corner with her hands on her head many times, but it's really hard because she is so funny and quick. But you can't let the class see you are laughing.

"Millie Luckhurst  is the cleverest and has lovely handwriting, but I don't think she gets much encouragement at home. We tried to get her sister Cissie to take the exam for the Grammar school, but her parents aren't interested. We can't send her, they say, we have another four to think about."

"Jessica Mullins is bright enough, but she doesn't seem to be able to spell. I can't understand why the word "carrot" is beyond her, especially after I've made her write it out fifty times," Miss Garrett interjects, "I used to rap her on the knuckles, but she used to get her left and right muddled up. So, I made her wear an elastic band round her left which sorted that problem out."

"If you see Susan Kelly scratching, she has impetigo again." Ena continues, "But if you see Sheila Williams scratching, she has nits. That family always has nits. Sheila is often off school looking after her younger siblings, as their mother works in the laundry, as their father is useless, always drunk. When Sheila does come to school, her hair is often tangled as there is no one to do her hair for her, poor thing."

"Are things like impetigo and nits common then?" asks Maisie, visibly shocked as there are few such cases in her home village.

"Some of the houses are very poor. It's only the dock workers that have a good wage and a pension," Ena responds, "You will need to keep an eye on the Tyler and Forest girls as I think they go without meals, so their younger siblings get fed. I always let them (and a couple of others) have what I've demonstrated in the cookery class, so I know at least they've had something to eat. More tea?"

Hattie asks, "Do you like going to dances, Maisie?"

"Father disapproved of dancing," Maisie responds. "He didn't let me accept invitations to the balls at the big houses in Chiddingly."

Hattie tries a different tact, "Do you play tennis? There are some lovely new courts in Grenville Road,"

"Father didn't think sports are ladylike," says Maisie, casting down her eyes in embarrassment, beginning to realise just how sheltered her life has been and how different it will now become. "I had to refuse invitations to the new tennis parties in the neighbourhood."

Hattie perseveres, "Do you enjoy going to concerts or to see films?"

"There was rarely any entertainment in Chiddingly. Father disapproved of films as he thought actresses were no better than harlots. Sometimes, there was a talk at the village hall by one of the teachers or another clergyman. Usually something about nature. Reverend Cummings liked to talk about his butterfly collection. He would bring some along in glass cases with their rare and beautiful wings pinned out. Mr Phipps, the solicitor, had once been to Italy with his wife, and he would talk about all the ancient sites they had seen in Rome, Florence, and Venice. He would show his slides with his magic lantern. He did this talk about once a year. I can safely say I now know as much as he did about the history of the Roman Forum!" Maisie answers wryly.

Hattie decides to take Maisie under her wing and introduce her to sport and local cultural events. She will also teach her to ride a bicycle, in order to give her some independence.

"What hobbies might you be interested in? We have a reading group on Thursdays, and we organise trips to places of interest in London and elsewhere," Hattie suggests, looking for a way to broaden Maisie's outlook on life.

"I'd love to travel and visit new places. I've hardly been anywhere," Maisie responds, without hesitation.

"How fortuitous!" Hattie exclaims. "Miss Garrett organises a holiday for us teachers every summer. This year, we caught the boat train to Dover, then across to the continent by steamer. We visited France and explored the South and Paris. Last year, we caught the steamer to Flushing, from right here in Queenborough and visited Belgium, and the year before that Holland."

Hattie continues with enthusiasm. "Miss Garrett doesn't opt for one of Mr Thomas Cook's tours. She works out the itinerary herself, using *Bradshaw's Continental Railway Guide*. She researches the railway timetables and routes, and corresponds with the hotels to arrange dates and prices. Then, she presents us with the schedule she has arranged.

"We usually spend a day or two travelling to our destination, then two or three weeks to discover what our surroundings have to offer. We buy a Cook's ticket, as it promises to take you anywhere on the South-Eastern and Chatham Railway, or even the world, so we can take a slightly different route home and see more of the countryside. You can join us! We are going to Lake Geneva in Switzerland next summer."

"Oh, I don't know. It must cost rather a lot," Maisie demurs, fiddling with her butter knife.

"Nonsense! We pay Miss Garrett a little each week, so it isn't a shock. I put away a few shillings in the Co-op to pay my expenses when we are away. You need to save about six shillings a week, but that includes all your meals. We always start saving at the beginning of the autumn term, so you will have to catch up a bit."

Maisie is torn; her salary is twenty-eight shillings, and she needs to pay Miss Garrett, and send a little to her mother. Six shillings will make a big hole in her wages. She also knows her mother will disapprove of her travelling alone without a male relative for an escort. But she has never been anywhere, and this is a wonderful opportunity to travel. She will find the right moment to tell her mother. Without further thought, she says, "Yes, I'd like that."

"Super, it's such fun," says Hattie, "And very educational," she adds, as an afterthought.

Monday morning starts fresh and is bathed with golden October sunshine. Maisie walks with Miss Garrett to the Girls' Broadway School, ready to start work. Her heart is beating fast with a combination of first day nerves and the excitement that comes with a new job. They arrive earlier than the children, to prepare for the day ahead. Miss Garrett takes Maisie straight to Miss Morrison's office and then goes off to her own classroom.

The headmistress is tiny and buzzes around like a gnat as she greets the new recruit, and takes her on a whistle-stop tour of the school ahead of the girls arriving for their lessons. The classrooms have high ceilings, with long windows to let in the light, but these are all placed above head height to stop the children looking out and getting distracted. There are inspiring pictures on the walls: His Majesty the King, from his Coronation in 1910, Holman Hunt's *The Light of the World*, together with landscapes showing the beauty of Britain, which looks nothing like the industrial dockyard town of Sheerness.

Miss Morrison takes Maisie to the staff room and introduces her to the rest of her colleagues, "This is Miss Fitch, she has a fair hand on the piano. This is Miss Lynstead, she is very talented," but Miss Morrison doesn't say at what. "This is Miss Briggs, whom you have met, she is very good at measuring out ingredients," she continues till she has damned them all with faint praise.

Maisie knows she won't remember all her new colleagues' names on her first day. She also knows she has little or no hope of remembering what subjects they specialise in. Miss Morrison introduces her saying, "Miss Kendall speaks French," even though it is not a subject on the curriculum. Some of the other teachers look impressed, and Maisie guesses this may have been why Miss Morrison has done so, as she has so little experience of teaching compared to the others. But a couple of the older women give Maisie a sneering look, which suggests that they see no value in her skills at all.

There are fifteen staff for over four hundred girls. The school is divided into juniors and seniors, each headed by a mistress. Below her, the classes are taken by an assistant mistress, of which Maisie is one of three in the junior school. Pupil teachers help out in the classes by taking those children who need more support. The infants attend a separate mixed sex school.

Married women are not permitted to be teachers, so all the women are spinsters. Very occasionally, one might be a widow – but this is rare. It is a choice of marriage or career. The same rule does not apply to men who are permitted to wed and have families. It seems a little odd that mothers will trust their daughters' education to women who have no children of their own.

As Miss Morrison takes Maisie back along the corridor to the school hall, Maisie notices a collection of framed photographs of the students. The headmistress enlightens her, saying, "When a bright girl comes into the school, we invest extra time and resources into her. Our hope is to get her through the entrance exam to gain a place at the County Grammar School when she is old enough. That way, she may get to college to become a teacher herself. Otherwise, she may become a clerk, or a typist, or even a telephonist. Employment opportunities are so limited for women, even educated ones. These girls are the centre of the Universe to us teachers here," Miss Morrison says, pointing to the students in the framed photos. "They afford us the opportunity to teach them the wider subjects needed to pass the exams: literature, instead of just reading; English composition and grammar, rather than just writing; and mathematics, rather than just arithmetic. Successful girls usually give me a framed portrait of themselves, but it never ceases to be a surprise to me that they do," she explains, waving at the photos, with the bright faces of the clever girls illuminating the dark corners of the ignorance of the lesser students.

In no time at all, the children start to arrive for the morning and the teachers take up their places in the hall for assembly. Once the bell is rung at nine o'clock, the girls invasively tumble through the doorways like so many wind- blown weeds. The soapy smell of the freshly washed pupils mixes with the smell of boiled onions and floor polish that permeates the corridors.

There are so many girls at the Broadway School, many more than has been at Chiddingly. Maisie looks at the sea of faces as they come into the hall. The girls are dressed in hand knitted cardigans, and grey or dark blue serviceable skirts and dresses. The whole ensemble is covered by a crisp white pinafore, lovingly made by mothers and grandmothers from dad's old shirts or the worn-out marriage bedsheets. The sleeves are ruffled, the fronts smocked, embroidered or pin tucked, and the hems generously large to allow for growth. The pinafores are boil washed with a little "dolly blue" to bring out the whiteness, then starched and ironed ready for the school week. Maisie notices how all the girls' long hair is tied differently to keep it out of their eyes. The only exceptions are when an infestation of nits resists the comb, and the hair is sacrificed to be regrown again once the intruders have gone. The girls all wear sturdy boots, designed to last until they are outgrown and passed on to the next child. Re-heeled and resoled, re-stitched and relined. They are polished with military care every Sunday by their dads, who feed the leather to keep it supple for running about, skipping, and jumping.

As the other teachers greet the girls by name as they line up in the hall, Maisie wonders how she will ever tell them all apart.

Hattie points out some children who group together as they come into the school hall and are ignored by the other girls. "They are the boarded-out orphans and deserted children from the workhouse," she explains. "You can tell by the unadorned uniform of the parish they wear. They are looked after by foster parents who are paid to care for them. But they miss the security of a real family. When they are ten years old, they have to return to the workhouse. They always seem so forlorn."

Assembly begins with the hymn *Jesus Bids Us Shine,* which Miss Fitch plays on the piano, whilst Miss Lynstead conducts the girls. As she sings, Miss Lynstead has the unfortunate habit of spitting. The word Jesus is the worst, and so, at the beginning of each verse, the girls in the front row try to duck the flying spittle without attracting attention from the teachers standing sentry down the side.

After the *Lord's Prayer* is said, Miss Morrison asks Maisie to come to the front, and introduces her to the school as Miss Clark's replacement. Dozens of expectant faces turn towards her, trying to work out if she is a knuckle rapper, a leg smacker, or shaker until your teeth rattle.

Maisie smiles back, trying to alleviate their fears, whilst feeling slightly daunted herself as they file out to their classrooms. But she decides to take her class in the same fashion as she has in the village school and make the day as much fun as possible.

She ushers the girls into the schoolroom and begins with the register to learn their names. More than one child shares a surname with a cousin of the same age in the same class, the family resemblance strong on their little faces. Most have sisters in classes above or below them, as the average family contains at least six children, giving the whole school the feeling of a girls' only village.

Maisie turns to the blackboard and starts with some basic sums to test their ability.

"How many nails do I need to build this boat?" she asks, drawing a quick sketch of a boat including chalky dots for nails along the frame.

"Is it steel or wood?" asks one student. "If its wood, you use pegs, and if it's steel, you use rivets."

"Let's say it's steel," Maisie replies.

"Then you need thousands," responds the same, snub-nosed girl. "My dad's a riveter, and each plate needs dozens, and there are dozens of plates in a ship."

"Right," says Maisie, doing her best not to get flummoxed by this superior knowledge. "Okay, let's just think of one panel then." She rubs out the boat and draws a rectangle. "So, if we need ten rivets across the long side on the top and bottom, and five along each short side, how many do we need in total?" She adds more chalky dots to mark the rivets.

A sea of hands goes up, and it is established that thirty are needed.

"And if we need ten panels for one side of our boat?" Again, the hands shoot up - three hundred rivets.

"And to make the second side?"

All morning, they calculate rivets and draw boats, each girl applying the arithmetic to what they understand about ship building for the British Navy which has been learned from their fathers and older brothers at home.

At lunchtime, Hattie suggests Maisie join her and another teacher, Rosie Dale, for lunch together at Ena's house. "We can talk about how your first morning has gone," her new friend says. There is a rota for dinner duties for the few girls who remain in school with a packed lunch and need supervising, but as it is Maisie's first day, she is not called upon to cover just yet, and so she gladly accepts Hattie's invitation.

"What is your specialist subject?" Maisie asks Rosie as they walk to Hattie's lodgings, having already forgotten what Miss Morrison had said that morning.

"I help Hattie out with physical education. We play tennis doubles in the summer, although I'm nowhere near as good as Hattie," she laughs at herself, a trait that some older teachers, like Miss Garrett, find very annoying; they think she is like some silly, giggly girl in the playground.

Rosie's clear eyes sparkle when she laughs, and Maisie thinks this is very attractive. She likes her new friend's hair which is somewhere between blonde and ginger, hinting that she is a little bit feisty, but it is tempered with her ready smile.

" I used to be a pupil at the Broadway School," Rosie continues, "My sister Betty was also a pupil teacher before me. We both started teaching when we were thirteen. I applied for a position of Assistant Mistress, and Miss Morrison took me on as an "uncertified teacher." She said it is because I am so good with the girls, being one of them."

"That must be nice to know the school so well, I'm finding it all a bit daunting this morning. It's so much bigger than the village school where I used to teach. Have you lived in Sheerness all your life?"

"Yes, Betty and I still live with our mum and our little sister. Our dad is in the merchant navy. He rarely shows up at our door, sometimes we go two or three years without seeing him. He only sends money home occasionally, so mum has always worked to keep the family together. Our gran looked after us when we were small. That's why we are so independent – it puts the men off though. Which is probably why neither of us is married yet, and I'm twenty-five already! Gran looks after our little sis now we've grown up, though she gets confused at times since she was widowed and came to live with us. She's only in her mid-sixties, but you'd think she was much older."

As soon as they get in, Hattie assembles a lunch of bread, cheese, and eye-wateringly sharp pickled onions from the Barnes Best Pickles range, served on the everyday crockery. They eat at the clothless kitchen table, whilst Hattie's cat, Tibby, winds round their legs trying to hypnotise them into sharing the cheese. The cat bulges in the middle where she is carrying a full complement of unborn kittens causing her to sway majestically from side to side.

Between mouthfuls of bread and biting off small corners of cheese to feed Tibby, Hattie says, "This is her third pregnancy; she is due soon. She hasn't started nesting yet, but she usually takes herself off under the stairs. Ena will probably arrange for all but one kitten to be drowned, otherwise we'd be overrun with cats. The local midwife comes and does it. I'd like to keep them all, but I know it isn't practical."

Maisie hasn't thought about this before, as there were hardly any cats sharing the villagers' homes like this in Chiddingly. Most cats live outdoors in the barns and work sheds and are welcomed for their rodent control skills, which is also their main source of food. It has never occurred to her that people would seek to control their numbers.

"Won't she miss her babies?" Maisie asks.

"Well, if you don't leave her one, she will. The midwife sexes them first, and keeps back a tom. And cats come into season again and get pregnant straight away. But what else can you do to keep her from having more babies? She has no morals; she's just a cat! She doesn't have a regular boyfriend! Last time, she had two ginger kittens, two tabbies, and a black one. She must have got friendly with at least two old tom cats, maybe three!" Hattie exclaims.

Hattie uses the conversation about Tibby's love life to delve deeper into Maisie's past. "Do you have a young man back home?" she asks, as she cuts herself another slice of bread.

Maisie blushes and shakes her head. "There aren't any young men that my parents considered suitable."

"Any 'unsuitable'?" Hattie counters, teasing her new friend.

47

Maisie bites her lip and drops her eyes. She didn't know any young men in the village well, so no one had paid her court. A young Irish doctor had tried engaging her in conversation sometimes when she bumped into him, but her parents did all they could to ensure the two young people were never alone. He was a Catholic and her father would never consent to such a relationship. Then, one day, Dr MacManus left Chiddingly and another older, married doctor, replaced him. She never knew why he left or where he had gone to. She had missed him and his lilting accent, as he had provided her with the only possibility of romance and escape through matrimony, even though she wasn't sure that she would have wanted to be his wife as he had a squint and skin pock-marked by acne.

"There are lots of young men here, suitable, and unsuitable. If I can get myself a young naval officer, I'd give up teaching these brats tomorrow!" Hattie laughs.

"Me too!" responds Rosie. "I don't want to end up a dried-up old spinster like some of our colleagues. I want to live my life, have children of my own instead of trying to teach other peoples the three R's."

"Not sure that I would have kids of my own, if I can choose otherwise," muses Hattie. "I'd like to be financially secure, but not have to look after children, and a naval husband would be away at sea, so I can get on with my own life."

Maisie is so taken aback that she sits for a moment with her bread and butter halfway to her mouth. She can't decide if she should be shocked at this joke or not; she decides to ignore it, and concentrates on asking, "Don't you like being a teacher?"

"Up to a point," Hattie responds. "I like that it gives me choices in life. If I don't get married, I can support myself. I get satisfaction when we can get a girl to grammar school and know that she too will be able to lead an independent life. But I want to be loved too – but on my own terms, I don't want to be some man's drudge. But we women have so few options that teaching is the only thing you can really do to be independent."

Rosie decides to steer the conversation onto a subject much dearer to her own heart. "There's a *Bachelor's Dance* next weekend. Hattie and I plan to go, so you can come with us if you want. They sell an equal amount of tickets to men and women, and there are refreshments and entertainment in the interval. They are the best dances!"

Maisie has a moment of doubt when she wonders what her mother might think. But the thought is quickly suppressed by the excitement of a dance, and she responds, "That will be lovely, but I don't have anything to wear, and I don't know any of the latest dances."

"We can sort all that out," is the reply from her two new friends.

## November 1913

The School Board orders the classrooms to be fumigated over the weekend, as there is an outbreak of Scarlet Fever in the town. Some parents keep their children home, as the disease is a killer. Miss Morrison clucks around saying, "I'm not convinced that the cleaning has been done to the standard it should be. That new caretaker is so slap-dash. The school is so often dirty since he arrived." She complains to all the teachers about his slovenliness, but doesn't report him to the Board.

Despite the dirt and risk of infection, Hattie and Rosie set to work on Maisie. They stay in the classrooms after school to practice dancing and alter her clothes. Rosie plays the piano, whilst Hattie teaches Maisie basic dance steps – the Waltz, and the Turkey Trot. Although Rosie's playing of Ragtime lacks some of the vigour needed, Hattie suspects that the playing at the dance will be similarly sedate. Hattie holds Maisie in her arms and takes the lead, giving her encouragement as she attempts to teach her to dance.

Fortunately, Maisie learns quickly, and they decide to leave it at those dances which are the most popular at the moment. The Tango has arrived in London, but is yet to make it to the provinces, and the local band won't know what to play for it anyway.

The women also put as much effort into altering Maisie's clothes ahead of the big night. The school owns a number of sewing machines, sleek black, gold embossed Singers. Gleaming, proficient, humming. Skirts are narrowed, sleeves de-puffed, hems shortened. With the aid of *Woman's Own,* which offers "dress tips every week," Maisie is transformed from country parson's daughter into girl about town.

When Rosie helps Maisie select an outfit from her limited wardrobe, she discovers her friend owns an evening dress of dark blue velvet.

"Shall I make this into something more elegant and revealing?" Rosie offers.

"I don't think I'm quite ready to go that far," Maisie responds.

Always sensible, Hattie says, "It's not really the thing for an ordinary dance, Rosie. We don't want Maisie to look out of place."

In a fit of pique, Rosie sets about making herself a new dress fit for a potential naval officer's wife instead, leaving most of the alterations of Maisie's clothes to her two colleagues. A suitable outfit is made ready for the dance; a moss-coloured skirt and soft blouse. Maisie practices her dance steps whilst wearing it, so that she will be comfortable.

Saturday arrives, and the three young women meet up outside the Masonic Hall in the damp autumn night, before going in together. The large room is decorated with balloons and streamers. The central chandelier is sparkling with its recently installed electric lights. The chairs and tables are pushed back around the edges, revealing a parquet dance floor. The musicians are grouped around the upright piano, a violin and bass completing the ensemble. The refreshment room is to the side, serving teas and ices, and the hot fragrance of the urn bubbles across the dance floor, which already boasts a number of couples moving to a rhythm for the "Grizzly Bear," imitating the actions of the animal and laughing as they shout, "It's a bear!"

Hattie waves to a group of people across the room, and goes over to join them, introducing Maisie as they approach.

"This is Maisie. She started at the Broadway School at the beginning of last week. Maisie, these are my friends. Bill West and Alf Streeter work at the Boys Broadway School. You know Rosie's sister, Betty; and Susan works at Blue Town Infants."

Bill is usually to be found where Hattie is. He doesn't dance, but comes for the female company and makes himself useful by fetching refreshments and holding coats or bags, as necessary. He is pleasant looking, with a shock of wavy hair and a cleft chin. He makes the effort to chat to all the women, so no one feels neglected. Alf is relatively new to the group and generally tries to dance with all the girls, especially as there always seems to be more women than men. Alf has the handsome, swarthy looks of a pirate and the gait to go with it. He has inherited his physiognomy from his maternal grandfather who transferred from the navy to the dockyard from elsewhere in the Empire, and married a local girl. They shake Maisie's hand, and she thinks it strange to meet men as equals and unchaperoned. Alf is extremely popular with the girls, who all want to be his dance partner. That evening, he chooses Betty to be his first, so Hattie, Susan, Rosie, and Maisie regroup ready to accept or repel advances.

Sub-Lieutenant Edward Prescott's steward, Greenleaf, brushes his jacket and trousers, irons his shirt, and polishes his shoes. He shaves him and helps him dress, opting for the normal uniform rather than the smarter dress uniform. This is done to attract the ladies, of course. No lady's maid could have taken more care for a young girl's coming out ball as Greenleaf does of Prescott for this *Bachelor's Dance* in the town.

Edward looks in the mirror and is pleased with the result. He is average height and build, but his shoulders are broad from swimming, and his muscle definition shows against his shirt. It is a shame to cover this with a jacket, as he knows that the eye of many a lady traces his biceps through the crisp white cotton. He realises that he is not conventionally handsome, but his wide grin, which he practices in the mirror, and the twinkle in his eye, mean he is not unattractive to women. Certainly, his friendly persona makes him popular. But a more observant person might spot the wariness to be drawn into intimacy hidden behind his eyes, like a mistreated dog sold to a new master.

Edward's father, Captain Prescott, died of yellow fever off the coast of Africa. He received a burial at sea, but no widow's pension was paid from the Royal Bounty, as he was not killed in action. So, Edward's mother, Dorothea, lost no time in looking for a new husband to support her and her little boy upon her widowhood. She was still young, pretty, and petite, but without a private income or any useful skills with which to earn her own living and support the child, marriage was her only option. She knows that a boy needs a father, but nobody has told her it isn't necessarily so that a man needs a stepson. She soon married a naval acquaintance of her late husband, Captain Shrubsole, in the belief that he would care for her, the widow of a fellow officer, and her son.

Shrubsole had not been the only man whose eye the young widow had caught, but he moved the swiftest, surprisingly so for a man of his bulk. He looked more like a prize fighter than an officer of the Royal Navy. He made his offer of marriage within a few weeks of Dorothea receiving the letter from the Admiralty telling her of the death of Captain Prescott, but decency meant they must wait till her mourning is over. This enabled him to build a loving facade to show to the world, as well as Dorothea and her offspring, whilst waiting to make her his wife and chattel. She didn't heed the warning signs; didn't see how little interest the captain took in Edward, nor heard how he spoke of changes to come. She blithely believed that it would all be fine.

Not long after the wedding, and their removal to the captain's house, Edward heard a puppy whimpering plaintively. He hoped that his new stepfather had bought him a dog for companionship, as he often found himself alone in his new home. The boy went in pursuit of the sound, climbing the stairs and calling, "Here puppy, here!" But when he tracked the sound down to his mother's bedroom, he saw her crushed under the bulk of the captain. Tears were escaping from the eyes that met Edward's over the mass of the man's shoulder, and she motioned for him to leave with her hand that was hanging loose over the edge of the bed.

Later, she came and found him hiding in the nursery. She whispered, "I'm all right; it is just a game the captain likes to play. You mustn't worry. He isn't hurting me." She held Edward in her arms, but he could smell where the captain had engulfed her, and he wasn't comforted.

Captain Shrubsole had also been aware that the boy had come into the bedroom, and wasted no time placing him into the Royal Naval School at New Cross, as soon as he was ten. And from there into the Osborne College at thirteen, to prepare him to become an officer once he transferred to the Cadet College at Dartmouth. This enabled the captain to rape his new young wife, Dorothea, every night, in the name of conjugal rights. She considered herself lucky to have a roof over her head, as she stared up towards it whilst the nightly ritual went on.

As the boy never came home for holidays, he never saw his mother again, after she waved him goodbye at New Cross. When, after several miscarriages, she died trying to deliver a premature stillborn baby, she gave herself up willingly to the afterlife in the belief that she had done the best for her son.

Edward embraced the tough life and, like his mother, learned never to cry. He determined to do well and become a naval officer, like his own father. He wanted his parents to look down from heaven and be proud of him. He would also have the prospect of supplementing his pay with Prize Bounty Money for the capture of enemy ships. This will enable him to set himself up for life outside the navy.

He put himself forward for everything, and set about making himself as personable as possible. Being well liked opened more doors than just talent alone. He also learned how to ensure he volunteered for the showier tasks rather than those that go unnoticed by the training officers.

Edward only ever made one enemy at Osborne College; a lad called Matthew Baker. One Saturday afternoon, during some free time in Portsmouth, he heard a commotion in the side alley next to Gieves, the Naval Outfitters, and saw Baker, a chunky, sandy haired boy, had cornered the pretty shop girl Mary there. He was pressing himself up against her and Prescott heard him say, "Go on let me. If you don't, I'll tell everyone you did anyway." The girl kept saying no and trying to extricate herself. She knew if she caused too much fuss the shop manager might come out to investigate, the cadet would save his own skin by lying and saying she had led him on. But, if she allowed the boy to take liberties with her, he would tell his friends and they would try the same thing. Luckily for her, Prescott saw it all and intervened to stop Baker; a fight ensued. Edward got the better of the other boy, but Baker never forgot, and bore a grudge from that day forward.

When Edward graduated at eighteen, his stepfather came to his passing out parade with his new second wife, and passed him a brown paper parcel containing a handful of possessions left by his mother. These included her wedding and engagement rings from his real father, a gold cross, and her Bible with the family names in it. Finally, there was a studio portrait of his mother taken before her marriage to Captain Shrubsole.

"I don't need her stuff," the captain said, as hard as a coffin nail, as he handed it over. After that, Edward never saw his stepfather again, for which he wasn't sorry.

On leaving the Naval College, Edward spent five years of sea duty as a midshipman, prior to promotion to sub-lieutenant. He hopes to gain promotion to lieutenant soon, and has volunteered to assist with a project at a shore base, which he hopes will present him with the ideal opportunity to network and prepare the ground. He has done an earlier stint ashore in Portsmouth. He found this was excellent for placing him in the way of his superior officers, where he can impress them with his grasp of tactics when playing cards at their evening soirees and show his leadership skills when organising important banquets.

His current posting is assisting Rear Admiral Bennington, who is Superintendent of Sheerness Dockyard. He arrived in mid-October, for a month's assignment. There is no prize money to be made ashore. However, once he is promoted, his share will increase, so he sees it as a way to speculate to accumulate.

Edward lives in the officers' quarters with nine other officers and their stewards. It is comfortable enough for a man who barely remembers home comforts. The stewards keep it clean, do the laundry, and prepare meals. He has nothing to worry about and can study for his naval exams in solitude, or join in with the others if he wishes.

Most of his fellow officers have passed through the same training regime as he has, but some have families who at least write to them regularly; others make trips home for the holidays. But, without a shred of love in his life, Edward has developed a protective shell around his real self by appearing personable and happy to join in with his fellow officers. So, when his friend, Lieutenant Peter Barnes, invites him on a trip to the *Bachelors' Dance* in town that Saturday, he accepts.

Edward joins his fellow officers in the mess for a quick drink, before heading into town. He only knows Barnes well, having served with him previously a number of times and been in the same peer group at Dartmouth. Peter has a face like a Lewis Chessman, long and dour, combined with the long-limbed angular body of a heron. Edward also knows Lieutenant Fredrick Dollan and Lieutenant Simon Jones from college, but they are a couple of years above him. But the camaraderie of the navy means everyone is prepared to rub along, and pretty soon they are laughing and looking forward to some female company.

Once they arrive at the Masonic Hall, they find a strategic position that enables them to survey the ladies and any hostile enemy action. There is a brief flutter of interest from those women for whom an officer's uniform might prove a draw, and a repositioning to ensure sight lines are at their best.

Maisie and her companions see the group of officers arrive as the band strikes up a waltz. One of the naval officers, Fred, approaches the bevvy of teachers, steering a course for Rosie. She smiles and joins him on the dance floor. The women close ranks like a Saxon shield wall.

Edward surveys the wallflowers around the hall and decides to follow his companion Fred to the same group. He hasn't quite made up his mind whether to ask the girl in the green skirt or her companion in blue, but as he makes his way over, another gentleman comes in left field and takes one of them by the hand, leaving him with green skirt.

"Would you like to dance?" he asks Maisie, offering her his hand.

She exchanges a quick glance with Hattie, who mouths, "Say yes," and she smiles at Edward.

"Yes please, but I'm not very good," she says.

"Well, that makes two of us then," he responds, leading her onto the dance floor.

Maisie manages to dance as if she learned many years past, not just two weeks ago. She smiles and makes small talk, and is generally pleased with herself for being so modern. She pushes away the thought that her father will be turning in his grave at such wanton behaviour. She likes the look of Edward; she feels right in his strong arms; he smells of the sea, and she enjoys his little jokes.

Edward decides he has got the better end of the bargain between the blue and green skirts. He likes Maisie's shiny hair, her blue eyes, and her ivory skin. She smells of violets and warm milk, and her laugh is hesitant and rewarding. But most of all, she fits into his arms as though she has always been there.

Edward and Maisie adjourn to the refreshment room, with its tables set with virginal white cloths. He orders two teas and some cake, and finds them some empty seats.

"I can't help thinking we have met before," Edward says, looking at her intently as he tries to place where he might have seen her before. "How long have you lived in Sheerness?"

"I've only been here a couple of weeks," Maisie responds, and she tells him how she and her mother became homeless, which led to her now working as a teacher and living with Miss Garrett.

"No, I'm sure I've seen you before. Is your landlady a severe looking woman?" he asks, cocking one eyebrow quizzically. Maisie says yes and he exclaims, "That's it! You were at the station! I offered to help you with your trunk, but your companion said no. I knew we had bumped into each other before!"

Maisie laughs. "Yes, you are right, I remember you now. I felt mortified that she was so abrupt. She disapproves of the services!"

After that, she asks what made him join the navy, and he tells her about his mother and his stepfather. He surprises himself that he tells her so much, it is not something he generally speaks about. But there is something about Maisie that makes him open up and feel comfortable.

They move on from their families to talking about everything under the sun: his career prospects, and how she is finding teaching at the much bigger school than in the village of Chiddingly. They talk about what they are reading and which composers they like.

In what seems like no time at all, Hattie and Rosie appear beside Maisie. "We should be going home now. It's getting late," says Hattie producing Maisie's hat and coat from the cloakroom in readiness.

Edward stands up to help Maisie with her coat and simply says, "I hope to see you again." But he doesn't make any firm arrangements as he goes to re-join his colleagues to walk back to the dockyard.

Maisie just manages to say, "That will be lovely," as Rosie and Hattie set off towards the exit, leaving her to trail behind them.

Once they are outside, the two other young women can barely contain themselves and start pumping Maisie with questions.

"What's his name?"

"How old is he?"

"Where does he come from?"

Maisie finds she doesn't know some of these basic facts, despite having spent over two hours talking to him. Rosie and Hattie nearly despair when it becomes obvious that no further meeting is arranged.

"We will go to the dockyard church for Sunday service," schemes Rosie.

"Yes, you can accidently bump into him there. If not this week, he will be there at some point," agrees Hattie.

Maisie has no memory of walking home; her head is so full of the handsome officer there isn't room for anything else. But a firm date is made for church the following morning between the women.

Rosie and Hattie appear at Miss Garrett's front door promptly at half past nine the next day. Church services in the dockyard church are not until eleven o'clock, but they want to ensure Maisie looks her best in a demure and God-fearing way. When they get to the church, they will select the best vantage point to see the young officer enter.

Maisie is just finishing her breakfast of a boiled egg and toast when Miss Garrett ushers the others in. The older woman looks none too pleased, and her disapproval of their going on a jaunt to the dockyard church is almost palpable. She can't decide if she is more offended about this blatant sortie into enemy territory, or the fact it is an Anglican service led by a naval official.

Miss Garrett hovers in the dining room as the girls discuss their plans, using the pretext of offering tea and toast to the visitors. Her curiosity gets the better of her when she hears Maisie has met a young man, but has failed to secure him for a second meeting. She finds herself uncharacteristically hurrying Maisie along and offering to help Mrs Bills with the clearing up so the younger woman will not be late.

Rosie and Hattie chivvy Maisie upstairs to her room to perform the necessary adjustments to ensnare her prey at church. It doesn't take long as Maisie's stock of clothing and accessories is small, but a cross and chain is found together with white gloves and the right hat to show off her face whilst projecting an air of devotional piety. These items are added to her usual Sunday best, which has already had the skirt transformed in an earlier operation to update Maisie's clothes.

Rosie grabs Maisie's Bible and says, "Hold your Bible like this in your lap when you sit down. It will make it look like you have a serious Christian mind. You can look down at it if you need to cast your eyes away from Edward. You will then be able to look at him from beneath your lashes like this," she demonstrates, "Plus, any small notes can be concealed within its covers, if such an item is passed to you," she finishes gleefully.

Maisie is amazed at the martial precision with which Rosie and Hattie undertake all these tasks. Every eventuality is considered and planned for. It is a wonder they are both still single themselves, despite the level of attack they bring to catching a suitable man.

They set off together at quarter past ten to ensure a good place in church. Miss Garrett reverts to her usual self and sniffs her disapproval as she fastens the door behind them and prepares for teaching Sunday school in a conforming way at a non-conformist chapel.

Rosie and Hattie chatter brightly, once again asking Maisie for all the details of her encounter with Sub-Lieutenant Prescott. It is a debriefing of almost military standards, designed to trigger any details that may have been shared with Maisie, but forgotten in the excitement. At the end of the twenty-minute walk to the church, only one additional fact is revealed; Edward is an only child, like Maisie.

The dockyard church is a grand Georgian affair with a large Ionic portico, square central tower, and arched windows. It was built by the Navy Board, just outside the perimeter walls when the dockyard was being developed, as the dockyard workers were required to attend church by law. There was also the perceived threat of non-conformism, which might bring a more egalitarian Christianity to the workers, which the Navy Board sought to discourage. On top of this, naval officers didn't rent pews in their new parishes as they only spent short periods at any establishment. This meant they were not given the status some would have felt they deserved. To encourage both officers and workers to attend church, the Navy Board gave them one of their own, grand enough to show the importance of the navy to both the town and God, in case the latter should ever forget.

The church stands at the end of a terrace of elegant Georgian homes, the like of which are usually found in more salubrious towns like Bath or Cheltenham. These house the senior officers of the dockyard, along with the Chaplain and the Chief Engineer. As the houses face away from the toil and dirt within the walls, the wives and daughters can pretend that they are posted somewhere grander than Sheerness. Their younger sons are usually away at Naval College and the older ones are serving officers already, so their opinions on the gentility of the street do not matter and are not sought.

Immediately inside the church, there are twin cantilevered stone staircases leading up to the gallery. Rosie and Hattie head straight up the left hand one and go as far forward towards the altar as they can get and commandeer the front pew. Maisie follows obediently behind them. This gives them the vantage point they require to see the front door, without needing to turn their heads one hundred and eighty degrees. They can also see down into the nave and check that Sub-Lieutenant Prescott has not yet arrived.

"You sit with your back to the door, Maisie, then we can look towards you and see who is coming through the main entrance. That way, you will seem less keen and appear more nonchalant when Prescott arrives," Rosie insists, as she organises the seating for the little group of friends.

Although the pews are not rented, it is quite evident that there is a hierarchy to how they fill up. Naval officers wear their dress uniforms, and the more senior they are, the further forward they sit. Similarly, the senior dockyard staff take up their places near the front. Most dockyard workers still attend their local churches, but those with an eye on promotion to the likes of shipwright file into the back, with their wives and families turned out in their Sunday best. The less senior naval officers sit towards the rear and fit themselves in around the other worshippers, as they rarely have any family with them. Finally, the ratings climb the stairs as though they are climbing the masts to keep watch and position themselves in the gallery, along with lesser dockyard workers such as labourers or storemen. There are a few other lone women dotted in the gallery, the girl friends and prospective sweethearts coming for a glimpse of their loved ones, or matrimonial target, depending on their status.

Most of the servicemen will arrive following church parade, but some will arrive independently, according to their duties that day. As the women know Prescott is shore based, it is thought that he will be amongst these arrivals who usually slip in at the back.

At nearly ten to eleven, their quarry finally appears, framed in the doorway. The suppressed giggling of her friends is enough to alert Maisie. She takes a breath and turns her head to see Edward looking every bit as handsome as she remembered him. At that moment, he glances up and their eyes meet. The slightest of smiles passes quickly across his face, and then is gone like it has never been. He inclines his head almost imperceptibly in acknowledgement of her. In return, Maisie raises her hand a fraction in a wave, and allows the corner of her mouth to lift in a nervous smile.

Edward finds a place in a pew near the back of the church and settles down. During the service, he exchanges several glances with Maisie, who uses her Bible with as much aplomb as a courtesan might use a fan. Hattie and Rosie continue to whisper and nudge each other like schoolgirls, and silently congratulate themselves on the success of their manoeuvres.

70

When the service ends, the congregation begins to file out. At that point, their clever positioning at the furthest end from the stairs, turns against them as they have to wait whilst the gallery empties out before they can leave. Hattie and Rosie fidget as they wait impatiently for the crowd to thin out. Maisie sits demurely, as the butterflies in her stomach feel more like elephants blundering about inside.

Hattie whispers, "I hope he hasn't left without saying goodbye."

It seems like the entire navy is crammed upstairs, and the ratings wait obediently, whilst the officers and their wives leave the church first. When they finally find themselves outside at the top of the stone church steps, it is with relief Maisie sees Edward is standing with the tall officer he attended the dance with, as the servicemen assemble to march back to their ships. As she emerges out of the shadows, Edward takes a step towards her and says, "Hello again, I didn't know that you worshipped at this church?"

Maisie is slightly on the back foot, but quickly responds, "As I'm new to the town, I plan to visit all the local churches to see which congregation I should join."

Edward smiles unconvinced. At that moment, Peter Barnes gives a little cough. "Where are my manners," says Edward at this prompt, "Maisie, this is my colleague and friend, Lieutenant Barnes."

Maisie nods and repays the compliment. "How do you do, Lieutenant Barnes? May I introduce my friends, Miss Roberts, and Miss Dale – Hattie and Rosie."

"Please, call me Peter," says Lieutenant Barnes. "Pleased to meet you. We are just going for a cup of tea in town. Would you like to join us?"

They all chorus their agreement and walk together through the closed Sunday High Street to find an open café. Maisie and Edward fall back slightly from the others to gain a little privacy.

Edward says, "I was pleased to see you in the congregation this morning. I didn't get the chance to say goodbye to you properly last night, when your friends arrived to collect you."

Maisie smiles, and realises her heart is thumping as she does her best to appear relaxed. "Yes, it's the first dance I have been to since moving here, and they wanted to ensure I got home safely."

Edward grins. "I hope they don't see me as threatening?"

They both laugh, and he continues, "I have to go back to Portsmouth this week. My assignment here is only for a short while, and then I will be sitting my exams for promotion to lieutenant. I am due to return here in the New Year, but I don't have a date as yet." He hurries on. "So, when I said I hope to see you again, I do, but it won't be for some weeks. Seeing you today so unexpectedly is a welcome bonus."

Maisie is taken aback. This scenario has not been played out with Hattie and Rosie, and she realises that it is probably a more realistic situation for a naval officer; here one day, gone the next.

"I see," she manages to say. "Well, that is just my luck; meet a young officer, only to find that His Majesty has other ideas of where he should be," she jokes, whilst at the same time hiding her disappointment.

"If you will be kind enough to give me your address, perhaps I can write to you and let you know when I am returning," Edward says, as he smiles and rummages in his pockets for a pencil and a piece of paper.

By now, they reach an open café which is busy with people on Sunday outings. The windows are steamed up from a mixture of body heat, hot tea, and expectations. The little party enter, and Peter heads straight to the counter to place their order.

Maisie does her best to redeem the situation with Edward as she sits down at the nearest free table, saying, "I have paper. What kind of schoolteacher goes about without the tools of her trade?" She produces the necessary equipment from

73

her bag, in the form of a leather-bound notebook and pencil. She tears a page out and carefully writes her address on it, folds the paper, and passes it to Edward, who puts it in his inside breast pocket and gives it a little reassuring pat.

Hattie and Rosie follow this without a word, and under the table Hattie squeezes Rosie's hand with excitement for her friend. Maisie avoids their eyes and behaves as though she is just giving the officer a shopping list. She knows that any acknowledgement from her will lead to muted triumphalism from the two girls.

The small group are soon comfortably swapping stories, and Hattie launches into telling them about the kittens Tibby has given birth to yesterday. The cat has chosen a narrow cupboard, where she has found a hole to crawl through into a void in the eaves of the bay window. "It's impossible to get to her," Hattie rattles on. "The midwife can't get the new-born babies. Obviously, Tibby has got wise to her and outwitted her on this occasion." Hattie stops momentarily to sip her tea, "If I stand on a chair, I can just see into the hole where the kittens are. I heard them mewing and I've left food and milk inside the cupboard so Tibby can feed." Rosie quickly changes the subject, as she knows Hattie will talk about the kittens all day otherwise.

After tea, and following much repeated good wishes, the women depart with waves and smiles, walking towards their homes, whilst the two naval officers set sail in the opposite direction towards the dockyard.

As soon as it feels that enough distance has appeared between them, Rosie and Hattie start cross-examining Maisie on what passed between the couple.

"He is going back to Portsmouth in the next day or so," Maisie tells them.

"Oh, no! How disappointing!" cries Hattie.

"When will he be back? Did he say?" asks Rosie.

"He doesn't know yet, but he has promised to write," says Maisie with excitement, but her friends take little comfort from his promise, as such pledges are easily broken. However, they have all made a new friend in Lieutenant Peter Barnes, who has agreed to join them for the forthcoming reading circle meeting at the Congregational church hall later that week, with the additional undertaking to bring other like-minded officers. All might not be lost.

They have enjoyed Peter's company during tea. He isn't handsome, having a long face and the stick like limbs of a wading bird, so much so that he seemed to fold himself into his seat, and sharp corners of him stuck out to catch passers-by unexpectedly; but he is funny and has an engaging way. When he talks, he seems genuinely interested in you. They are all looking forward to seeing him again, even if he is not dashing like his colleague, Sub-Lieutenant Prescott.

Peter is an entirely different kettle of fish to Edward. He is kind, intelligent, and thoughtful. He is known for his generosity and, as an officer, is renowned for putting the welfare of his men first.

His family are not seafaring folk, as they own a pickle factory near London Bridge where they live in an adjoining house built by the original owner. It came completely out of the blue to his parents that he wished to join the navy, after reading stories about Nelson.

The pickle factory is famed for the condiment – *Barnes's Brown Sauce* which was originally the only product they made. Over the last one hundred years or so, Peter's extended family has built up the business from employing under fifty staff to now employing around three hundred. They manufacture pickled gherkins, walnuts, and hard- boiled eggs, as well as the famous brown sauce and piccalilli. Peter's father inherited the company from a cousin and had not been raised to run the factory. As a result, it had begun to get into difficulties following some bad decisions, but fortunately Peter's two sisters, Margaret, and Edna, have stepped up to the mark and saved the business. It is they who keep London in piccalilli, as they are now the power houses in pickles. It is the two sisters who keep the accounts, manage the staff, get in the orders, and ensure that the quality of the products is always the highest. At the same time, they skilfully let their father believe he is still in charge, despite all the evidence to the contrary.

Peter's parents accepted his decision to join the Senior Service, as it would help him climb the social ladder, and possibly help find husbands for his two sisters, as they are in danger of becoming old maids, although in reality it is already too late for his siblings. Originally, it was planned that he would be educated at a minor public school (the first of their family to attend such an institution), but when it became certain that he was determined to join the navy, he was placed in Osborne College. But his father made it clear to him that one day he will have to take over the pickle factory. His sisters keep him fully updated about the current state of the condiments industry, so he can step in should it ever be required. However, they know Peter fully intends to leave the running of the business to them, when the day came, as he knows he has no more of a head for commerce than their father has.

The Barnes family are close knit and Peter's sisters adore him. They are considerably older than him, as he is a "menopause" baby. Whenever Peter returns home, he is treated as a returning hero with the best foods prepared and guests invited to meet him. As London is only an hour by train from his current land-based posting, this is a frequent occurrence. He hopes one day to meet a girl who will make him feel as loved and cherished as his sisters make him feel.

When next he pops home to admire the new bottling line set up for pickling cauliflower, he can't help mentioning he has met some new people.

"What kind of people?"

"Do you mean a girl type people?" the two women ask, one after another.

"Well, yes," responds Peter, somewhat coyly. "Well, a little group of girls — teachers actually. Edward met a girl at the dance we went to, and we ran into her and her friends at church. We all went for a cup of tea," Peter confides.

"How nice," Margaret says.

"What are the names of these teachers?" Edna asks.

"Maisie," Peter says, wistfully. "Maisie has a very pretty smile and has such an infectious laugh. Edward talked to her all night at the dance, I can see why. She is a very nice girl," he finishes, lamely. "I do hope we will see her again soon, and her friends, of course. Prescott is returning to Portsmouth, but I do hope she will be with her friends at a reading group they invited me to."

The two sisters, using their business opportunism, decide Peter should make the most of his friend being out of the way to woo Maisie, and set about coaching him in talking to his new friends.

"Where does the reading group meet?" Edna asks.

"What sort of books do they read?" questions Margaret.

"Oh, I don't know," he answers vaguely. "I will have to find out."

"You need to impress her with your knowledge of the classics."

"Yes, tell her you read Dickens and Kipling."

"You can't let her know you only ever read the latest cricket almanac."

"You must give us a full report on how it goes."

Finally, they make suggestions as to which colleagues he should take along with him. By the time he walks back into the officers' mess later that day, he is ready to present himself as a literary man.

The evening of the reading group arrives. Hattie, Maisie, and Rosie are joined by other teachers, including Miss Garrett and Ena, as well as

Will and Alf from the boys' school. There is a scattering of other readers: clerks and shop girls wanting to improve themselves, and spinsters and bachelors looking for company. They meet in the Napier Road Hall, which hides itself amongst the terrace houses trying to blend in. This means it is easy to miss.

Inside, the hall opens out, to be much bigger than it seems from the outside. Its large window arches and the lantern windows in the hammer beam roof provide wonderful illumination during the daylight hours. But, on November days, it lets in the blackness which the gas lights struggle to chase away. Some additional oil lamps stand on a table to help with reading at this time of year, and the stove is banked high by Mr Moss, the caretaker, to banish the cold to the far corners.

The reading group sit in a wide circle around the stove to keep warm. They sit on a selection of ill matched chairs. Some are wooden, some are cane, and some have sea grass seats that are repaired by the girls' club that met weekly, and are given small repair jobs such as sewing curtains, reupholstering seats, and other such DIY activities for the hall, in the name of recreational crafts.

The reading group has read Mrs Gaskell's *North and South,* and are quite animated about whether Margaret Hale's description of the South is a true portrayal. Certainly, Maisie can identify with it as, like Margaret, she is a pastor's daughter from a rural parish. However, the rest of the company have lived so long in the dockyard town of Sheerness that they identify more with the description of the North. One of the dockyard clerks is holding forth on the similarities between the streets of terraced housing, when the door bursts open to reveal Lieutenant Peter Barnes and a second officer.

"So sorry we are late," he apologises, "but we didn't realise there are two Congregational churches, each with its own hall! We've had to escape a meeting of the local ornithology society to be here! We nearly missed this hall as it blends in so well with the street."

Everyone laughs, except Miss Garrett, who clearly did not welcome the interruption as Peter introduces himself and his companion, Lieutenant Harris. The circle widens, and Maisie and Hattie make space for the two naval officers to grab a chair and join them. Miss Garrett sniffs and draws her chair away from the interlopers.

Samuel Harris has a complexion of boiled ham, and fists to match. He has clearly been dragged by Peter to the meeting to provide him with the cover of "literary man," as a front to meet up with the three young teachers again. However, having been reluctant to come at first, Harris seems more than willing to sit next to Rosie (to her delight) and share her copy of the book as the conversation progresses.

Neither Peter nor his companion have read Mrs Gaskell, and Miss Garrett is not convinced they have read anything beyond what is necessary to pass their officers' examinations, but the two men gamely join in the North versus South debate, as though they might have read it.

It is agreed to read Emily Post's *The Title Market*, for the next meeting, and compare and contrast it to the universally acknowledged dull *The Portrait of a Lady* by Henry James, which they read earlier in the year. The two naval officers are at a disadvantage, neither of them having read the first book, but Lieutenant Barnes promises that he will read both by the next meeting as they chat over tea out of thick white cups and saucers, served at the end of the meeting from the small kitchen area at the back of the hall by the lady members. Miss Garrett supervises as she rarely does any menial tasks herself.

Lieutenant Harris manages to position himself between Rosie and the rest of the group like a blockship in a port, but she seems quite happy to listen to his conversation about ships, the sea, the Royal Navy, and the dockyard. Peter Barnes chats to Maisie and Hattie, and keeps up a string of amusing stories about his clumsiness. Both women find him to be the best company and, as people start drifting off, it is only their small group left behind with Mr Moss, who jingles his keys meaningfully as he waits to lock up.

"We'd best go," says Hattie, moving towards the door, in the hope that the others will follow.

"Have you heard from Sub-Lieutenant Prescott?" Maisie asks.

"Not yet," Lieutenant Barnes responds, "but a colleague came up from Pompey the other day and reported having seen him. He has passed his exams and will take up a lieutenant's post shortly."

A small "oh" escapes Maisie, and she looks deflated that Edward has not written to her to tell of his promotion, but she covers it quickly with a congratulatory smile. Barnes realises that perhaps Maisie has hoped for a different answer and says, "Not much time for writing in the navy, I'm afraid. I'm sure he will write when he gets a moment to tell you his good news."

"Of course," Maisie replies, and manages a forlorn smile that seems to put a slight dampener on the evening. Only Hattie notices how Lieutenant Barnes also looks disappointed as they go out into the cool November evening air.

## December 1913

A few weeks after the reading group meeting, the postman brings Maisie the long-awaited letter from the newly created Lieutenant Prescott. It is chatty, and apologetic for the delay in writing. He talks about his new quarters and his sporting activities, but doesn't say if he missed Maisie, or even thinks about her. It could have been written by a brother rather than a possible suitor. Maisie read it and reread it, trying to find the smallest indication that Edward is thinking of her, but she can find none. This sets the tone for her reply, as she knows she must respond in like manner. She can't tell him how much she likes him, or how good looking she thinks he is. She thinks long and hard, and finally decides on what to say:

*Dear Edward,*

*May I take this opportunity to congratulate you on your well-deserved promotion to Lieutenant.*

*We have been enjoying Lieutenant Barnes's company at our reading group. He keeps us all amused with his stories of the pickling factory. Lieutenant Harris has been coming with him, but I suspect he has never read a book in his life. He pretends he has forgotten to bring his copy of whatever we are reading, just so he can sit next to my friend Rosie and share hers. They are inseparable now.*

*The weather here has been getting colder as the nights draw in. I wonder if we will have snow for Christmas.*

*Nurse Noble, or "Nitty Noble" as the children call her, visited the school on Monday. She makes the children queue to have their heads examined for vermin, and any child found to be "alive with nits" is sent home. It's always the same ones, she tells me.*

*We have been following the activities of the suffragettes in the newspapers and are looking forward to hearing of their success. My friend Hattie is friendly with a local firebrand and has said she will invite us all to tea soon.*

*I hope we will soon see you if you are posted back to Sheerness.*
*Regards*
*Maisie*

Again, she waits for a response from Prescott, but the postman resolutely fails to bring her one.

Christmas is rapidly approaching, and Maisie decides to send a "Christmas Greetings" card to Prescott, despite not having had a reply to her last letter. It isn't polite etiquette for her to write again, but

85

she reasons that a Christmas greeting will be the exception to the rule.

Once school ends for the day, she sets off through the gathering dusk to Cheeseman's, the stationers in town, as she thinks they will offer the best selection of cards. She doesn't tell Hattie or Rosie her plans and has slipped out quickly before anyone notices her departing. Hattie is too wrapped up with trying to find homes for Tibby's kittens. She has managed to persuade Ena not to request their disposal, with the promise that she will find them all homes as people will want them as Christmas presents for their children, so she has not noticed Maisie acting furtively.

The shop window is crammed with all kinds of cards, maps, books, pens, and examples of printing – menu cards, invitations, and business cards. Inside, stands a young spotty-faced shop assistant dressed in a long, navy-blue calico apron and matching oversleeves to protect his clothes from any ink stains, but his hands are less fortunate, as the ink is ingrained into his nails. Before the shop doorbell stops ringing, he asks Maisie, "Can I help you, madam?"

"I'm looking for some Christmas greetings cards," she responds.

The boy produces a number of card templates to add a printed message to. Maisie has to dash the lad's hopes of a big sale saying, "I'm sorry, I'm looking for individual cards." He has shown her the kind of card sent out by the dozen from the local tradesmen to their business associates and loyal customers. They are not the sort for a young woman to send a gentleman friend. With slightly less interest and care, the shop assistant pulls out some drawers filled with examples of Christmas cards to which a handwritten message can be added.

Maisie spends an age selecting just the right card. She wants a humorous one, but the fluffy kittens getting into hilarious Yuletide scrapes don't quite hit the mark. So, she settles on one with a scene of a small girl dressed as Mary, wearing a blue head scarf, whilst holding a doll dressed as the baby Jesus, reminiscent of the school Nativity play which is being rehearsed daily. Inside, the card has a quote from Dickens: *"May the wings of friendship never moult a feather,"* which Maisie feels sets just the right tone.

She selects another (of the kitten variety) to send to her mother and aunt, and pays the shop assistant for her purchases. She then pops into the post office to buy two penny stamps to see her cards safely to their respective destinations. She returns home walking along the already darkening, wintery promenade where the lights from the naval ships glitter on the Bible black water. The solitude enables her to enjoy a little story in her head of Edward receiving her card and immediately penning a reply. There isn't much screen time in this imaginary story dedicated to her mother also receiving a Christmas greeting in the post.

As soon as she returns home to Miss Garrett's, she goes up to her room to write her cards. She pens a brief note to go inside Edward's:

*Can't resist this card as I am tearing my hair out trying to get Millie Luckhurst to learn her lines for the Nativity play next week. I hope you have an enjoyable Christmas. I am going to spend it with my mother and aunt. If you are posted back to town, it would be lovely to see you,*
*Best wishes,*
*Maisie.*

She ensures that her aunt's address is included, just in case Edward might write to her whilst she is away.

She seals the card reluctantly, having removed it from its envelope more than once to check if she has missed anything. She then adds the address, and affixes the stamp. Meanwhile, she simply writes, "with love, Maisie," into her mother's card, and prepares that for posting. She grabs her hat and coat and walks back into town to post the envelopes at the pillar box outside the Post Office, to ensure she catches the last post of the day, before once again walking home.

But as Christmas rapidly approaches there is no further correspondence from Edward.

Maisie packs the smaller travelling trunk that Miss Garrett lends her ready for her trip to her aunt's house. She is in agonies that a letter might arrive from Lieutenant Prescott whilst she is away.

"You will forward my post onto me, won't you, Miss Garrett?" she asks her landlady.

"Of course, I will, but you are away for less than a week. Are you expecting an important letter then?" she pries, whilst trying to seem helpful.

"Oh, no, I just want to stay in touch," Maisie responds airily, to which Miss Garrett gives an unconvinced sniff.

By the time Maisie boards the train on Christmas Eve to travel to West Meon, she knows in her heart of hearts that Edward will not write.

Maisie's mother, Evangeline (Evie) Kendall, was born the third child to a gentleman of good country stock. The daughters were expected to marry well, and it was believed that there was no need for them to earn their own living. She had no skills or money of her own, and was totally unprepared when Reverend Kendall died unexpectedly at fifty-eight, from typhoid, leaving her and Maisie penniless and homeless. With no other means of support, Mrs Kendall had no choice but to move in with her widowed sister, Mrs Euphemia (Effie) Monkson, in her home in West Meon, Hampshire.

Effie is in better financial circumstances than her older sister, having been left a small cottage, and an even smaller private income from her late husband's estate, the rest passing to his son from his first marriage. She likes to call herself "The Dowager," as she firmly believes her husband should have been Sir Ernest; even though the Monksons' fortune is little more than the sum of a large farm. In reality, the family are non-titled landowners, but it is enough to give them the front pew in the local church and a high status in their village. Effie also likes to call her cottage on the estate "The Dowager House." It makes her feel slightly better, as she only has a life interest in the property which will go to her stepson upon her death. As she has no children of her own, she doesn't have anyone to leave the cottage to, but she feels the absence none the less. Effie's stepson provides his stepmother with a maid and a cook to look after her, and he supplies her with ample food from the farm. Evie Kendall hopes her sister will outlive her, or she will have nowhere to go at all.

Now, the two sisters live in genteel poverty together in the tiny cottage. Aunt Effie's stipend is supplemented by the small allowance Maisie sent regularly to her mother and the gifts from the estate. It is an uneasy alliance. The two sisters have never been close. Evie is too self-righteous to be an easy companion, whilst Effie finds it hard not to be her sister's social superior, despite her own impoverishment.

Maisie's mother makes it her business to fuss over her daughter as much as she is able to for the duration of the short holiday. She scores points over her childless sister by saying things like, "If only you hadn't been barren, you too would have enjoyed the love of a daughter," or "Maisie is such a comfort to me in my widowhood. It's a shame the Lord didn't bless you with a child."

But when Maisie arrives at the cottage for Christmas, Mrs Kendall is shocked to see how her daughter has changed in just a few months. She is more confident, looks smarter, is more fashionable, and she talks on a wide variety of subjects that would have horrified the Reverend Kendall. She has opinions on everything: votes for women, the Irish Question, working conditions for the dockyard workers, housing the poor and, most surprisingly, German expansionism. Evie has never heard anyone in polite society discuss these subjects, and thinks they are more appropriate for men to discuss after dinner with their brandy, than for a single young lady.

There is another change in Maisie; she now drinks port. She asks her Aunt Effie for a glass after they have eaten their dessert. It seems some of her teaching friends will serve a glass of port or sherry at dinner, if it is a special occasion. Her landlady, Miss Garrett, is a non-conformist and teetotaller, but she too stretches the point on high days and holidays and serves sherry. Maisie doesn't mention that occasionally she and her friends will go into the parlour of a local public house and occupy a little snug bar, to take a glass of port or sherry. That would be more than her mother can take.

The whole non-conformist issue is also a concern for Mrs Kendall. Although Maisie tells her mother she has joined the local Trinity church, the egalitarian ideas of the Congregationalist are freely discussed amongst her new friends. Maisie seems to be sharing some of their views, including why can't women be pastors? She cites how women are assistant pastors and in some small Congregational churches are in fact THE pastor.

And is that red lipstick she is wearing, like the suffragettes are reputed to wear? The late Reverend would not have approved of this new Maisie.

Maisie has yet to tell her mother about the planned trip to Switzerland in the summer. She has avoided the subject, as she knows her mother will think it an extravagance. She also knows her mother will worry about her travelling with just a group of other women across Europe. But she has to tell her, and decides that the conviviality of the evening will perhaps help.

"Have I told you that I am going to Vevey in Switzerland for a few weeks in the summer?" she asks, knowing full well she has not.

Her mother opens her mouth, but no words come out. Effie responds with, "How lovely, travel broadens the mind. My late husband and I loved to travel on the continent." As an afterthought, she adds, "And it will give you the opportunity to practice your French."

Evie continues to say nothing, but just stares at her daughter.

"Yes," says Maisie, pretending not to notice her mother's reaction to this news, "I hope we will be able to travel around Lake Geneva and see Lausanne and Montreux. We hope to be able to spend a few hours in Paris on our journey too."

"I loved Paris, it's so gay!" exclaims her aunt, enjoying her sister's discomfiture.

But Paris is too much for Evie, and she splutters out, "Are you mad? A young woman travelling alone! To Paris, of all places!"

"But I won't be on my own, I'll be with Hattie, Ena, and Miss Garrett." Maisie decides she should change the subject and, as she sips her ruby port, she confides in her mother and aunt that she has met Edward, but nothing seems to have come of it. Aunt Effie is delighted that Maisie is enjoying her new life, but her mother is aghast and says, "You've been out meeting young men, unchaperoned?"

Maisie laughs. "Oh, mother, I am always in the company of a group of people when I am with him. I am never in any danger!"

"Yes, Evie. Leave the girl to enjoy herself. What harm can she come to with all her friends there?" Effie asks. "We were all young once, and Maisie isn't getting any younger, is she? She's already twenty-six!"

Maisie doesn't think her aunt needs to be quite so gleeful when stating her age.

Maisie's mother remains unconvinced. "There is no shame in life as a teacher."

"As an Old Maid!" Maisie retorts. "Surely you don't want me to stay a spinster till I die!"

"I wish your father were still alive, he would know what to say to you," her mother replies, struggling to deal with her daughter's newfound outspokenness.

"Then, I definitely would have died a spinster!" Maisie gives a hollow laugh, which doesn't put a sparkle in her eyes. The port emboldens her to say, "If father were alive, I would still be living in his shadow, and have no life of my own. I would never get to meet any young men!"

"How can you! He's not been gone a year!" Evie says, as she rushes out of the room in tears. Maisie realises she has overstepped the mark.

"I'm sorry," she cries, half rising. But it is too late. She hears her mother's bedroom door bang shut.

"Oh, dear," says Aunt Effie. "Your mother is finding it hard to cope as a widow. I think she envies you your new life, so like my own used to be. You are able to look after yourself and make your own choices. It's a freedom Evie never had, nor ever looked for, unlike me. And it's too late for her to use her independence now. Leave her to have a little cry, then apologise." She continues conspiratorially, "From my point of view, I am happy you are meeting suitable men. My widow's income will not be enough to support all three of us. So, if you can marry a naval officer, then that is good news for all of us."

Maisie sits quietly finishing her port, whilst gazing into the fire and wonders how she can make it up to her mother, but at the same time she knows there is no going back to their old lives in Chiddingly.

In the morning, the three women exchange Christmas gifts. Maisie has embroidered handkerchiefs for both women, and is pleased with their reception. Evie has made pin cushions in the shape of strawberries. She had initially intended to say that she had not been in the right frame of mind for presents, following her widowhood, but thought better of it.

But Aunt Effie manages to console her sister Evie, and calm her niece with some well-chosen gifts. She went through her wardrobe and picked out some items to give to her family. It looks like an act of generosity. However, since her own widowhood, she has nowhere to wear such things, and her income does not run to the purchase of such items new. She gives Evie a beautiful Indian shawl. It is of a Paisley design, in purples and blues, and of the finest wool from Kashmir. Her sister is delighted with the gift and immediately wraps it around herself saying, "That will keep the draught out from this old cottage." Effie has several such shawls, and gifting one is no loss, so she bears her sister's snipe without comment.

She gives Maisie a beautiful green kimono style wrap. Effie bought the garment following a trip to Paris with her late husband. It exactly matched her mood at that moment, but seems too flamboyant to wear as a dowager. Anything Japanese is still the height of fashion, and she thinks it will suit this new Maisie down to the ground. But, following the argument the night before about Paris, she makes up a story that an arty friend has given it to her. She doesn't want her sister to think she might be less than respectable buying such a racy item of clothing and gifting it to her niece; it might seem like she is encouraging Maisie to be too Bohemian in Paris.

Maisie is delighted with it. It is beautifully embroidered with exotic birds in colourful silks. The faint scent of her aunt's expensive perfume clings to it, a perfume her aunt can no longer afford to buy. She puts it on and almost dances around the room.

"Thank you, Aunt Effie! It is the most exquisite thing I have ever owned."

"I'm so glad you like it," Effie responds, but she can't resist adding, "You can wear it when you go to Paris," just to annoy Evie.

After Christmas dinner of a capon, with all the trimmings provided by Aunt Effie's stepson, the women sit round the fire and enjoy a glass of sherry together. Effie asks Maisie to tell her more about her new friends and particularly the young men whom she has met.

"Are there any other naval officers beside Lieutenant Prescott in your circle?" she enquires, as marrying an officer is still a very desirable thing, and she hopes Maisie might improve her situation by doing so.

"Yes, my friend Rosie is extremely attached to Lieutenant Harris. They are inseparable. We hope to hear wedding bells. And, of course, there is Lieutenant Barnes. He is a lovely man, but is very tall and gawky. His family make *Barnes's Brown Sauce.*"

Effie sits up and takes notice at this revelation.

"He is very funny and so kind. He wanted to buy oranges for Christmas for all the girls in my class, and asked me whether he should buy one or two boxes. I told him it would be unfair on the other girls in school, so asked him not to. Do you know what he did?" she asks her mother and aunt, not expecting an answer. "He contacted the pickle factory's fruit supplier in Covent Garden and arranged for a dozen boxes to be sent by train. Every girl in school got an orange for Christmas. Isn't that sweet of him?"

Effie says bluntly, "He's the man you should set your cap at!"

Maisie laughs, while her mother and aunt exchange meaningful looks, for once in accord.

## January 1914

After Christmas, the group of friends starts meeting regularly, both at the reading group and elsewhere. There are trips to tea shops, walks along the promenade and other outings. They all now attend the Congregational church where Hattie and Rosie help with Sunday school. There are forty teachers and four hundred children attending classes at different times of the day, so any help is gladly accepted. Twenty years before, one of the teachers had left to be a missionary in China, and it is still talked about as being both a loss to the church and a feather in their cap. The two naval officers and Maisie muck in, but don't lead any classes. However, it enables them all to have some tea and a chat together on Sundays. When it is necessary for the officers to attend the dockyard church for church parade, the whole group will change their religious allegiance together, reverting back the following week.

Maisie looks forward to seeing Peter. He really brightens her day and can switch from being amusing to talking seriously with her about any concerns she has at school. He will offer to help with outings for her girls, and she will never forget his kindness when he bought her whole class an orange each for Christmas.

Peter Barnes tactfully avoids the subject of Lieutenant Prescott whenever Maisie asks if he has heard from his colleague. Peter subtly deflects Maisie away by telling another amusing story about what has happened in the officers' mess or some other incident he is involved in.

He also has a string of stories from his family's pickling factory to regale them with. His two sisters feature greatly in these tales. The latest example is how they forgot to cook their own turkey for Christmas dinner. The bird was too big to go into the oven at home, so they took it to the factory to cook in the large oven there. But they ended up cooking so many turkeys and geese for their staff that their own remained uncooked. Peter had leave to go home for a few days and had been looking forward to a festive banquet, but had sat down with his family to a meal of cold cuts, pickles, and boiled potatoes instead of the traditional fayre they have promised him. His sisters Margaret and Edna had remembered to put their own Christmas pudding on to steam in the factory, but had left it too long, so the water boiled away, and the pudding burned. The household cook, Mrs Clements, was so cross with them for spoiling the Christmas dinner that she took herself off to bed on the pretext of a headache, leaving the sisters to do what they could to prepare a feast for the family with just the help of the kitchen maid. Maisie laughs so much that it is only afterwards that she realises that Peter didn't respond to her question about Edward.

"You must bring your sisters to meet us," Rosie urges one day. "You talk so much about them; we feel we know them."

"They never get a day off, there is only Sunday when the factory is closed," Peter responds.

"We can go to London to meet them!" Hattie suggests. "Do they get a half day on Saturday?"

Peter concedes that they do, so it is immediately agreed that on the next free Saturday, they will all get the train to the city to meet the Barnes sisters for the afternoon.

Maisie is as excited as a child at the prospect of going to London, as she has only been once before as a girl with her parents. She doesn't count the railway journeys where she has to change trains at Victoria, as she never goes beyond the station concourse. She desperately wants to go again and see the sights, but is unsure of where these might be in relationship to the pickling factory. She also wants to go on the Underground which she has never been on before, and asks Miss Garrett to help her plan a route in anticipation.

They arrange to meet Peter's sisters, Margaret, and Edna, at London Bridge Station at three o'clock on Saturday 17 January, with the hope that the weather will be good. So far January is either wet or dull, but suddenly it changes, and the temperature drops, leading to what starts as a bright crisp day where everything sparkles with a heavy frost, a precursor to the snow that will come the following week.

The group of friends catch an early train so they can do a little sightseeing and have lunch before meeting the sisters. Maisie has commandeered the window seat so she can get the first glimpse of the city centre as they come through the suburbs. She chooses the left-hand side of the train so she can see Rochester Cathedral as they pass through towards the river Medway. Peter sits next to her and offers Hattie the other window seat. Rosie and Sam sit on the right-hand side. Once or twice, Maisie reaches across and squeezes Peter's hand in her excitement. He squeezes hers back, captivated by her child like enthusiasm.

The train pulls into Charing Cross Station well before eleven o'clock. Rosie and Lieutenant Harris stun everyone on arrival as they have some plans of their own. Announcing that they will meet the group at London Bridge at three o'clock as arranged, they disappear into the London crowds before anyone else can say another word.

Peter, Hattie, and Maisie look at one another at a loss before Hattie takes charge and says, "Where shall we go first?"

They agree to walk along the Strand towards Fleet Street and then to St Paul's Cathedral. Maisie has never seen so many grand buildings. She is overwhelmed by the opulence of the many hotels and theatres. She doesn't know what to look at first. She is also amazed by how many omnibuses and other carriages there are, not to mention motor cars, of which there are dozens; she thinks it must be some sort of rally. The noise is almost deafening: the rattle of the carriages, the engine noises, and the clatter of hooves on cobbles make it difficult to carry on a conversation.

Maisie suddenly says, "Look! There's Rosie and Samuel going into that hotel! I wonder what they are up to?" She points towards the bevelled glass doors of a swanky hotel. "Do you think they are going for an early lunch?" she asks innocently. She is just about to raise her hand and wave when Hattie and Peter usher her away.

"I think they want to be alone," Hattie explains, as they hustle Maisie past the hotel foyer. Hattie glances in and there, to her consternation, is Lieutenant Prescott with a pretty young woman, evidently just leaving.

Lieutenant Harris greets his colleague and exchanges conspiratorial looks as they pass one another with their lady friends. Prescott doesn't recognise Rosie who does her best to hurry Harris on. As Prescott turns towards the exit, his eyes lock with Hattie's through the glass doors as she quickly seeks to distract Maisie from looking into the hotel interior for Rosie.

Hattie realises that Peter has also spotted Prescott, as he finds another amusing anecdote to gloss over what might prove a difficult moment. He is laughing and smiling with Maisie, but not before a look of anger has pass fleetingly across his face. Between them, they manoeuvre Maisie past the danger towards St Mary-Le-Strand church which straddles the road.

When eventually they arrive at St Paul's, Hattie thinks it safe to suggest stopping for some lunch in a chop house. She and Peter exchange looks conveying silent information about what they have both seen, knowing it will devastate Maisie. Hattie takes a silent vow to keep it from her.

By three o'clock, the whole group reassembles on the south side of London Bridge and look out for Peter's sisters. Rosie and Samuel arrive only moments before, looking flushed but happy. Hattie has by now found a moment to explain to

Maisie why the pair wanted to be on their own, and it is not raised again. It never ceases to amaze Hattie how naive Maisie can be.

Meanwhile, Rosie explains to Samuel about Maisie and Prescott, and he too knows not to mention seeing his colleague in the hotel. She manages to draw Hattie aside and whispers, "We saw Lieutenant Prescott in the lobby. He was with another woman. Samuel says he recognised her as she works in the naval outfitters in Portsmouth. He says it is rumoured in the mess that Edward has been seeing her on and off since he was a young cadet at Osborne College."

"Peter and I spotted Prescott with her when we saw you going into that hotel," Hattie quickly explains. "Fortunately, Maisie didn't. She will be heartbroken if she knows. Please don't tell her."

Right at that moment, Peter starts making a noise and flapping his arms like some giant seal. They quickly realise he is hallooing to his two sisters who have just hove into view.

The two new arrivals are dressed in superior quality clothing, both kitted out in hard wearing tweed skirts with fox fur collared coats. Edna wears dark blue, whilst Margaret wears brown. Maisie thinks how shabby her own grey woollen coat must look. She wears a knitted yellow beret, made for her as a Christmas present by one of her students. It keeps her ears warm and her hair in order, but she feels under dressed as the sisters wear very large flamboyant hats with a combination of ostrich feathers and artificial flowers. Indeed, Edna's seems to include some wax fruit, but Maisie doesn't want to stare so can't be sure. The two sisters are both in their early forties and have a no-nonsense aura around them.

The siblings acknowledge Peter's greeting with some hallooing of their own, much to Maisie's disbelief; they don't look like the kind of women given to such displays. They pick up their skirts and break into a trot to join their brother and his friends. There then passes several minutes of introductions, hand shaking, and broad grins shared by both parties.

"Let's walk towards Southwark Cathedral," Edna suggests,

"We can have some tea," says Margaret, linking her arm through Maisie's and Hattie's whilst Edna links hers with Peter. Rosie and Samuel are inseparable, so no attempt at arm linking is made there.

Maisie hopes for a view of the ships on the wide river Thames which eventually joins the sea at Sheerness, but the warehouses are packed in tightly around them so that it is impossible to see. They pass the medieval cathedral in its tiny precinct, hemmed in by so much commerce that the story of

Jesus in the Temple springs to Maisie's mind. This is quite a different London to the one just over the river, where all the grand hotels jostle with glittering shops selling expensive luxury goods.

Maisie would very much have liked to be holding Peter's arm rather than his sister's as some drunken sailors explode out from one of the pubs in a hail of fists and swear words; she knows he will make her feel safe. "Just like home," Hattie laughs, somewhat nervously, as they pass the protagonists at what Maisie thinks is not enough of a safe distance.

They walk past flower sellers on the pavements offering small posies for a penny, past dray carts replenishing the pubs, past a group of ragged children playing football with the skull of a sheep. A stray dog scratches in a pile of rubbish, looking for a meal, whilst a mangy cat that even Hattie would be reluctant to stroke, sits high on a wall looking down on the scene below.

Men stand around smoking pipes, swearing, and spitting. One takes himself off to urinate in an alley, without the least concern that the ladies will see him. A couple of gaudily dressed, hard eyed women stand on the corner attempting to show a little flesh, despite the cold, in a bid to attract some custom from the sailors. They twist and turn to show off their wares to the music of a barrel organ being played across the street, whilst giving the seamen the "glad eye." Maisie averts her gaze and wonders where there can possibly be anywhere suitable to take tea, when they stop outside a small café which looks lost amongst the pubs and warehouses.

"This way," says Margaret.

"In here," Edna says, ushering the party in, as though leading them to safety.

Inside is an oasis of calm amidst the maritime battle raging outside between the different nationalities of seamen and the locals. It is just everyday life, so close to the greatest port in the world. The owner comes over and shows them to a large table bedecked in a red and white checked cloth.

"Wonderful Francesco." Edna thanks him as he pulls out the chairs for the ladies. "He's Italian," Margaret explains, as though the party from the coast will not know. However, in their own town of Sheerness, there are several Italian families running ice cream parlours along the promenade. But they don't want to appear rude to Peter's sisters by saying they know an Italian when they meet one.

Margaret and Edna have pre-ordered earlier that day and a selection of Italian dainties are produced along with teas and coffees. As they all tuck in, the sisters set about quizzing Maisie about herself, but almost ignoring the other women.

"So, what school do you teach at?" Edna asks.

"The Broadway school," answers Rosie.

"How long have you been there, Maisie?" Margaret continues.

"Only since October, but Hattie and Rosie have been there a lot longer," Maisie responds.

"Yes, I started as a pupil teacher," says Rosie proudly.

"Really," interrupts Margaret, "And what is your specialist subject?" She directs this question to Maisie, by slightly turning away from the others.

"French, but it isn't on the curriculum," Maisie replies.

"Mine's physical education," Hattie tells the sisters, "I run a swimming class for the girls."

"How interesting. Do you swim, Maisie?" Edna says, glossing over Hattie's response.

Every time Hattie or Rosie answers, they quickly turn the conversation back to Maisie. It is like they are interviewing her for a position in their business.

Fortunately, they are skilled at appearing to chat, as they use this as a cover to run the pickle factory when, in fact, they are shrewd businesswomen in a world of men. They decide Maisie will make a suitable wife for Peter, and they vow they will do everything they can to make it happen.

Soon, it is time to go, and Margaret and Edna insist that they walk back to London Bridge station via the factory, so that they can say goodbye to them there. But really, they want Maisie to realise Peter is a man of substance, in the hope she will see him in a new light.

Margaret shouts, "Do keep in touch, Maisie,"

"Yes, please write," Edna adds, as they disappear through the front door of the factory amid many good wishes from the rest of the party. Peter leads the group back to catch the train home. This time, Maisie ensures she links arms with the tall, imposing officer, and, with Hattie on the other side, they pass through Borough Market without incident.

## February 1914

Miss Riviere, the local suffragette, eventually keeps her promise and invites Hattie to tea and encourages her to bring along some like-minded friends, so Hattie invites Rosie, Betty, and Maisie. The party catch the omnibus to Eastchurch village, and Miss Riviere arranges to meet them outside the church. To their awe, she is waiting in a shiny new red Riley motorcar that she drives herself. None of them know any other lady who can drive.

"Get in, girls," she calls from the driver's seat. She is dressed in a motoring costume: a long wool coat covering her skirt and blouse, and she wears a knitted sweater for extra warmth which gives her more manoeuvrability than a jacket. Directly under her coat, she wears an all-covering smock to protect her clothes should she need to look at the engine for any reason, not that she has any idea of how the internal combustion engine works. On her head she wears a visor cap secured by a long silk scarf against the wind.

"I need to drive myself to my other home in London where I help out at *WSPU HQ*, so I bought this little jalopy," she explains at their incredulous looks. "I've had five driving lessons from Mr Cross. Most people only have two or three, if any, but I like to do things properly."

They all squash into the red leather seats and hold firmly onto their hats. Miss Riviere drives them all to her bungalow in about five minutes flat, whilst keeping up a constant narrative about what a wonderful invention the motor car is.

Miss Riviere's bungalow is situated on her large productive farm. Living in a bungalow is a symbol of her Bohemianism. The contemporary style of home has become the building type of choice for the aspiring upper middle classes seeking an affordable second home in which to enjoy "the weekend." Miss Riviere is taken with this latest trend, so whilst her main residence is in London enabling her to attend the *WSPU HQ* offices easily, she needs somewhere to live on her farm. She visited Birchington to see where the famed artist Dante Gabriel Rossetti had been living at the time of his death in 1882 and, like many others, she had been delighted at the modern layout of the "*Rossetti Bungalow*." She immediately chose the style for her residence on her farm on the cliff top at Eastchurch. She magnanimously allows her estate manager to occupy the ancient, cold, and draughty farmhouse with his family.

As well as the farm, Miss Riviere owns other property around the country. She also has a substantial private income. She joined the *Women's Tax Resistance League,* when it was founded in

1909, and every year she refuses to pay her taxes, quoting the League's motto of, *"No vote, no tax!"* Not quite as catchy as the American War of Independence motto of *"No taxation without representation!,"* but they don't want to copy a bunch of men. Once again, the tax collector, Mr Mottson, has taken out a distraint order on her goods for the fifth successive year and plans to sell them in May at the Clarence Road Bethel church hall, to cover her debts if payment is not received in time. But every year, her taxes are paid for her by "friends," to save the embarrassment of the sale.

As an ardent campaigner of women's suffrage, Miss Riviere never misses an opportunity to promote the cause and argues eloquently with anyone who cares, or doesn't care, to listen. However, despite the work of her fellow activists, the Government remains stubborn in its attitude to votes for women. After *The Parliamentary Franchise (Women) Bill* is narrowly defeated in 1912, Miss Riviere has become radicalised and joins the *Women's Social and Political Union (WSPU)*.

This local firebrand regularly reports on the suffrage meetings she attends in *"The Vote"* and *"The Suffragette."* She'd been particularly happy with the last meeting she organised, when on the *WSPU* annual summer caravan tour. It was the first in Sheerness. Her message is well received by the local men, as well as by the women, as forty per cent of men are also unable to vote, and there are a lot of disgruntled, disenfranchised working men in the town.

It is at this meeting that Hattie first met Miss Riviere. She had gone there with Rosie and her sister Betty. Afterwards, Hattie stopped to speak to Miss Riviere and has subsequently met her a number of times for tea in the town. She even attended a big rally in Chatham as part of that lady's party. It is Miss Riviere who introduces Hattie to red lipstick. In 1912, Elizabeth Arden handed out red lipsticks to women marching for the vote on New York's Fifth Avenue; the British suffragettes also adopted it as a badge of honour and defiance. Miss Riviere is an advocate of the cosmetic and now Hattie wears it all the time outside work, and encourages her friends to do the same.

Miss Riviere parks outside the bungalow and ushers them through the front door into the sitting room where tea is already set. She disappears into the kitchen to ask her cook to boil the kettle and get her maid to assist her in removing her motoring garments in the bedroom. Miss Riviere is only really interested in emancipation for the better off classes, so keeps a number of staff, including a "chauffeur come gardener" who keeps the car running and does most of the driving – especially the long trips to

114

London. The staff reside in two former tied cottages next to the bungalow, whilst the chauffeur lives over the garage, which was formerly a stable.

When she returns, she launches straight into her agenda, "I'm glad you have come. I wonder if you might be interested in getting more involved in the cause?" she says, whilst pouring the tea that the maid sets before her.

"Certainly," Hattie responds immediately. "I'm happy to give out leaflets and help at meetings."

The other schoolteachers say nothing.

"Well, I am hoping you will be a bit more active. *'Deeds not words'* is our motto after all," Miss Riviere replies.

"What kind of deeds?" asks Betty.

"Well, something to grab the newspaper headlines," Miss Riviere says, appearing to concentrate on the teapot.

The women look at one another. They have all read about the suffragettes exploits and know they face imprisonment for their actions. Miss Riviere has previously been arrested, but the same "friends" who pay her taxes always pay her fines. So, to her feigned disappointment, she has never been imprisoned in Holloway or force fed, although she maintains that she is always willing to do so for her beliefs. She boasts that she covets the *WSPU* prison badge, which she sees as a medal won for the cause. No one knows who these friends are who thwart her ambitions, but it is believed to be her brother, a rich businessman who married into minor aristocracy, and is always looking to avert any scandal.

"There really is no risk," Miss Riviere clarifies dismissively, handing round the teacups.

"How is there no risk?" asks Hattie. The others look at her in alarm, as engaging in the conversation can lead to engaging in the action.

"Well, the *WSPU* have been setting fires to grab headlines, so I thought we could set fire to the odd haystack or two," she responds, as she passes the milk jug to Betty.

"But how will that be risk free?" Hattie persists.

"They will be my haystacks," Miss Riviere states, without fuss.

Hattie exchanges looks with the others; they remain unconvinced, but she nudges Maisie and says, "Go on, it will be an adventure. We will be real suffragettes."

Miss Riviere spots a weakening in the group and jumps in, "We can burn two or three of my haystacks, then retreat back here. If anyone is caught, I will say I don't want to press charges, but it will make the papers, which is the whole point."

Hattie starts to laugh and claps her hands together, "Why don't you and I do it, Maisie?"

Maisie's eyes are as wide as saucers, "But what if someone is injured?"

"There won't be anyone else around. Just us and we will be careful," Miss Riviere responds, closing down any argument.

"Well, I'm in!" says Hattie, whilst the other women remain silent.

"Good," responds Miss Riviere, "We will do it next Sunday night when there is a full moon to see by."

Hattie wears Maisie down with her talk of adventure and real suffragettes, and she agrees to go to Miss Riviere's bungalow on Sunday evening. February's weather is exceptional with warm south westerlies bringing unseasonably balmy conditions, but it starts to change to something more wintery in the late afternoon.

Maisie meets Hattie on the main road into town where Miss Riviere has promised to pick them up in her Riley motorcar. Hattie is carrying a large leather bag. A wind has started to get up, and the winter stars are hidden behind thickening cloud.

"We won't be able to set fire to anything if it rains," Maisie whispers, hoping the mission will be called off.

"It's not raining yet," replies Hattie, keyed up for her first suffragette adventure.

"What about the wind? That will make it difficult, won't it? Wouldn't it be better another time?"

"We will be fine. Miss Riviere has done this kind of thing before."

Just then, Miss Riviere's car comes into sight, and she halloos to them, waving, and not really paying much attention to the road. She pulls up beside them shouting, "Hop in!" After performing a nineteen-point turn in the road, they speed away, back towards her farm.

"Did you bring a change of clothes?" she asks, peering at Hattie through the driver's mirror.

"Yes, my friend, Will, from the Cricket Club lent me some clothes to disguise ourselves with. Plus, men's clothes are more practical," Hattie responds for both of them, indicating the cricket bag that she is clutching. "We can never run in a hobble hemmed skirt, no matter how fashionable!" she jokes.

"The weather is changing. I think it will rain. We can't set fire to your haystacks in the rain," Maisie bursts out.

"Nonsense!" says Miss Riviere dismissively. "Haystacks are always dry under the top layers."

"I mean the wind will blow out our lucifers," responds Maisie still trying to bring the conversation back round to reason.

"We will soon get a good blaze going!" says Miss Riviere, obviously intent on fulfilling her mission.

When they arrive at her bungalow, Miss Riviere's cook has a hot beef stew waiting for them in the modern gas cooker.

"Tuck in," Miss Riviere commands, inviting the women to sit at the dining table as her maid brings in steaming plates of food. "You will need to keep out the cold." She pours them each a large measure of whisky to help with the insulation process.

Maisie struggles to eat anything as she is so nervous, but drinks two large glasses of whisky which makes the adventure a bit less scary. Miss Riviere explains which three haystacks are for burning. "That partial stack, over there, has been left from last year and has gone musty. My steward tells me it can't be used for animal bedding because it might lead to respiratory problems if the animals inhale the spores from the mould, so it will be no loss to the farm. It should burn quite nicely. The second one is also partly used. It's that not- so- tall one over there," she says, as she gesticulates vaguely towards some black bee-hive shaped lumps in the distance. "The third is a bit further away. I dare say you will find it easily enough as I have left a red bucket next to each stack so you will know if it's the right one. You should be able to reach the top without too much trouble as they are only partial stacks, so you can set the fires more easily. There, I think I've thought of everything," she helpfully points out.

"Where will you be when we are setting fire to your haystacks?" asks Maisie, realising that Miss Riviere is not coming with them.

"Back here, of course. It simply won't do if I am caught at the scene. Everyone will know it is me and it will be a fruitless gesture, as they are my haystacks. It will never make the newspapers," she responds, as though Maisie should have worked that out for herself. "Now, wrap up warm in your men's disguises, it's cold out there."

Maisie feels slightly piqued; Miss Riviere will be safely indoors, whilst she and Hattie are assigned to do the "*deeds not words.*" She was ridding herself of her musty old stacks, which she will claim on the insurance, leaving her in pocket rather than out of it. At the same time, she will gain herself merit marks with the *WSPU*.

Hattie and Maisie withdraw to the bedroom to change. Miss Riviere's maid follows them to assist, but they decline her help.

120

"Are you sure about this, Hattie?" asks Maisie, as she wrestles with the alien clothing Hattie has given her, whilst attempting to hide her hair under a workman's cap. "We are risking injury and possible imprisonment for Miss Riviere, and she is not risking anything, not even her musty old haystacks. It's not like you to be reckless. You are always the sensible one."

Hattie begins to have doubts, but can't see how they can back out now. It is almost ten o'clock and the omnibuses will have stopped running by the time they walk back to the village. They are dependent on Miss Riviere to take them home or face a six mile walk in the dark. She tries to settle her own nerves and Maisie's by saying, "It will be fine. Members of the *WSPU* are doing much bigger and more dangerous missions than this all the time!"

Miss Riviere gives them another glass of whisky each to keep out the cold and to give them Dutch courage as she provides them with all they need – lucifer matches, suffragette leaflets, and a new-fangled flashlight with the latest tungsten bulb. She switches off her electric light in the hallway of the bungalow, points to the dark humps of the haystacks in the distance, and sends her foot soldiers off to do their duty.

The flashlight is useless as the battery can only produce light for a short time, then it needs to be switched off to rest before it can give out light again. The two women run across the fields in darkness as the thickening clouds obscures the almost full moon that should have lit their way that February night.

They reach the first stack and find the red bucket; it is the right haystack. Hattie loosens up some of the dryer hay from under the top layer, whilst Maisie holds the temperamental flashlight for her.

"Here goes!" says Hattie, striking a match and shielding it from the wind as she reaches up to the tinder she has arranged. It catches immediately and the two women quickly withdraw to a safe distance to watch it take hold. They remember to leave their leaflets in the red bucket, far enough away to be out of danger of catching fire. "Okay," says Hattie, satisfied that their first target has been achieved, "Now, to find the second."

This is easier said than done as it is much further from Miss Riviere's bungalow, and it hadn't really been clear where she meant. Once more, they run across the fields in the dark past the landmarks that flag their way. There is still a third haystack to be found somewhere too.

They come into the village and can see the second partial haystack some distance away, not far from the new Royal Naval Flying School. There is no red bucket when they get there, but there is a red watering can. They decide it must be the right one as there is no other partial stack in sight. This one is much closer to the road than the other and they feel more vulnerable to being spotted.

As they start on their second mission of the night, they can hear men's voices getting louder as they get nearer. Hattie and Maisie retreat behind the haystack to see a party of four naval officers walking back down the road to the Flying School from the local pub, laughing and smoking as they do so.

"I'm just going for a jimmy!" calls one of the men, as he veers off towards the haystack, cigarette in hand. Hattie and Maisie crouch behind the stack, their equipment ready for their deed as the man lumbers around, almost falling over them. It is Lieutenant Peter Barnes.

Maisie and Hattie shush him, pulling him down beside them. "What are you two doing here?" he asks under his breath, dropping his cigarette end on some of the loose hay Hattie has dislodged.

"Just out for a stroll," hisses back Hattie. Barnes' colleagues keep chatting and laughing as they walk towards the camp. Hattie watches them like a cat. "When I say run, Peter, you run. Okay?" she says, as she starts to busy herself with the task in hand.

"What's going on?" he tries to ask, but Maisie quite unlike herself and feeling the effects of the whisky, suddenly kisses him full on the mouth to shut him up.

Just then, Hattie jumps up and throws some lighted tinder onto the stack, and shouts in a stage whisper, "Run!"

At first it doesn't catch light, but the inner heat from the stack makes the whole thing easily combustible and up it goes with a whoosh. Peter's cigarette has also started a small blaze on the scattered hay. The dancing flames light up the sky making a beacon that can be seen from the distant Flying School and alerts the officers who are walking in the opposite direction, that something is amiss.

Hattie, Maisie, and Peter run towards the main road beyond the village, whilst Peter's companions, hearing the sudden roar of the fire, turn back. They start calling Peter's name, fearing he might be caught in the inferno as he was last seen disappearing behind it, and wondering if he has accidently set it alight with his cigarette. Maisie turns and shouts at Peter, "You had better go back. Say you tried to catch us, but couldn't." And with that, the two women run as fast as they can in their men's trousers, under the cover of darkness.

Peter stumbles and picks himself up as one of his colleagues starts running towards him. "I'm okay," Peter shouts, "They got away. Just some kids. I must have disturbed them."

"No," says his colleague, Lieutenant Jones. "Look at this, there are leaflets everywhere. They are some of those bally suffragettes."

Barnes and Jones run back to the burning haystack, which is now truly alight, setting the sky aglow as the smell of burning fills their nostrils. The first haystack can be seen burning in the distance, and the officers are concerned the fire pump can't deal with both fires at once, so a number of men from the Flying School are called upon to surround the fire and attempt to put out the flames by forming a bucket chain to a nearby pond, whilst waiting for the pump to be brought from the village.

Hattie and Maisie run back to the bungalow, where Miss Riviere is waiting.

"I only saw two sets of flames," she queries, as she lets them back in through the front door.

"We were nearly caught by some officers from the Flying School," says Hattie.

"You shouldn't have been that side of the main road. That's not my haystack!" bemoans Miss Riviere. "You had better come in and get changed, and I will take you home, although I don't know what I can say to Mr Beasley tomorrow, now you have burned his haystack. Honestly, I should have done it myself."

They drive back into town in silence as Miss Riviere sulks at the incompetence of her foot soldiers. Hattie and Maisie hang their heads, wondering what they have done.

The weather is extremely wet and boisterous the next day. Hattie and Maisie sit in a corner of the staff room to eat their lunch together and discuss the evening's events. It was late when Miss Riviere dropped them at their respective homes, and they haven't had a chance to review things till now.

Hattie is very unhappy with the mission. Miss Riviere has made it clear she blames them for setting fire to the wrong haystack, and she will have nothing to do with them should there be any comebacks on that one.

Lieutenant Peter Barnes had practically fallen over them, and his companions have seen the two women running away. They are convinced they will be caught.

"If we go to prison, we will lose our jobs, we won't be able to pay our rent, and we will end up having to throw ourselves on the mercy of our families," Hattie says mournfully. "None of my brothers will want me."

"Miss Garrett will chuck me out and my aunt has made it very clear that her stipend won't support both Mother and me. I don't know what I will do," responds Maisie.

"Miss Riviere is only concerned with herself. She is showing very little sorority now."

"Let's hope the local police don't question her."

"Do you think Peter will say it is us?"

"No, I think they will have been here by now if he has. Arson is a serious crime."

"I so wanted to be a real suffragette! I went to Emily Davis's funeral with Rosie last year. I was really inspired. I was so pleased that Miss Riviere singled me out and invited me to tea at her home and asked me to bring like-minded friends. You can be so wrong about people, can't you," Hattie sighs. She bites her nails with worry, "I'm sorry I dragged you into it. You were right to be cautious."

"When are we due to meet up with Peter next?" asks Maisie.

"Thursday, at the reading group," responds Hattie.

"I hope Peter doesn't think less of us for this. I would hate for him to end up in trouble because of us."

"I'm sure he won't."

There is a pause as Maisie considers what to say next, then she blurts out, "I kissed him to keep him quiet whilst you set the fire," she says, with a suppressed giggle.

"What!" gasps Hattie, "You didn't say!"

127

"There wasn't a right moment."

"My goodness! No wonder he didn't blow our cover. He's been sweet on you from when he first met you," Hattie says.

"I'm sure it was the whisky Miss Riviere gave us that made me so bold! We'll have to see what Thursday brings," Maisie laughs, covering her face with her hands to hide her blushes.

In the end, they have worried unnecessarily. The Eastchurch village policeman assumes Miss Riviere is responsible as her suffragette sympathies are well-known. He telegraphs her brother who arranges to pay damages to Mr Beasley, averting any proceedings. As the other haystack is Miss Riviere's, no charges are brought and the constable completes the station log saying the fires are set by, "Persons unknown, possibly suffragettes from London."

When the schoolteachers meet with Lieutenant Peter Barnes at the reading group on Thursday, there is a moment's embarrassment as he struggles to find what to say. He picks some imaginary dust from his trousers before he eventually says, "I hope you ladies are well since I last saw you?"

"Yes, very well thank you, Peter," responds Hattie, "We are keeping warm as best we can this winter in front of a lovely fire."

Hattie and Maisie start to giggle, and soon Peter joins them.

"You must tell me all about it," he laughs. Inwardly Maisie and Hattie sigh with relief. "I told my sisters how I bumped into some suffragettes recently; they are most interested. They are strong advocates for women's suffrage but are a bit more moderate."

"I think these two local suffragettes are also likely to be moderate from now on," Hattie responds, still smarting from Miss Riviere's fickle behaviour towards them.

After the meeting, Peter catches Maisie's arm and draws her to one side, "I wonder if you might care to come to tea with my sisters one Sunday?" he asks.

Maisie's stomach knots. She can see the look in the lieutenant's eyes, and knows he hopes there was more to their kiss behind the haystack than she feels. She doesn't want to lead him on, but at the same time, she really likes Peter and wants to stay friends; they enjoy the same things and share a sense of humour. He makes her feel safe. So, she says, "Yes, that will be lovely."

Peter's face brightens considerably. "I will arrange a Sunday, but it may not be for a couple of weeks as I'm being temporarily assigned to the Flying School for a little longer and it's more difficult to get away."

The arrangement is left open ended, much to Maisie's relief.

**March 1914**

Lieutenant Barnes returns from his secondment to the Flying School early in the month and decides to woo Maisie in earnest. She is the loveliest girl he has ever met, and she is kind, intelligent, and fun to be with. What is more, he thinks he has a genuine rapport with her; they like the same books and music, the same kind of outings and share a sense of humour.

He reasons that she must feel something for him, otherwise why did she kiss him behind the haystack which she and Hattie were firebombing? But she seems distant whenever they meet up and always has some reason why she can't come to tea with his sisters. Other outings he arranges to the theatre or a trip out on the train will always end up including Hattie or Rosie.

One day, he came into the reading group to find Maisie in tears.

"I'm sorry to cry like this," she explains, as she folds and refolds her handkerchief, trying to find a dry spot. "Little Penny Maloney, one of the girls in my class has died from diphtheria. Her little heart failed. Everyone at school is so tearful, it is so sad. She was such a dear sweet thing and so pretty. We will all miss her."

"Why don't I take you out at the weekend to cheer you up?" Peter suggests. "We can have a trip out to see Rochester Cathedral."

"That would be lovely, I know that Miss Garrett is very keen on Dickens. And you always say he is your favourite author too. And I'm sure Ena, and Hattie, will like to come as they will all feel the need for a treat after such a sad week at school," she concludes. Poor Peter once again finds himself unable to get Maisie on her own.

It is a lovely early spring day, and Miss Garrett is very knowledgeable about Charles Dickens and his connection to Rochester. She organises a walking tour to see where he lived at Gads Hill, then on to Restoration House that features as Miss Havisham's house in *Great Expectations,* before finishing at the Six Poor Travellers Alms House which appear in Dickens' Christmas short story *The Seven Poor Travellers.*

They go for luncheon at the Royal Victoria and Bull Hotel, where it is reputed Dickens stayed on many occasions and included the hotel in two of his most famous works, *The Pickwick Papers,* and *Great Expectations.* Miss Garrett reads the extracts from Dickens' works for a full half hour to the others to prove her point.

Afterwards, the ladies all thank Peter for a wonderful day. Miss Garrett says, "What a lovely idea of yours to organise it, we really needed that little pick-me-up after the week we've had." But all he wants is to be alone with Maisie. He just can't seem to get her to himself, so that they can talk and be together.

When he next visits his sisters, he explains his predicament, and how Maisie has kissed him. Edna listens patiently and exchanges glances with Margaret.

"What kind of kiss was it, Peter?" she asks.

"Was it passionate or just a kiss as a greeting, like the continentals do?" asks Margaret.

"It was passionate, she meant it. But now she seems to be avoiding me," he laments.

"Well, if the mountain won't come to Mohammed," starts Edna.

"Then Mohammed must go to the mountain!" finishes Margaret.

"We will visit you next Sunday, and we will go to tea together then."

"If necessary, with all her friends," the two sisters conclude.

A plan is devised where Peter will arrange tea with Hattie and Maisie at a local café the following week, after Sunday school. Edna and Margaret will be there already as the two sisters will say they want to see their brother's naval base and decide to surprise him.

Meanwhile, Peter decides to take some direct action. Hattie let slip that it is Maisie's birthday, and he decides to buy her a small present. Once or twice, Maisie has mentioned how she admires Ena's jewellery. He thinks a small trinket might be acceptable.

On his next free afternoon, he goes to the local jewellers in The Crescent, opposite the rather ostentatious cast iron town clock which is said to be the tallest in Kent. It was built in 1902 to celebrate the Coronation of King Edward VII and rang out the hours. It is where the group of friends assemble for their outings as it is in the centre of the town. It is also the focal point for his colleagues to gather when they come into the High Street to do their errands. Peter is concerned that someone from the naval base might walk by and see him going into the jewellers, or one of his friends might see him there. Eventually, Peter screws up his courage to go in and enquire about what might be a suitable present.

Inside, the shop is filled with glass fronted cabinets containing silver photo frames, clocks, ladies and gents fob watches and velvet trays of more delicate things, like rings, bracelets, pendants, and earrings.

The jeweller asks him, "What kind of lady are you buying for, sir? What are her likes and dislikes?"

Peter thinks hard and says, "She's a suffragette!"

The jeweller looks on disapprovingly. He is one of the many people who see suffragettes as being unfeminine, disruptive, and simply undesirable. However, a customer is a customer, He is not above taking their money, so has stocked a few items made with white, purple, and green stones for sale to any militant lady who might cross his threshold. He reaches into a cabinet and produces a tray of brooches to show the lieutenant.

"This may be just the thing," he says, and points to a dainty gold brooch set with tiny seed pearls in a crescent with peridot and amethyst stones along the bar. The jeweller explains that the stones are the colours favoured by suffragettes. Purple stand for loyalty and dignity, white for purity, and green for hope.

It is the prettiest thing Peter has seen and he immediately buys it, knowing it will appeal to Maisie.

The jeweller places it in a small black leather box lined with watered silk, which Peter puts into his breast pocket ready for the right moment to give it to Maisie.

The following Sunday afternoon, the weather continues cold and wet with wintery showers, so their regular plan of a walk along the promenade after

Sunday school is abandoned. Visibility is so poor that Southend is just a bruise-coloured smudge across the estuary.

"It's too cold to walk today. Let's go to the tea shop now," suggests Hattie to the rest of the usual Sunday gang of Maisie, Betty, Rosie, and the Lieutenants Barnes and Harris.

This throws Peter into confusion as his two sisters need to get to the café first. He sets about trying to stall them by saying, "But there are some interesting ships in at the moment. I'd really like to see them from the shore here."

But the inclement weather means his companions are unwilling to stand around and pass the time of day. Even Lieutenant Harris cannot manage to be interested as the wind is making his eyes water.

They set off along the High Street, passing the blank closed shop fronts as quickly as they can to get out of the sleet. Their favourite tea shop welcomes them with a pool of reflected yellow light on the wet pavement where slushy puddles gather icy particles. The door yields with a cheery ring of the bell and the warm smell of fresh toast hits the party, as the hot steam from the urn spirals lazily to the ceiling.

"Fancy seeing you here," calls Edna from a strategically chosen table for two, next to a much larger table ideal for the six friends.

"Please join us!" calls Margaret.

"Lovely to see you again, Maisie."

"Do come and sit next to me."

Maisie finds herself seated next to Edna and across from Margaret, as the café owner obligingly pushes the tables together. They manoeuvre Peter into sitting beside Margaret and position the rest of the group at the other end of the table.

Edna and Margaret swing into action and begin to subtly interrogate Maisie.

"Do tell us about your suffragette activities."

"We are very keen on women's suffrage ourselves."

"Looking back, it was so scary, but fun too!" Hattie exclaims.

"I bet it was!" says Edna.

"Were you scared Maisie?" asks Margaret.

Whenever Hattie ventures any remark, they quickly turn the conversation back to Maisie, just as they have done when the party went to London.

Then, with a killer blow, Edna asks, "And what happened behind the haystack?"

The rest of the party watch as Maisie blushes scarlet and mumbles something inaudible. But this is news to Rosie who is not prepared to let it go. She jumps in with, "What did you say Maisie? Why are your cheeks so red?"

"Peter and I kissed," Maisie blurts out. "It is a mistake! Miss Riviere had given us whisky for Dutch courage. I forgot myself in the excitement. I'm sorry."

Poor Peter wishes the ground will open up and swallow him whole. He has hoped his sisters will find out how Maisie feels about him, but instead, it seems Maisie is doing her best to forget all about it. He wants to find the right moment to give Maisie the brooch he has bought for her birthday, but it will not be possible now.

The two sisters realise their error, and make light of it saying, "These things happen in the "heat" of the moment!"

"I'm sure you were all "fired" up!" alluding to the firebombing of the haystacks.

But Rosie and Betty are enjoying Maisie's discomfiture for a change and decide to rib her about it mercilessly. "Oh, Maisie, you were canoodling behind the haystacks!"

"What will Miss Garrett say?"

All of a sudden, Maisie stands up and says, "I'm sorry, I must go and prepare for school tomorrow," upsetting her teacup as she does so, and leaves them to it. Hattie and Peter, leap up after her, but Edna grabs his hand and whispers, "Let her go." He sinks back down, and Hattie goes after her friend alone out into the cold. Betty and Rosie make their apologies for overstepping the mark and say they too need to prepare for school. Lieutenant Harris leaves with them, offering to escort them home and leaving the siblings to discuss the fallout.

## April 1914

Rosie and Lieutenant Harris get engaged in April when she discovers she is pregnant. Counting the days, it was probably their outing to London that is responsible for this accident. When Rosie realises she has fallen, there is much discussion between the friends as to the plan of attack to ensure Lieutenant Harris will do the right thing.

Rosie is sure Samuel will stand by her, but these things are by no means certain. Rosie's younger "sister" is in fact her niece, a product of a brief encounter between Betty and a soldier who went off to serve the Empire and died of Malaria before he had the chance to return.

Mrs Dale had sent Betty to stay with a "sick" aunt in Suffolk, and at the same time, her mother started to "fill out" with a later life baby, which arrived unexpectedly whilst she was visiting her daughter and her sick sister. New mother, daughter, and baby return together. Betty relinquished nursing the sick aunt to another cousin to assist her mother with the new baby, surprisingly named Alberta. Some people mentioned that Betty's young man was called Albert, but they learn it is a family name and just a coincidence that the names are similar.

There are also those who whisper that Betty and Rosie's father, the errant merchant seaman, hasn't been seen in his home port in more than two years, so even the most overdue of babies should have arrived before Alberta did. But it isn't in the least uncommon for families to have one infant whose arrival is a miracle of arithmetic. Only single mothers are seen as "fallen women." Where creative solutions are arrived at, the woman's reputation is saved.

Lieutenant Samuel Harris is steady and reliable, not to mention, as a naval officer, a good prospect. On learning that Rosie is to be a mother, he immediately seeks permission to marry, buys a ring, and does his duty. He writes to his family in Plymouth, who are all seafaring folk and tells them the happy news, inviting them to the forthcoming wedding.

Rosie says yes without hesitation and starts planning the event with the help of her friends and family. As her father is not around, it is arranged for one of her uncles to give her away. Lieutenant Harris could have paid for a wedding breakfast, but as it is traditional for the bride's family to pay and Mrs Dale has her pride, the teachers rally round to make food for the reception held in the Napier Road Hall, following the service in the nearby Congregational church. Ena helps organise the menu using the school's new domestic science classroom to provide enough ovens for the baking, and she undertakes to make the wedding cake herself. Miss Garrett intends to stay away as she disapproves of shotgun weddings. However, her nosiness gets the better of her and, in the end, she can't let herself miss out.

Rosie gives her notice in at school to fulfil her wifely duties. Her colleagues club together to buy her a silver toast rack and the children contribute their pennies to buy an electroplated egg cup and matching spoon, just the one, as they don't know Lieutenant Harris, so don't feel the need to buy him a present.

The school children, wearing their Sunday best, form a guard of honour outside the church and make posies of wildflowers (and some gathered from the municipal gardens), to scatter before Rosie and her new husband. Daisy Scott and her sister Florence have not been to school for a few days as neither has any boots to wear. However, they arrive at the church wearing what are obviously their two older brothers' boots, lent to them for this special occasion so they can join the guard of honour. But not before they delight in sending up sparks from the Blakey's set in the boys' boots – a treat usually denied to girls.

Samuel and Rosie engage a photographer to capture their big day for posterity. To many people's amazement, the studio sends a woman apprentice instead of a gentleman. She is remarkably confident and more tactful than a man might be. She helps Rosie to strategically place her bouquet of roses and gypsophilia or as it is more commonly called, *Babies Breath*, over her growing bump.

Afterwards, the happy couple depart for the train station in a friend's car for a short honeymoon to Plymouth, to meet the rest of the groom's family. Lieutenant Harris intends to take a property near his family home for them to live in when he is next posted, but this might alter depending on where that posting will be. So, Rosie is initially going to remain living with her mother, whilst Samuel is still stationed in the dockyard. Until the move happens, her life will be one of local domestication, and her friends continue to treat her as they did when she was single.

Lieutenant Peter Barnes attends the wedding with his fellow officers. It is the first time he has seen Maisie since the awkward tea party with his sisters. She sits with Hattie on the bride's side of the church. She looks so pretty in a pale blue blouse that matches her eyes. She has her best hat on, to which she has added some bluebells, and these too bring out her eyes, he thinks. He tries not to stare at her, but it is almost impossible.

She looks up from her hymn book and catches his eye. She gives a little smile, which Peter returns and is rewarded with a bigger smile.

After the wedding reception in the church hall, the young people decant to a pub near the sea front. There are tables and chairs in the adjoining garden which enables the customers to enjoy the sea view. It is still a little cold, but the sun is shining, and everyone is in a holiday mood. Maisie and Hattie sit at a table with Will and some other colleagues drinking lemonade as the men smoke cigarettes, when Peter comes over and asks if he might join them. The other naval officers return to the officers' mess, and he is alone. They make space for him to pull a chair across, and he sits down near Maisie.

"I'm so sorry about my sisters," he manages to say, not looking either woman in the eye, but staring at his big feet.

Hattie and Maisie, both smile. "Please don't worry about it," says Hattie reaching across to place her hand on his.

"I'm sorry too," says Maisie, but not mentioning what it is she is sorry about. "I'm glad we are all friends again."

Peter stares balefully into his beer, accepting this is the best he can hope for; the birthday brooch remains in his pocket as the group chats about how lovely the wedding was.

## May 1914

It is the first cricket match of the year between the schoolteachers and the navy. Lieutenant Peter Barnes arranges it with Bill West the schoolteachers' captain. The boys' teachers are keen for a little respite following the dockyard exams. All the boys' schools across town are geared up to this annual selection. Those students who pass will be offered apprenticeships according to where they are placed in the results table; the high scorers getting the skilled jobs leading to careers as draughtsman or shipwrights, and the low scorers offered jobs as labourers or storemen. It will be a job for life, leading to a pension with medals for long service and paid holidays. It is always a relief when the process is over, and a friendly game of cricket is just the tonic needed.

Hattie is officially twelfth man, and when the team and their supporters turn up at the navy's ground, there are slight rumblings from the other officers about her appearance, not least because she is wearing trousers. However, Bill points out they were completely open that Hattie is a woman when the fixture was arranged, and the navy men, as gentlemen, accept. After all, they are a team of officers not men. Luckily, Lieutenant Barnes talks them round and some think it will be good sport to show the teachers how superior they are, especially a team "handicapped" by having a woman on their team.

As usual, Hattie replaces one of the other team members who is "injured," so she goes out to bat. She, of course, wins the grudging respect of the officers for hitting three sixes and scoring forty runs before being run out by her partner. Maisie has gone along to support her dear friend as usual, and as Lieutenant Barnes is playing for the navy, it presents an ideal opportunity to meet their friend together with other young men.

At tea, many of the officers come over to shake Hattie's hand and ask her where she learnt to play so well. Maisie is so proud of her friend's ability that, at first, she doesn't recognise Lieutenant Prescott amongst them.

Edward comes over to Maisie and strikes up a conversation with her, as though it is only a week or two since she has last seen him.

"How have you been? Are you enjoying the game?" he says, and that is that really. It's as though they have never been parted.

Over the next weeks and months, Maisie and Edward go everywhere as a couple. She becomes his "plus one" for official functions, watches him play cricket instead of watching Hattie, and chats to Edward about the books she has read instead of talking to Peter and the rest of the reading group. She only has time for Edward.

All the other young officers start to treat Maisie as Edward's intended; they think she is "the one" for him. Poor Peter feels very forgotten.

Edward volunteers to help out on a school ramble to Borden, which Peter has initiated. Peter, generous as ever, has agreed to treat the whole party to tea, with cakes and buns for all the girls. It is much talked about back in the officers' mess. It is known that Barnes bought some oranges to give out at the school before the Christmas holiday; he is very thoughtful, although some colleagues speculate that he is more interested in one of the teachers than being kind to the local children.

The school party sets off on the afternoon of the Friday designated to be Empire Day, and they catch the train at half past one. Upon arriving at their destination, the group head out towards Borden to visit its fine church and the Tudor houses in the village.

Many of the orchards are still in blossom, although they are starting to look a little bedraggled following some heavy rain earlier in the month, and are now past their best, but it still makes for a pleasant walk. The pink and white petals carpet the ground like wedding confetti.

Maisie and Betty have chosen around twenty girls whom they feel have made most progress that year and have good attendance. Letters have gone home to their parents, and the tea arranged at a small tea shop in the village.

Edward decides to join the expedition to ingratiate himself with the Rear Admiral's wife, Mrs Bennington. She has thrown herself into the local community and is chairing almost every committee, from building a cottage hospital to an organisation with the unwieldy name of *The Society for Befriending Women and Girls*. The ratings joke it is the *Fallen Women's Express*, as anyone befriended seems to disappear, to be married off in the far-off colonies of Australia or Canada. These are the lucky ones. *The 1913 Mental Deficiency Act* enables unmarried mothers to be categorised as "moral imbeciles" for having a child out of wedlock. Those who have more than one child find themselves assigned to the local lunatic asylum outside Canterbury, where they will be treated with electric shocks to help them mend their ways. Mrs Bennington feels they have a moral duty to the people of the town not to increase the population with the illegitimate children of the sailors under her husband's command, and to relieve any poverty the burden of the navy might inflict on the town as a consequence. She is a firm believer that the men should take responsibility for their actions.

Maisie thinks Edward has volunteered because of her and is flattered that he wants to help her out. But Edward doesn't really care for children, never having had any siblings. Nor has he any experience of how to engage with the girls, as he has not had a father figure in his own life. But he is a quick learner and copies the horse play of his colleague, Peter, giving piggyback rides and playing at chase where he is a monster making the girls squeal with delight. He helps Peter serve the teas to the girls and buys them each a penny stick of toffee for the journey home.

After tea, the girls pick wildflowers to press, whilst the adults sit in the shade chatting. Betty says, "It's funny at home now that Rosie is married. Samuel is around and we're not used to having a man in the house."

"My sisters never let me be in charge," responds Peter. "They let my father think he is running things, but he isn't. I think women are very capable."

"I'm sure some are," replies Edward, "But I prefer a woman to be a woman. These suffragettes are nothing but trouble. If you married one, she'd want to wear the trousers, and that would never do.

Like your friend Hattie in her cricket whites! You need the right kind of wife to get on in the navy."

"We teachers do the same work as men, but we are paid less and get no say in how the government runs the education system. That can't be right!" Betty retorts. "Don't you agree, Maisie?"

Maisie is caught off guard. Since arriving at the Broadway School, her outlook on life has changed. She is more independent and no longer takes her cue from what her father used to tell her is right; she now makes her own decisions. But she doesn't want Edward to think her a militant suffragette either. She catches Peter's eye and hopes he will keep her secret safe about the fire-bombed haystacks before she answers, "Well there are probably other ways that women can contribute to the debate, without being too political about it."

"That's my girl," Edward responds, before changing the subject to the latest Keystone film being shown at the Oxford Cinema that week, featuring the hilarious Charlie Chaplin and Fatty Arbuckle. Betty says nothing, but gives Maisie a hard look for being disloyal. Maisie drops her gaze to her lap, slightly ashamed.

On the return train ride, Betty sits with the girls and ignores the others; she is so cross about Maisie's betrayal.

Maisie sits next to Edward and does her best to snuggle up to him without bringing attention to herself from her pupils, and says, "You will make someone a wonderful father one day." She adds, as an afterthought, "And you too, Peter."

Edward just smiles and squeezes her hand discreetly, whilst Peter averts his eyes and stares out of the window.

## June 1914

It is with trepidation that Maisie and Hattie set off on their duty call to Miss Dobbs, after receiving an invitation to tea. Miss Morrison has sent them as sacrificial lambs on behalf of the school. All the head teachers in town ensure that Miss Dobbs has one visitor a week; that way, they know that she will happily donate to their various fundraising activities.

Miss Dobbs did not enjoy good health. If ever there is a danger that she was found in good health, she immediately sought out some chill or stomach disorder. She prefers the warm glow that being unwell gives you when you receive visitors from the comfort of your day bed. They always come with some little gift to make you feel better. Whereas should you have the misfortune to be in rude good health, people expect you to visit them.

She has a pale wan complexion that speaks of illness, but which, in truth, she keeps topped up with a little face powder to hide her ruddy cheeks, the smell of which can be detected when she invites her visitors to kiss her. She rarely leaves the house, but regular tots of brandy for purely medicinal purposes give her face too much colour.

Miss Dobbs sees it as her duty to answer truthfully and fully when anyone enquires after her health, to the point where friends and neighbours dread to ask. If you have a cold, she has flu; if you have a cough, she has pleurisy; if you have a boil, she has a tumour. The only mystery is how she never dies from any of these maladies.

Upon receiving a substantial legacy, Miss Dobbs gave up working for a living as a teacher and became a full-time invalid, with a nurse and servants to look after her. She was happy to make the career move and takes delight in explaining to her visitors that keeping a class of forty urchins in check is more than her delicate health can take, although she loved the work dearly and misses it so.

Miss Dobbs is keen to promote dental care to the school children and has purchased a quantity of toothbrushes and powder for distribution, having lost a tooth to decay caused by eating too many sweets. She now has a gap in the front of her mouth that she conceals with her hand whenever she laughs in company. She has made several donations to schools, and even got her nurse to talk to the children about how to brush their teeth properly. She has considered going herself, but her health will not allow it.

Hattie and Maisie go to visit Miss Dobbs straight after school, on Wednesday afternoon. They bring a gift of some strawberries from Miss Garrett's garden, and some rhubarb jam that Ena has made. Ena sees jam making as a form of alchemy that her scientific brain can engage with and prides herself on her ability to get even the most difficult fruit to set.

The young women are ushered into the parlour where Miss Dobbs reclines on her sofa in readiness, with her little bug-eyed pug dog, Phoebe, by her side. She is slightly out of breath as she has been busy playing fetch with the dog, but upon hearing the visitors at the door, she has taken up her position of repose in preparation to greet them.

Phoebe has recently been in season and has been confined to barracks to keep her away from any undesirable attention from the stray dogs that roam the streets. She is now showing signs of a phantom pregnancy and is lactating. The little creature goes through the same imaginary travail every six months or so. She is restricted to the garden for her exercise, under the watchful eye of one of the maids. Once, one of the girls was distracted by the attentions of the butcher's boy, and a mongrel managed to find his way in and paid court to the little pug. The maid kept silent about her lapse, but when it became evident that the dog's pregnancy was real, an inquest was held, and the girl dismissed without a reference. It was almost like the maid had become pregnant herself, so great was the shame. Phoebe went on to have four large and common puppies, with all but one meeting a similar fate to Tibby's previous litter of kittens. The vet had been called to help with the difficult delivery caused by the enormous size of the offspring from the brute who compromised Phoebe. Quite an exceptional case for a man used to attending the dockyard horses.

The little dog has been forgiven her wantonness by Miss Dobbs, who watches over her even more carefully than before. Phoebe is on her mistress' wide lap amongst the many ruffles of lace on the woman's dressing robe, being fussed over as though she has just delivered a dozen pedigree puppies, rather than once more imagining the results of the attentions of the back street mongrel she has given her heart and everything else to.

Miss Dobbs invites them to sit down and asks after their pupils. Hattie at once begins lamenting about the current number of absentees.

"Numbers are starting to fall as some families have already left to go fruit picking. I don't know how they all manage to live in those little huts for the season. I know some families move from farm to farm until the late summer, when the hops are picked. It must be so disruptive. The harvest doesn't end till the hops are in. It's only after that they return to their homes and send the children back to school. It's such a shame for their education."

Maisie joins in the subject that has become dear to her heart, "The farmers like the child workers, as their small hands don't damage the fruit. Child labour is supposed to be illegal, but so many children work through the summer. I know that to many families; their income is a welcome addition. It's crucial to the poorer families as the work lasts for so long. But it's sad that many parents have to make the choice not to educate children who can earn their own keep."

Miss Dobbs nods in agreement, before calling to her maid for the tea to be brewed. When the girl appears, it is Alice McDonald, a small, freckled girl barely twelve years old and one of Hattie's class of seniors. There is a moment's embarrassment from the girl, before she drops a slight curtsy, puts the teapot down, and leaves. Hattie and Maisie exchange looks, but bite down on their outrage at Miss Dobb's hypocrisy about child labour. It is not uncommon for girls to go into service before they are twelve years old. However, the two women think that a fellow teacher should not encourage the practice of depriving girls of schooling.

As soon as it is polite to do so, the teachers make their excuses to leave. Once outside, they debate what to do about Alice.

"We should report it to the school attendance officer," Maisie argues, "They will take action and Alice can finish her schooling, not clean up after Miss Dobbs."

"It's a lost cause, Maisie. The family won't thank you as they'll be deprived of her income. And if the case goes to court, the family will be fined and be even worse off financially. They might then take the next child out of school prematurely too."

Hattie stops to stroke a friendly ginger cat who is sunning himself on a windowsill, when a figure appears at the corner of the alley and beckons to them. "Miss, miss!" she calls in a stage whisper. It is Alice.

Hattie and Maisie go over to speak to the girl.

"Hello, Alice," says Hattie. "I didn't know you worked for Miss Dobbs."

"My dad said I should leave school and help out. Miss Dobbs' last girl was dismissed for dawdling when she was sent to the doctors to pick up the mistress' orders," the girl responds. "Our Cathy is expecting, and her boyfriend is away with the army."

"Isn't Cathy only fifteen?" asks Hattie.

"Yes, but Wilf says he loves her and will marry her as soon as she is old enough. My dad went to see him with my Uncle Ginger. They asked to see his commanding officer. He told dad Wilf will be back in December with the rest of his unit. Cathy will be sixteen by then and the banns will be read."

"When is the baby due?" asks Maisie.

"We think about September. You won't report me will you Miss? My dad'll give me such a whack if

157

I lose my place here," she says, wringing her already permanently work roughened hands in her starched white apron.

Hattie and Maisie exchange looks and make a silent pact. "Well, I don't envy you working for Miss Dobbs," says Hattie. "I hope it all goes well for you and Cathy."

"Thank you, Miss," responds Alice, as she ducks back down the alley before Miss Dobbs has time to notice she is gone.

"Poor Cathy," says Maisie. "A mother at fifteen. No life at all."

"We are so lucky to be independent women," replies Hattie. "Having the vote won't change much for the likes of her in our lifetime."

The whole town shuts for the dockyard holiday of the King's official birthday. All the workers and their families make the most of the summer weather by visiting the businesses on the promenade or taking a trip on the train for a day's ramble in the countryside. Spackman's Omnibus and Tram Company puts on extra services to reach the other end of the island, so that people can enjoy the views from the clifftop downs at Minster, or the sands at Leysdown Bay.

Hattie decides to organise a picnic to visit Eastchurch to see the remains of Shurland Hall, and to visit All Saints church with its elaborate Jacobean tomb to the Livesey family. She feels it is now safe to return to the scene of her foray into being a militant suffragette.

The party consists of Maisie, Edward, Peter, Rosie, Samuel, Bill, and Betty, with little Alberta as well as Hattie. Alf has been invited, but he is otherwise engaged, much to Betty's disappointment. Mrs Bills and Ena have indulged in a competition to see who can make the most food, whilst Mrs Dale has concentrated on making all the things Alberta likes. It is agreed to buy bottles of beer and soft drinks once they arrive in the village, to save carrying it from Sheerness.

Having walked themselves near to dropping in the early summer sunshine, they decide on a hillside picnic spot peppered with vibrant blood-red poppies, buttercups, daisies, and cornflowers. It overlooks the new aerodrome and Royal Naval Flying School, so they can watch the planes taking off and landing.

The men go to buy the crates of beer and lemonade and carry it to the picnic spot, whilst the girls spread out the tablecloths on the grass and unpack the potted meat, hard- boiled eggs, cheese, and ham sandwiches, along with the fairy cakes Ena has made. Mrs Dale has made Alberta a pastry man with currents for eyes and coat buttons, and some

159

cheese straws together with some sausage rolls. She has purposefully not made any jam tarts, one of Alberta's favourites, as they attract wasps.

Whilst they are eating, Peter comes into his own as he is able to identify the various models of aeroplanes which all have nicknames like *Birding*, *The Vacuum Cleaner*, the *Field Kitchen*, and a twin-engine monoplane called the *Double Dirty*.

"The Admiralty jumped at the chance when they were offered two aeroplanes on loan back in 1911. It was a fantastic opportunity for some officers to learn to fly," Peter explains. "They put a call out for volunteers and, not surprisingly, over two hundred officers came forward. Only four lucky ones were selected. They learned every aspect there is, including undergoing technical training at the Short Brothers factory. But more exciting than that, they visited the French Military Aeroplane Trials at Rheims, and studied foreign developments in aviation. Lieutenant Samson persuaded the Admiralty to buy two training machines and selected twelve naval ratings to form the basis of the first British Naval Flying School, right here in Eastchurch.

"Aeroplanes will be the next big thing if there's a war, and I think there will be," Peter concludes, gazing wistfully down at the airfield. "I'm too tall to fly. I can't fit into the cockpit, but I'm thinking of asking for a transfer to work on the control side of things."

Edward counters with, "Yes, but the planes are so flimsy, they won't provide any protection to the pilot. You'll be a sitting duck. Give me the sea any day."

After they have eaten, Edward asks Maisie if she would like to walk over the brow of the hill to see the view of the Swale. Maisie has not been to this part of the island before and readily says yes. As they walk, Edward picks some lilacs growing wild and presents them to Maisie saying, "I will always think of you when I see lilacs." Maisie is much taken with the uncharacteristic romantic gesture and carries the flowers like a wedding bouquet.

Once they are out of sight of the others, Edward takes off his jacket and spreads it out, and invites Maisie to sit beside him whilst looking at the channel glittering in the sunshine below them. The Thames barges pass serenely along, carrying bricks, or fruit and vegetables up to London, and returning with rubbish for dumping. Their red sails swell like pregnant bellies. Overhead, a marsh harrier hovers, scanning the ground for prey. Its dark wing tips spread like fingers reaching into the sky. Maisie lays back and shields her eyes for a better view.

"Isn't it amazing that humans can now fly! And Peter says he had a ride in a twin seater!" she says.

"Yes," responds Edward, immediately looking for a way to turn the conversation back towards himself, "but he is too clumsy to fly, unless it's like a heron does with its long legs dangling behind him!"

Maisie laughs at the image this conjures up.

"You're so pretty when you laugh," says Edward, bending over to kiss her soft mouth. The tall cow parsley makes a lacy curtain around them and hides them from sight. Maisie relaxes as Edward holds her tight and the kiss becomes more intense. She runs her hand over his biceps and round his back into the deep muscles there. They begin to forget where they are, when, suddenly, little Alberta's voice calls out, "Auntie Maisie, where are you?"

They leap apart as the sound of the approaching child draws nearer. They can hear Betty's voice from somewhere behind calling, "We ought to be getting back now."

Edward stares intently at Maisie, but she can't read his thoughts. "We're here!" he calls to the little girl, "Shall I give you a piggyback up the hill?" And he stands up to carry little Alberta, without assisting Maisie to her feet.

## July 1914

As the holiday to Switzerland draws nearer, Maisie no longer wants to go; she doesn't want to leave Edward. In her dreams, she is Jane Austen's heroine Anne Elliott from *Persuasion* and Lieutenant Edward Prescott is her Captain Frederick Wentworth. He is so dashing in his uniform and is highly thought of by Rear Admiral Bennington. He knows everything going on in the dockyard. He is so knowledgeable, and has talked about the possibility of war for weeks. Maisie feels so important when she accompanies him to official functions at Admiralty House. When the ladies retire from the dining room, as the men have their port, brandy, and cigars, she sits with Mrs Bennington in the blue drawing room. Everyone wants to meet the Rear Admiral's wife, because she is clever and beautiful and has the loveliest clothes. Maisie loves the reflected glory of seeming like she is part of the inner circle of naval wives. She is happy to fetch Mrs Bennington's wrap or pass her reading glasses to look at photographs of the officers' children that their proud mothers show her.

Edward is always talking about what he wants to do in the navy, where he wants to travel to. He often says the right wife can really make a difference to an officer's career prospects. Maisie does her best to be just like the Rear Admiral's wife. She has altered one of her blouses to look like one of Mrs Bennington's. She has let Rosie alter her velvet evening gown too. But as she needs more formal clothes for all the functions they attend, she has gone to Bon Marche, the dress shop, to order a new evening gown for a ball that they are having at Admiralty House in September. Edward has promised to take her if he hasn't been posted away by then. She also keeps her newly formed opinions on women's rights to herself. Mrs Bennington makes it clear that a naval wife's role is to support her husband's career, not to have one of her own.

Maisie was thrilled when Mrs Bennington showed an interest in her teaching and visited the school. The Rear Admiral's wife sat in on her class and listened to her pupils reading. She said she was impressed with the standard of the girls' essays and asked to borrow one to show her husband. Maisie thinks it is clear that Mrs Bennington sees her as a suitable wife for an officer as her teaching skills are so good, and she is excellent with children; the Rear Admiral's wife has almost said as much when she was in class.

But Maisie committed to this holiday last autumn and has given Miss Garrett money from her wages every month to pay for her train ticket and hotel bill. Miss Garrett is so looking forward to it, as is Hattie and Ena. Maisie doesn't feel she can back out now, and she certainly can't afford to lose the money she has paid up front.

Edward is very understanding. He says improving her French will be particularly useful if there is a war with Germany, and France is our ally. Edward has lots of plans for the future and talks to her all the time about how every sailor needs a wife to come home to. She is sure he is going to propose at any moment. It just hasn't happened yet. But she thinks he should say something to her before she leaves on her rapidly approaching holiday.

Edward knows it is wrong. He didn't mean to get in so deep. It is important to find the right wife to further your career. You don't have to love her, or be attracted to her even. She has to be intelligent enough to hold a conversation with your superior officers and their wives. She has to be pretty, but in a non-showy, girl-next-door way. Someone your colleagues will envy, but not lust after. She will need to be sensible and the type of girl who will stay faithful whilst you are away at sea. She will need to be prepared to "muck in" and help with the Rear Admiral's wife's pet charities, be a homemaker and good housekeeper. Sweet, bright Maisie is many of these things, but not all of them, although he can't quite put his finger on what it is that she lacks, although once or twice she has ventured opinions on women's rights with which he does not agree.

Edward has kept company with two young ladies during his last posting to Portsmouth. Sadie is the daughter of a senior officer. She is almost right; she has all the breeding he is looking for, and she knows how to be a navy wife but, in the end, she just isn't pretty enough and has an annoying laugh. He can't see himself wanting to return home to her for years to come, so after a couple of official functions, he didn't ask her to be his partner anymore and allowed things to just fizzle out.

But there is always the possibility of keeping a mistress, which in effect is what he has done. Mary Andrews is a shop assistant in the naval outfitters. He had first met her when he was a cadet at Osborne College, and they were both too young to do much about it. She is prepared to give herself to Edward and make no real demands in return. But being a gentleman, he always gives her a little present each time he sees her. These are small trinkets or if he forgets, he leaves her a few shillings and tells her to treat herself. He only meets her for walks or for a drink in a local pub. Sometimes, he takes her to the picture house to see the latest films from Keystone. Once he took her to London to celebrate after he was promoted to lieutenant. They nearly bumped into Maisie and her friends on that occasion, which could have been very difficult to explain had he not reacted swiftly and suggested some tea in the hotel lounge. He is genuinely very fond of Mary; she is curvy and lively and has hair the colour of a new conker, but she is too common to marry, with her Hampshire hog accent and will not advance his career. She understands this, so the two women together, Mary and Sadie, made for a perfect love life.

But the dockyard town of Sheerness is much smaller than Portsmouth. Having two girlfriends is not possible without everyone knowing, because in a small naval base, everyone already knows your business. For the past few months, he has only walked out with Maisie. Pretty, sweet Maisie. She of many qualities, but chief amongst them is her sex appeal. She is completely unaware of it, and yet you can see the men's eyes turn to her as she walks by. Since he has started walking out with her, several of his fellow officers try to engage her in conversation, so he has to steer her away. He is annoyed when one of them returns from an expedition into town and reports seeing Maisie for a long chat. He knows that if he gives her up, one of them will step in, and he isn't prepared to do that until his next posting comes along. And that won't be long, with the outbreak of war.

Her month's holiday away in Switzerland will be ideal to make the break if he is posted. He can write to her without having to deal with her face to face. He will find it hard to watch her blue eyes fill with tears as though they are melting. In his own way, he is rather fond of her. it is just that she isn't quite right.

Rear Admiral Bennington and his wife are very taken with Maisie. Mrs Bennington has visited Maisie's class at school and has come away extremely impressed with her skills as a teacher. She has said as much to Edward when she saw him next. The couple ask after her constantly. The Rear Admiral will bluster when he sees the two of them together.

"When are you going to make an honest woman of her?" Edward will laugh it off, but he is aware that Mrs Bennington never laughs, but just fixes him with her eye.

So, he keeps company with Maisie, and does his best not to compromise himself, whilst keeping watch on the greater prize, his next posting.

The whole school is in a state of excitement as *Chief Wild Wolf's Wild West Show and Circus* is in town for one day only. In recent years, the new cinemas have brought films of the Wild West to the people of Sheerness, films like *The Great Train Robbery, The Hold Up of the Rocky Mountain Express* and *The Sheriff of Stone Gulch*. The

Western style circus is hotly anticipated with its spectacle of sharp shooting and lasso tricks, midget horses who perform manoeuvres unknown to the working drays of the back street carts and wagons and, finally, the show boasts that most Western of performing animals, a real-life elephant called Sugar.

There is nothing sweet about Sugar's temperament and, as a result, she has a chequered history, having killed her handler about two years earlier, reputedly when he beat her once too often when he was drunk. However, she is such a valuable beast, that a new handler is found, and nothing said of her murderous past. Most children have never seen an elephant before. The exception being those few boys and girls whose parents have served in HM Dockyard in Trincomalee, Ceylon, where teams of elephants are used to haul heavy objects. This makes Sugar the single biggest draw of the circus.

As a result of the anticipation, about a third of the school are absent from class on the afternoon of 23 July. But not all, as the cheapest child's ticket is one shilling, the same as an adult ticket. The more expensive seats start from half a crown, but are half price for kids. Only the better off families go to the circus. But everyone can watch the free parade through the town, timed especially for the dockyard workers' lunchtime.

The circus arrives by train the night before. The animal cages and performers' caravans are wheeled off the freight wagons, then pulled by the midget and full-sized horses to the fields just outside the town. The big top is erected as soon as they arrive, with the colourful sideshow stalls of rifle ranges, boxing and strong-man exhibitions and food kiosks being arranged in such a way as to funnel the crowds into the main arena. It is all up and ready by midday when the parade assembles.

Maisie and Hattie meet Rosie and her sister Betty at lunchtime. Betty brings along their youngest family member, Alberta, to watch the parade. They stand in the crush of the town centre under the heat of the midday summer sun, as the swell of the brass band and other carnival-like noises come rumbling towards them. Hawkers sell sweet smelling toffee apples and nuts from trays, whilst others sell flags and gay coloured paper streamers. Alberta is getting a little too big to be balanced on Betty's hip, but she and Hattie take it in turns to ensure the little girl can see the parade. Rosie is, by now, seven months pregnant and is flagging in the July heat.

The atmosphere is electric as the spectacle trundles past. There are feathered, headdressed Red Indians with war painted faces walking on silent moccasined feet carrying their tomahawks, bows, and arrows. Burly cowboys ride high on piebald horses, shotguns balanced across their denim clad legs. Clowns with their painted smiles and brightly coloured costumes perform japes for the crowds as they pass by. Acrobats in spangled clothes turn cartwheels and somersaults as the people gasp. The lions and tigers are pulled along through the town in their cages, the bored animals barely looking up at the crowd. Bringing up the rear of the parade is Sugar, the elephant. She is exotically decorated in crimson and gold cloth, which is studded with bosses of gold. Her ears are dressed with large silver tassels (Alberta innocently asks if they are Auntie Ena's earrings, making them all laugh), and to finish the ensemble, the elephant wears a headdress of gold, ornamented with scarlet ostrich feathers.

"Please can we go and see the show, Auntie Betty? Please, please!" Alberta begs. Betty can deny her nothing, "I suppose it will be okay for you to stay up late on this one occasion. Every little girl deserves a treat now and then," Betty says, giving in to her illegitimate daughter. "Who else would like to come?"

"I'm too tired," says Rosie rubbing her round belly as the baby kicks inside her.

"I'd love to come with you if Edward doesn't offer to take me," responds Maisie.

"I'm game too," says Hattie, chucking Alberta under the chin, "we can all go together!"

"I can go and get your tickets for you for the evening show, save you a little time after work," offers Rosie.

They arrange to meet up at half past five, so that they have enough time after school to walk to the circus and look round the stalls with Alberta before the show starts. It is possible to see the menagerie for just tuppence beforehand, and the child is especially excited to see the wild animals. She loves the elephant as it has captured her imagination. The little girl is only slightly bothered by the raw smell of animal dung combined with the iron smell of the meat fed to the big cats, none of which distracts her from the joy of seeing the elephant or eating a penny-lick ice cream from a well-used glass that has only had the most cursory of rinses before being refilled for the next customer.

Maisie is slightly out of sorts and, from what they can gather, she hopes to see Edward before they leave for Switzerland, when school breaks up later that week. Whilst they queue for the different sideshows, then for the menagerie, she is constantly hanging back and looking around, in case Edward should appear. There is a brief moment of respite when she spots the tall frame of Lieutenant Peter Barnes, head and shoulders above most of the crowd, but even this turns to disappointment when it is not him, but another officer of similar stature.

Inside the big top, they spot Susan and Edith from school, and decide to join them by the ringside. The two parties settle to watch the show together. It is so spectacular that they don't know where to look as jugglers, fire eaters, stilt walkers, lion tamers, and clowns take turns to entertain them.

It is quite breath-taking, and Maisie temporarily forgets her woes and becomes absorbed in the magic of the circus. Nothing like this ever visited the small village of Chiddingly where she lived with her parents, and when the more famous Sangers Circus visited Hailsham, her father denounced it as the work of the Devil, as the women performers were scantily clad and were no better than they should be.

When Sugar the elephant comes into the ring, Alberta is beside herself with excitement and consequently wets herself. Betty sighs and says she will take the little girl home during the interval; she is already fighting desperately to stay awake, but is really half asleep as it is well past her bedtime. Hattie offers to accompany her, saying, "I'll help you carry her."

"I'll come too," says Maisie, jumping up.

"No, you stay with Susan and Edie. I saw the circus a few years ago when Sangers came to town, but I know you've never seen one."

After several "are you sures?" Betty and Hattie leave, carrying the now all but sleeping Alberta.

The second half of the show is dedicated to the equestrian displays. Women and men dressed as cowboys and Indians perform acts of daring horsemanship, sharp shooting, knife throwing, and lasso tricks. One act consists of Indians capturing a very handsome cowboy, dressed only in his leather chaps and white Stetson hat. They tie him up to a stake from which he has to escape before a candle burns through a rope, which releases a heavy weight to fall on a saloon girl. She is also tied up and guarded by the Indian chief, who theatrically ogles her in her sparkly costume that shows off her legs. The cowboy flexes his naked muscles as they bind him, then relaxes them to give himself the room he needs to wriggle free from the bonds around his chest. He then grabs a discarded bull whip to flick out the candle left burning under the rope. He rescues the saloon girl by lassoing the Indian guarding her, before untying her. The finale is a big battle between the cowboys and Indians, including the elephant rampaging across to help with more theatrical rescues.

At the end of the show, Susan and Edith invite Maisie to visit the sideshows with them, and the three women set off together. Maisie has never been to a fairground, so is dazzled and confused by the flashing electric lights and loud music that now fills the warm night, all generated by a noisy steam traction engine chuffing away. Many of the visitors depart taking sleepy children home, but some people are still wanting to enjoy the late summer evening and are milling around the stalls selling cider, beer, chestnuts, ice cream, jellied eels, pies, and fried fish.

Somehow, Maisie is separated in the crowd and ends up behind the big top, where the men are already working on dismantling the seats and internal fittings. A cowboy approaches her and asks, "Are you lost?" Maisie recognises him as the one from the exciting rescue of the saloon girl. He remains stripped to the waist and is still wearing the buck skin leather fringed "chaps" from his costume, but has discarded his white Stetson hat. The sweat on his suntanned torso shines under the electric lights.

Maisie isn't sure what to reply. She is embarrassed by his semi-nakedness, but, at the same time, is fascinated that this is one of the performers she has seen only a short time ago performing tricks with a lasso and bull whip. He is tall and handsome, and there is an animal appeal to his bare chest and muscular arms. He has strong hands from wrestling horses and Indian riders to the ground

175

and his fingernails are black with grime, but she doesn't notice that. He has been so chivalrous to the saloon girl, a real hero. Eventually, she settles on replying that she is lost and thinks to herself how fortunate she is to be rescued by this man.

"Let me escort you back to your friends," he responds gallantly. His accent is strange to her; she assumes he must be American, when in reality he is from Wolverhampton. But as the silent films don't give voice to the on-screen cowboys and she has never met anyone from the Midlands or the USA, she knows no better. "Thank you," she replies, and innocently takes his proffered arm, touching his naked flesh.

He smiles down on her, and she is almost star struck as they walk together behind the circus wagons. He talks about life in the Wild West, as though he has actually been there. Maisie is mesmerised. The cowboy tells her his name is Jim and asks hers. "Maisie," she responds shyly.

"Mighty pleased to meet you, Maisie," he responds. "Can I show you the elephant and midget horses? They are right over here."

Maisie is about to respond that they have visited the menagerie earlier, but Jim grips her wrist with his work hardened hand and pulls her after him.

"You're hurting me! I want to go back to my friends," Maisie protests, but Jim pulls her on to where the animal cages cast dark ominous shadows, as they are lined up ready to hit the road again, well away from the bright lights and prying eyes of the sideshows.

"In a minute," says Jim, "There's something I want to show you. You don't want to offend a poor cowboy, do you?"

"No, sorry, I don't want to be rude, but I must get back, they will be looking for me."

"It won't take a moment. I'm sure you will enjoy it."

Jim pushes Maisie up against the back of the furthest cart and starts pawing at her breast, whilst forcing his tongue into her mouth.

Maisie tries to pull away, but Jim grips her tighter. She can't call out as his mouth covers hers. His hand reaches down and pulls at her skirt. She tries to push him off, but he sweeps her legs from under her. As she falls, he supports her body and follows her down all in one seamless movement; the manoeuvre perfected by flooring Indian chiefs in the circus ring. Her skirt is now round her waist as he pulls at the buttons of her blouse, squeezing her breast painfully.

"No, please!" she manages to cry.

"That's it little lady, say please," he says, in a pseudo-American accent, covering her mouth with his calloused hand.

Jim fumbles at his trousers and roughly penetrates Maisie.

"Please, let me go!" she sobs, as his body finally goes limp on top of hers and he relaxes his hold on her.

He rolls off her, and she jumps up pulling her skirt down and her blouse together. She staggers off as quickly as she can, half running, heading for the lights and the hope of finding Susan and Edith again.

She knows she can tell no one about what happened, as they will say she led the cowboy on. Only recently there was a story in the local paper of a married woman going for a drink with a sailor who was not her husband. The woman was raped by the rating and two of his shipmates. The judge said she was a woman of low morals who must have encouraged the sailors, because she had met up with one of them. Maisie won't be able to bear the shame.

She catches up with Susan and Edith as they are trying to win a prize on the hoopla stall. She swallows her tears and just says, "I want to go home now."

As soon as Maisie gets home, she locks herself in the bathroom and runs a bath. Miss Garrett knocks at the door and asks, "Are you all right? You don't usually bathe this late in the evening."

Maisie gathers herself together enough to call back, "Yes, fine. I don't know when we might have time for a bath before we leave for our holiday on Saturday."

She scrubs at her legs, her breasts, her arms, anywhere the cowboy has touched her. Blue bruises are already appearing on her wrists and breasts, and she feels like she has been kicked by a mule between her legs which bore the marks of where the cowboy has prised her thighs apart. The warm water soothes the sting where her flesh is raw.

She keeps thinking, "What if he has got me pregnant? I can't tell anyone. What will I do?"

When she eventually feels clean enough to go to bed, she cries herself to sleep. When she wakes up later, she is tangled up in the bedclothes, with tears streaming down her face.

# Part 2
# The Great War

## August 1914

"How lovely, Miss Garrett! I think you have surpassed yourself this year!" Hattie declares as they step off the train in Vevey. She thinks it is a delightful location and applauds Miss Garrett for her choice.

"Let's hope the hotel is as comfortable as Mr Bradshaw promises in his guide," Miss Garrett responds, a little smugly. She, in turn, wants the other ladies to enjoy their holiday in the knowledge that its success is entirely down to her. *Bradshaw's* says the town is in "a very fine situation on the Lake of Geneva," and promises, "much tobogganing," in the winter, though it is unlikely that has been the decider for Miss Garrett in making her choice. Vevey has its own railway station, which gives easy access to the cities of Lausanne, Geneva, and Montreux, with their cosmopolitan shops and cafés. The South-Eastern and Chatham Railway promises through trains to Vevey from Calais during the summer months. Miss Garrett thinks it is the ideal choice for the teachers' holiday. But much to her annoyance on booking, she finds that they need to go via Paris and change for a train through Dijon and Geneva to get to Vevey. The younger women are slightly peeved that the journey does not allow them any time in

Paris as they hoped, but with all the luggage it isn't possible to go far from the station, and certainly not as a group. Miss Garrett suggests it will be easier to explore Paris on the return journey once the luggage is booked onto the boat train.

The Swiss town boasts a small museum, with a gallery and natural history collection. Miss Garrett is very keen on history, so has marked this as a place to visit. To their delight, the town has a pretty onion domed Russian Orthodox church and an English church built in 1882, in the traditional Gothic style. Vevey features in Louisa M Alcott's novel, *Little Women* and is one of the two locations for the setting of Henry James' novella, *Daisy Miller*. At first glance, it is everything they could want in a picturesque holiday destination. It is also home to a huge, condensed milk factory belonging to Nestlé, which dominates that part of town and gives the air a permanent, sweet milky aroma which is somewhat sickly, but they choose to ignore that as they direct the man sent from the hotel to load up their baggage onto his cart.

The Hotel Pension Nuss isn't large, nor is it right in the centre of the town, but it is near the station, and it is only a short walk from the pleasure boat pier which allows them to explore across the crystal-clear waters of Lake Geneva, to the beautiful Alps around it. In the advertisement in *Bradshaw's,* the hotel boasts all the latest comforts. Pension rates are only six and a half francs, so it also meets their budget.

As *Bradshaw's* lacks an artist's impression of the hotel, Miss Garrett hopes for a delightful chocolate box chalet with fluted gables and window boxes containing colourful geraniums which send up their distinct fragrance when touched. She always thinks of greenhouses and the tiny gravel you find there when she smells them. But the hotel is more Italianate in its architecture. It still has balconies and flower boxes, so Miss Garrett isn't that disappointed.

The hotelier is Monsieur Eggenberger, a stout moustachioed man whose Teutonic name and build proclaim his ancestry as a plough owning bürger from the German speaking regions of Switzerland, which sit uneasily with the French title for "mister." That said, he has the most surprisingly dainty hands, decorated with elegant rings, which suggest not all his ancestors were farmers. He gives them the grand tour of the building, before showing them to their rooms.

There is a lovely salon with views across the gardens, or "terrace" as Monsieur Eggenberger calls it, where chairs and tables are set out and shaded by stripy parasols. A flight of stone steps leads down to a lower level where you can walk out onto the lake front. At night, coloured electric lights illuminate the garden in a fairground way, making it gay and continental to sit outside so late. The moths dance round the glass bulbs in ever decreasing circles in a more flamboyant way than at home, or so Maisie thinks. There are a couple of stray cats who bask in the sunshine and are happy to accept titbits from Hattie, so she is able to indulge her love of cats and not miss Tibby too much.

"Why don't Maisie and I share a room, that way our talking won't keep you two awake?" suggests Hattie. Miss Garrett is both pleased and annoyed; she quite enjoys Maisie's company, but, from past experience, she knows that Ena snores loudly and suspects this is why Hattie has made her proposal. However, once she is asleep, nothing wakes Miss Garrett, so she agrees, much to the two younger women's relief.

The bedrooms themselves are different to what they are used to. Instead of cosy blankets and a counterpane, each bed has a large goose down filled quilt, almost like a cloud resting on the bed. It is soft and warm and can be shaken to rearrange the feathers to make it cooler. The pillows are not made of lumpy kapok, but again of soft down, and are square in shape instead of oblong. The beds are made of pine and look like something out of a fairy story, with carved head and footboards. "I feel like

Goldilocks!" Hattie declares, when she first sees them.

There is a bathroom on the same floor as their bedrooms, which only their two rooms share, being on the top floor of the hotel in the attic rooms. The rear rooms under the eaves are used for storage. The modern electric lift doesn't go right to the top, so there are some stairs to climb, but the extra privacy afforded to the ladies is worth it. Their elevated position gives them spectacular lake and mountain views.

Breakfast, luncheon, and dinner are provided as part of the pension rates offered by the hotel. The Swiss food is quite heavy; designed to fill you up and keep you warm in the winter. Fondue is a revelation, everything covered in melted cheese. The breakfast is a selection of cold meats, hard boiled eggs, and more cheese, as though it is a high tea. There is sour curdled milk which Miss Garrett thinks ought to be thrown away, but Monsieur Eggenberger calls it yoghurt and serves it with runny jam which he calls compote; he claims it is very good for you. Another oddity is a cereal invented by a Swiss doctor who calls the new food muesli. It is made with uncooked oats, dried fruit, and nuts. Miss Garrett looks at it on the breakfast table and says, "I am of the opinion that if you want oats for breakfast, then you should have porridge," and with that she steers clear of the muesli whenever it is presented.

Maisie still feels unclean after her experience at the circus and wants to forget all about it. But the horror of it keeps rising up. So, when Hattie suggests hiring a bathing hut and going for a swim in the lake, she jumps at the idea.

There are several beach areas, and swimming is very fashionable, which Maisie is unaware of. There are all the usual amenities found at the seaside; a place where you can hire towels, and men and women's changing facilities and conveniences. Hattie has packed both the bathing suits she owns, and offers one to Maisie to borrow. It is a navy-blue two-piece made from good quality cotton fabric. It has a sailor's collar on the blouse which, along with the skirt, is trimmed with white braid, as are the knee length pantaloons beneath. It is very stylish, and Maisie thinks it very flattering.

Hattie has a newer costume she bought in London, modelled on the one worn by Annette Kellerman, or *The Diving Venus* as she is known. It is a clingy, one-piece black swimsuit that has no skirt, revealing her athletic thighs. She favours it because it is the kind of swimsuit the women Olympic swimmers wore in Stockholm in 1912. It is the one that she wears to teach the girls to swim in at school. Some other people on the shore stop to stare at Hattie's outfit, but she ignores them, feeling superior in her ability to swim like an Olympian.

When they go into the lake, the mountain water is so cold that it shocks Maisie and takes her breath away, but her body soon becomes accustomed to it. Hattie shows her how to do breaststroke, as she thinks this is the easiest stoke to do in the cumbersome old-fashioned swimsuit. Maisie is soon able to swim a few yards and tread water.

The clarity of the water made from the melted snow of the glaciers goes some way towards making Maisie feel clean. It clears her head and cleanses her soul. For the short duration of their swim, she almost feels herself again.

When they get out of the lake and return to the bathing hut to get dry and change into their ordinary clothes, Hattie notices that Maisie's wrists are covered in fading bruises.

"How did you get these?" Hattie asks, reaching for Maisie's hand. "I didn't notice them before; they look like they are at least a week old."

Maisie responds, "The lid of my trunk fell on me as I was packing for our holiday." But Hattie eyes the fading yellowy green marks with some suspicion; she is not convinced, as they circle Maisie's wrist, and she thinks she has glimpsed more bruises on her legs as she undresses. She realises that Maisie has been very careful not to let her see her body when they change in their shared room. She thought it was just modesty, but now she wonders if Maisie has been deliberately trying to conceal the bruises from her.

Maisie wraps her towel around herself as quickly as she can and turns away.

The two older women think Maisie is behaving in what can only be described as a skittish way. She is not as bubbly as usual, and Miss Garrett thinks she is a little withdrawn. A few times, she has looked like she has been crying. But when she thinks about it more, Miss Garrett is of the opinion that Maisie was out of sorts, even before they left. She has been acting oddly since the night of the circus, or maybe before, and has drawn away from people when they come near.

Miss Garrett wonders if it is because Maisie has been walking out with that naval officer Prescott for a few months, and is missing his company, even though he was noticeably absent at their departure. She doesn't consider a naval man to be a reliable proposition, despite how many others see an officer as a good prospect. You don't live in a dockyard town for fifteen years without reaching that conclusion.

Whenever Miss Garrett has seen the pair together, the young officer doesn't seem that attentive, often looking somewhat bored with Maisie's chatter. But Lieutenant Prescott needs a young lady to accompany him on official engagements, where wives are trotted out, so Miss Garrett suspects he has chosen the pretty and certainly respectable Miss Kendall, for her ability to fit in rather than because Lieutenant Prescott is in love with her. Since there was first talk of war clouds gathering, the lieutenant has begun speculating about what his next posting might be. He doesn't seem to be including Maisie in his plans. Everyone knows a war can be a fast track to promotion for a naval man. It is clear to Miss Garrett that he doesn't want to be just a Rear Admiral's aide whilst battles are being fought. But it is also apparent Maisie has firmly set her cap at him, and is likely to be disappointed.

Maisie starts to miss Edward, almost as soon as they depart from the train station. He said if he could, he would see her off and wish her *bon voyage,* but he wasn't there. She dawdles as the porter loads their trunks into the guard's van, then their travel bags into the carriage. The other women are busy flapping like so many crows that they don't notice her hanging back. She is last into the compartment, and

189

keeps leaning out of the window, craning to catch a glimpse of Edward should he come running onto the platform, but he never appears.

There is one small ray of sunshine; Lieutenant Barnes comes to the station to see them off. As the women settle into their second-class carriage, he dashes onto the platform hallooing and waving to them in his now familiar seal-like way. He gives them each a bag of sweets for their journey – Turkish Delight for Maisie, toffee for Hattie, humbugs for Ena, and acid drops for Miss Garrett. (Nobody asks if there is a code to these choices of confectionary.) He then slips Maisie a small box.

"Save it for Switzerland," he says, tucking it into her travel bag before waving and turning on his heel and dashing off just as quickly as he arrived.

The sweet treats cheer Maisie up, and for the rest of the journey she and Hattie are as excited as schoolgirls. Together they watch out of the window for landmarks like Canterbury Cathedral and the White Cliffs as they approach Dover. Once across the channel, they look out for the first glimpses of Paris, then the Alps as they travel through Europe.

But after the initial excitement of the holiday has worn off, Maisie has become more melancholy. Hattie is doing a sterling job listening to Maisie, whilst she sets out yet another daydream where Edward is posted far away and writes copious love letters to her. In all these fantasies he says they must be married as soon as he returns. These scenarios reveal to the others that Maisie very much hoped the lieutenant would propose to her before she left for Switzerland. This obviously has not happened and is probably a contributory factor in her despondency.

Before they departed, Maisie provided Edward with the hotel address so he can correspond with her, and she implored him to telegraph should he receive any news of a posting. She sends him postcards wherever they go, from Montreux, Lausanne, and Geneva; from the small lakeside villages they visit and when they go up into the mountains on the Star Train to *Les Pléiades*. These postcards are sent, care of the officers' mess, where Edward lives. She knows all his colleagues will also read them, but as he has no private address, Maisie keeps her greetings to things he won't object to the others seeing. There is little privacy in the navy. But no post arrives at the hotel for Maisie from Lieutenant Prescott.

Maisie feels so bereft and wonders what she has done wrong to upset Edward. That is when she is not trying to sink the idea of another young woman having sailed into his sphere of influence. After all, she is as old as Anne Elliott in Jane Austen's novel *Persuasion*, and Anne's peers in the narrative considered her an "old maid." She wonders if going on holiday with three other spinsters (well two and Hattie), makes people think that she is also happy to remain unwed. Did Edward think that of her?

Miss Garrett finds herself listening to Maisie's fancies with one ear, whilst reading her novel in the hotel lounge. She is reading *Madame Bovary* in French as she thinks it is appropriate whilst in a French speaking region. Just in case it turned out that their lakeside town was German speaking, Miss Garrett had packed *Effi Briest* to read in German. She feels it marks her out as cultured to the rest of the clientele that she can read novels in the language of the town.

Hattie finds an English newspaper that is only three days old with the hope of learning the cricket scores. Ena is doing her embroidery. She uses her free time to practice making items that her pupils will be able to copy: handkerchiefs with flowers in the corners to make excellent gifts, tablecloths for wedding presents and baby clothes for the inevitable hasty christening afterwards. She chooses her reading material in the same way. Currently, she is reading *The Secret Garden* by Frances Hodgson Burnett. "I think I'll read this aloud to my class when school recommences. But I won't be doing Dickon's Yorkshire accent," she proclaims. "It's bad enough that the girls don't speak English properly, without

192

them getting fanciful notions from story book heroes with words like "*graidely.*" Ena is not as in love with the gardener's boy's accent as Mary in the story has been.

Maisie is reading a rather racy novel by Elinor Glyn calls, *Three Weeks.* Miss Garrett disapproves; it is one thing to read a novel about a married woman having affairs if the woman is French, one expects it almost. However, reading a novel about an affair written by an English woman is slightly unsavoury.

"You should pop a different dust jacket on that book," Miss Garrett suggests to Maisie, who responds, "It's set in Switzerland," as though that answers everything.

The book currently lays forgotten on the sofa, whilst Maisie again laments the fact that Edward hasn't written. Hattie tries to console her by explaining, "Lieutenant Prescott's life must be terribly busy, he will have lots to do. He probably just hasn't had time."

Maisie is temporarily mollified and returns to her novel.

Over the next few days, this scene is repeated again and again, with it taking more work on Hattie's part to restore calm. She is now being called upon by Maisie, to give her opinion on Lieutenant Prescott's mind-set, as Maisie believes her friend

193

has an insight into how men think. Hattie always qualifies this by saying that she only knows what they think about cricket. And all the time Maisie's lower lip droops further and further as Hattie takes longer and longer to reach a point of reassurance that satisfies her.

In the fortnight before she left, at Maisie's insistence, she and Edward exchanged photographs. They attended Mr Whitehead's studio together, but did not pose for a photo as a couple as Edward thinks this silly. They have gone to that particular photographer on Rosie's recommendation, as the studio employs the woman apprentice, Miss Mitcham, who took the wedding photographs. The young teachers think this very progressive of Mr Whitehead and ensure they give him their custom. It is Miss Mitcham who takes Maisie and Edward's photographs.

Maisie buys three copies of her portrait, one for Edward, one for her mother and one she keeps. She wants to write on the copy she gives to Edward something like, "*To my dearest Edward, with love from Maisie.*" But Edward says it will spoil the picture, so she has not. And without barely looking at it, Edward takes it from her and pops it in his pocket.

Edward purchases two copies of his portrait; one he keeps, and the other he gives to Maisie, upon her request. He wears his uniform, and she dresses

194

in her navy-blue skirt, and the blouse she altered to look like Mrs Bennington's. She doesn't wear a hat as she wants to show off her hair, done in the latest Gibson Girl style, with some lilacs from the garden artistically pinned above her right ear. She and Edward have discussed the colour of the lilacs and he picked some for her from the gardens outside the dockyard offices. She wants him to remember the time he gave her some blooms on their picnic to Eastchurch whenever he looks at her photograph. But most of all, she wants him just to remember her and not have his head turns by some Louisa Musgrove type character who might jump in front of him the way Jane Austen's original did in *Persuasion*.

The photograph of Lieutenant Prescott now sports a silver-plated frame and stands on Maisie's bedside table in Monsieur Eggenberger's hotel. During her melancholy episodes, she sits gazing at it as though willing the facsimile of Edward to speak to her and tell her everything will be okay. But the black and white mouth remains resolutely fixed.

Meanwhile, Hattie sends postcards to Maisie's forgotten friends - to Rosie, now in the final weeks of her pregnancy, and to Lieutenant Barnes. Peter has also been given the address of the hotel and sends a postcard wishing them a happy holiday. It is addressed to both Hattie and Maisie, but Maisie barely looks at it. As their time away moves on, she asks to re-read it, scrutinising it for any news of Edward that she might have missed on her first reading. But there is none. She then starts asking if Peter has sent any more postcards, in the hope of gaining information about Edward, but he has not. Hattie has to remind Maisie that he too is probably caught up with preparations for the threatened war, and suggests that Maisie writes to him direct, they are such good friends. But Maisie declines.

As they sit together on the terrace, enjoying the view of the lake, Hattie remembers Peter's gift and hopes it might be something to cheer Maisie up.

"What is in the box Peter gave you at the station?" she asks.

"I never looked," came Maisie's doleful reply. "It slipped to the bottom of my bag, and I forgot about it."

Ena and Miss Garrett look up expectantly from their occupations as Maisie rummages through her bag for the small gift box. With a look of triumph, she pulls it out from the darkest corner and proclaims, "It looks like a box from a jeweller's shop. Do you think it's from Edward and he asked Peter to give it to me?"

"Probably not," says Miss Garrett bluntly.

"I'm sure Peter would have said if that was the case," responds Hattie, more tactfully.

Maisie opens the little box revealing the brooch Peter bought for her birthday.

"How pretty," exclaims Ena, casting her expert eye over it. "Suffragette colours, pearls, peridots, and amethysts. What a thoughtful gift." The semi-precious stones sparkle in the sunshine.

"Definitely not from Lieutenant Prescott," says Miss Garrett, with a sniff.

Maisie and Hattie exchange looks, remembering their encounter with Lieutenant Barnes when they firebombed the haystacks.

"Is there a note?" asks Hattie.

There is, folded neatly to fit into the little box. On it, Peter has written,

*I bought this for your birthday but haven't had the chance to give it to you. I hope it will remind you of your time as a suffragette.*
*Peter.*

"Put it on then," says Ena, wanting the gift to bring a smile back to the younger woman's face.

But Maisie can't hide her disappointment that it isn't from Edward and, bursting into tears, she thrusts the brooch in its little box back into her bag and runs upstairs to her room.

Having arrived in Switzerland on 27 July, it is unfortunate that Great Britain and her Empire declare war on Germany just over a week later on Tuesday 4 August, following Germany's declaration of war on Belgium, the day before. The two older schoolteachers think it really is rather tiresome, but refuse to be put out by it. When Maisie and Hattie suggest that they should cut their holiday short and return to England, Miss Garrett argues, "I don't know why you are fussing. Switzerland has declared itself neutral, so there is no immediate need for us to turn round and go home. Let's enjoy our holiday whilst we can." But Hattie and Maisie are unsure, so agree to ask the proprietor, Monsieur Eggenberger, for his advice on what to do.

They find the hotelier in his small office behind the reception area. He is surrounded by a number of newspapers; he is evidently concerned about the current situation and is not surprised that the English ladies have come to ask what is happening.

"Have you received any direction from your government as to whether or not we English tourists should end our holidays early? Should we return home now that France and Germany are at war?" Miss Garrett enquires.

The hotelier shakes his head; there hasn't been any advice as yet, and the government is keen that the tourist trade should continue, as is Monsieur Eggenberger, thinking of the loss of income.

"Please do not worry, the French authorities have promised safe passage for foreign nationals when you need to return," he reassures them. "The French are confident it will be over quickly, and they will be victorious. There are at least two hundred other British tourist staying in the region," he concludes, as if there will be safety in numbers, should the Germans prevail.

The English ladies return to the salon to discuss the matter further. Miss Garrett says, "I still say that there is no need to worry. We should just carry on as normal."

Ena agrees, saying, "Yes, if we leave now, we will just be caught up with the crowds of people who will flock back home."

"Indeed, Ena. Run along girls and enjoy your holiday," says Miss Garrett, treating them all as though they are in school, and she is the deputy headmistress of their free time.

Maisie and Hattie remain unconvinced that this is the right thing to do, but go along with her and don't argue further. Miss Garrett attempts to reassure them and calls out after them, "The French will get us out if necessary. We are British and should not let men fighting get in our way of having the good holiday that we have planned for most of the year."

Straight away, Maisie returns to the bedroom that she shares with Hattie and writes to her mother and to the headmistress, Miss Morrison, to explain their predicament. She does her best to put their minds at rest, saying that they are all right and in no danger, even though she doesn't feel that is necessarily so herself. She also writes to Edward as she is sure he will worry about her, even though she has heard nothing from him, despite her ensuring the address of the hotel is included on every postcard she sends him.

A few days later, Monsieur Eggenberger makes one addition to his earlier travel advice to the women teachers; the Consul has instructed him that all British tourists will require a passport. As rail tourism has developed across Europe over the previous sixty years, it put pressure on the existing passport and visa system. The speed and frequency with which trains crossed the borders made it difficult to carry out checks. France responded by abolishing passports and visas altogether in 1861. Other countries follow suit, so that by the time the teachers departed for their holiday, passports are all but eliminated across Europe. However, fears of national security raised by the war result in passports and visas being reintroduced at short notice.

Monsieur Eggenberger explains to the teachers that they will have to travel to Geneva to complete the paperwork needed for the documentation. Great Britain decides to take advantage of the developments in photographic technology to ensure the holder is who she or he say they are, and stipulates all passports are also to include a photograph. So, the hotelier recommends some studios in the city, so that they can comply with the new requirement.

A day is arranged when they will travel to Geneva. However, when they arrive in the city, all the studios near the consulate are inundated with work from other British travellers needing photographs. So, they have to find a photographer across town. Fortunately, they are able to do this all on the same day as Monsieur Eggenberger's list is quite helpful. But they then have to return again to the city, once the portraits are developed, so that they can be included in the documents. A further trip is then required some days later to collect the completed passports from the Consulate. This take three days out of their holiday, which annoys Miss Garrett, who keeps repeating, "I have travelled across Europe many times over the years without so much as a scrap of paper to say who I am. Never needed one before! And a photograph too!" Nevertheless, the Consulate staff work as quickly as they can to process the passports for British people in the region, so that their papers are ready ahead of their projected departure dates.

On the final trip to Geneva, Maisie is sick on the train. They catch an earlier departure in the hope of concluding their business as soon as the offices opens, so that they can use the rest of the day for sightseeing. Miss Garrett is keen to visit the recently opened *Musée d'art et d'histoire*, with its Egyptian and classical antiquities. However, Maisie is sick almost immediately they depart. It is fortunate Ena has a large paper bag with her, and they break their journey at the next station to wait until Maisie feels okay to travel again.

"Did I hear you being sick in the bathroom a couple of days ago?" Miss Garrett enquires, as they sit in the ladies' waiting room. "I hope you are not going down with something."

"Was that yesterday?" asks Ena, "I heard you being sick too."

"You must be mistaken, Ena, it was definitely Tuesday, as it was before we went to Montreux," Miss Garrett corrects her.

"I could have sworn it was yesterday," says Ena. "I wanted to change my blouse, but the laundry hadn't come back, and I only had one clean one left, so I rinsed one out in the bathroom to hang out on the balcony, and it is still there. I had to wait for Maisie to come out to do so."

"Yes, I wish you wouldn't do that, it lowers the tone," Miss Garrett says, with a sniff. "Nobody wants to see your dirty washing hanging about."

"I think it is the spicy Italian sausage Monsieur Eggenberger put out for breakfast. It is too rich for me," Maisie responds, averting her eyes and rummaging in her bag for a handkerchief to wipe her mouth with; she reapplies her red lipstick discreetly.

Miss Garrett gives the younger woman a hard look. She feels Maisie's mooning about is enough to bear, without the girl being unwell and possibly passing on a bug to the rest of the party. After some further discussion, they put it down to the brown trout with almonds which she ate for dinner the day before, as no one else is unwell and only Maisie ate the fish. Once they start their journey again, she is fine, and the day passes without any further incident.

As Maisie's mood swings continue over the next few days, Miss Garrett is increasingly irritated with her for spoiling their holiday. Having managed very nicely thank you without being married herself, she can't see why Maisie doesn't just consign the relationship with Lieutenant Prescott to the "what might have beens" of life. She has to stifle the little tsck noise that is beginning to rise to her lips each time Maisie returns to the subject of the post from England. Now, after more than two weeks in Switzerland, the little tsck escapes and is complemented with a raised eyebrow. It is soon joined by an exchange of glances with Ena, which accompanies Miss Garrett's little dismissive sniff.

They have yet to receive a response to the letters they have sent home, assuring every one of their wellbeing. There is no way of knowing if their letters have got through and Maisie is feeling on edge. She also sent out a number of postcards to let her friends know they are okay and have arrived safely. But despite everyone knowing where they are, they have heard nothing back.

There is also no reply to the special card she sent to Edward at the officers' mess. She tells herself that he is bound to be anxious about her, even though he didn't come to the station to see them off. But his lack of response just unsettles her further.

The situation isn't help when a letter does arrive from home for Maisie from her mother. It has no local news to impart that might include intelligence of Lieutenant Prescott or others in their circle. Mrs Kendall knows nothing of what ships are currently in port, or who might be coming or going. In fact, the letter contains no war news whatsoever.

Admittedly, there is little news anywhere of what is actually happening beyond Switzerland. Things are not going well for the Belgians, but what Britain and France are doing is still not clear. Miss Garrett and Hattie are keeping an eye on the newspapers, ready to mobilise their colleagues ahead of the end of their holiday, should they need to.

The following day, Maisie receives a letter from Miss Morrison, who advises that they ought to try to come home as soon as possible because they may not get a chance later, and the school needs them. Maisie brandishes the letter saying, "We should pack up now! We might not be able to get home at all and be stuck here!"

But Miss Garrett and Ena are still of the opinion that they are in no current danger. "We weren't advised by the British Consul that we should depart early when we got our passports," says Miss Garrett, as dismissive as ever.

Maisie throws down the letter and rushes to her room in tears. A very large tsck emits from Miss Garrett, with an exchange of looks with Ena. Hattie excuses herself, saying, "I'll go to her." Ena remains unshaken and gives Hattie's retreating behind a hard stare as she disappears after Maisie. She returns Miss Garrett's look with a roll of her eyes and goes back to her needlework.

Maisie throws herself on the bed and sobs. Hattie follows her in and sits on the edge of the bed, stroking her hair till the tears subside. "There, there," she keeps crooning, as though to a child. "Whatever is the matter? Things can't be that bad. We will soon be home. The French have guaranteed our safe passage, so Miss Garrett says there is no need to worry," she says, full of concern for her friend.

Maisie wipes her eyes and nose with her handkerchief and takes a deep breath. "I'm late," she says, in a matter-of-fact voice. "I might be pregnant."

Hattie also takes a deep breath, before asking, "How late?"

"Only a few days, but I'm worried. I've been sick a few mornings, and when I haven't been sick, I feel sick. I just don't feel right. I know it's too early to be sure. But how can I let Edward know? What if he's posted away whilst we are out here? What will I do?" This last sentence is accompanied by a fresh outbreak of sobbing.

Hattie resumes her crooning, whilst she considers the options. "Did Edward force you? Was it him that bruised your wrists?" she asks.

"No, I told you, I did it whilst packing," Maisie responds, averting her eyes.

Hattie remains unconvinced. "Has Edward made you any promises?" she asks cautiously. She is aware he has talked about marriage in general

206

terms around what a man should look for in a good naval wife, but that is different to coming to an agreement. She doesn't believe Edward will step up to the mark the way that Lieutenant Harris has for Rosie.

Maisie hiccups. "No," she says bluntly, "No, not in so many words and the more I think about it, the less certain I am he is considering asking me."

She looks at Hattie, takes a deep breath, and begins. "I thought I could force his hand if I submitted to him. These last few weeks we have become closer and when he held me to kiss me goodnight, I could feel his thing digging in me. He never did anything improper, but I wanted him too. We were never properly alone, so it wasn't really an option, but I was conscious he didn't think it was something he could ask me to do. Then, a couple of weeks ago, we went for a ramble, and the wheat was so high, the sun was so warm, everything was golden. We decided to sit down on the side of a hill to admire the view of the sea and Edward kissed me and I responded. He moved on top of me, and I allowed him to touch me. It was blissful. After a few moments, we heard someone coming and broke apart. We knew we had to find somewhere to be alone. I suggested to Edward that he should visit me when Miss Garrett was out at Girl Guides the following Tuesday and Mrs Bills went out to visit her married daughter. I used the pretext I wanted to lend him one of the books we read in the reading group. But it was never said what was on both our minds. We just knew that it was time.

"I couldn't wait for the day to come round. I prepared for ages. I bought a new face cream and perfume. I tidied my room. I suggested to Miss Garrett that she could pop in on Ena on the way back from Guides, so she could check that she was ready for our holiday. That way, Edward and I could have a little longer without being disturbed.

"Edward borrowed a bicycle and came down the back alley. I was waiting, pretending to read a book in the garden whilst the sun shone. When he came, I made a big thing of asking if he would like a tea, in case any nosy neighbours were watching. He brought me some late blooming lilacs, and I popped them in a vase in the kitchen, whilst keeping up a light conversation. We both knew what he was there for, but it seemed clinical just to go upstairs, like animals rutting. Edward was standing in the hallway and caught hold of me as I passed him to put the flowers in the parlour and pulled me to him. I could feel his manhood pressing insistently against me. My insides were turning to liquid, and I was melting into him. He took the vase from me and put it down on a table in the parlour. He took me by the hand and led me upstairs. His breathing was fast, but mine was just as quick. He asked which was my room, and I replied, and he pulled me into my bedroom and shut the door.

"I surrendered to him utterly. His hands, his mouth. Then, I felt a sharp pain as he entered me. I wasn't sure if I should try to stop him, but it was too late and anyway, I didn't want to.

"Then, he collapsed on top of me, and I knew it was over. He rolled off and sat up with his head bowed. He said he must get dressed. There was no declaration of love. He didn't even tell me I was beautiful. It felt like he had made a mistake, that he couldn't help himself, and then regretted it. I grabbed my kimono and put it on. I asked him if he wanted some tea now, but he said he'd better be gone. Then, I heard a key in the front door, and I knew Miss Garrett had come back sooner than expected. I ran down the stairs and met her as she came through the inner hall door.

"I asked if she had seen Ena, but she said Ena wasn't home; she knew she was out as her bicycle was gone. I garbled at her something about coming to look at the beautiful lilacs I'd picked and steered her into the parlour. I remember holding up the vase and whittering that I was looking for the best place to put them. She gave me one of her looks and said, "What, in your kimono?" I must have gone bright red, but I laughed and said I was doing last minute packing.

"I heard the creak of a stair, then a slight noise as the gate latch clicked, and Edward was gone. We never got to talk about what happened. I knew something wasn't right, but never having been in that situation, I didn't know how he should have behaved afterwards. But he hadn't said goodbye or made any arrangements to see me before we left on Saturday. I sent him a note to remind him we were leaving and gave him the hotel address again, but I got no reply. When Saturday came, I thought he might be at the station, but he wasn't. That's why I was so hopeful he might have asked Peter to give me that little jewellery box. I thought it might be a ring. I was so disappointed that it was a brooch from Peter. Then, I felt guilty for being ungrateful. But I felt so used and discarded by Edward, like an old rag."

Maisie starts crying again, "And to top it all, I've missed my monthly. What am I going to do? What if Edward won't marry me?" She says nothing to Hattie about how she was raped by the cowboy, or her fear that any baby might be his and not Edward's. The distress and shame of it is too much to share, even with Hattie. She doesn't even want to think about it herself.

Hattie feels an increased uneasiness in her stomach. Without any assurance that Lieutenant

Prescott will stand by her, Maisie could find herself with no means of support, homeless, her reputation gone, and with an unwanted baby to care for. They will need help from the others to sort this mess out.

Lieutenant Prescott thinks things got out of hand quickly with the arrival of summer. He turns over recent events and wonders what he should do.

He and Maisie had taken some nice rambles together, and when he kissed her, she had started responding in a way that resulted in him no longer being able to think straight. Possessing her had filled his brain, and it was only the lack of privacy that had stopped him going further.

Maisie was quite artless in her responses. She is past the first flush of youth, but somehow remains inexperienced. Her parents had sheltered her until her father died, after which she took this teaching post and moved into the old harridan's house. This meant her protective circle of friends and family are no longer with her, and the women she now associates with are strong, independent, and fearless of what other people will say.

On their last outing, Edward found that he had nearly lost control when kissing Maisie in the ripening wheat. He'd almost been carried away with the spontaneity of it all. He'd only been saved from going too far by the sound of voices, but Maisie had shown she didn't want him to stop. She talked about how the harridan went out to Girl Guides and she is alone in the house on Tuesdays as the housekeeper has the evening off. He found himself saying perhaps they could have a cosy tea together and she could lend him some book she kept talking about. There was only a week till she was off on her holiday, so he felt confident he wouldn't overstep the line and give Maisie the hope he will wed her, but he wished he could enjoy more of her.

He'd wanted that Tuesday to come round quicker. He'd gone to the barber for a shave and a haircut, and asked Greenleaf, his steward, to iron him a fresh shirt. He borrowed a fellow officer's bicycle and stopped to pick the last of the summer lilac on the way. Maisie had given him a photo of herself with lilac in her hair, and he thought it will be a nice touch to show he remembered. He'd cycled down the back alleys to avoid seeing any colleagues and arrived at the rear of Maisie's lodgings out of breath.

No sooner had he dismounted and touched the gate when it was opened by Maisie herself. She'd looked prettier than ever, with a slight flush on her cheeks and her lips an inviting ruby red. If he'd thought about it more, he would have wondered if it was lipstick as Maisie's friends associated with suffragettes who wore it as a badge of honour.

Maisie had invited him in for tea and enthused at the beauty of the lilacs, whilst all the time his brain had filled with the need to reach out and hold her close. The next thing, he had her in his arms and was kissing her in a hungry way, ready to devour her innocence. He'd pulled her upstairs after him. His eyes locked on hers and took her into her room which smelt of her perfume. It further assaulted his senses increasing his desire to a point where any sensible thoughts were rapidly disappearing.

He told himself they would just lay on the bed and kiss, but his hands were already pulling at her clothes. He told himself he would just admire the beauty of her body, but his mouth was on her breast softly nuzzling. He told himself he would just stroke her milky thighs, but his hands were already seeking out her secret place. He told himself he would not penetrate her, whilst all the time his manhood strained against his clothing. He told himself he would withdraw, "get off at Fratton[1]," as the men say, but once he had entered her, he could think no more.

When it was over, his brain fired up, and he asked himself, "What have you done? Why didn't you buy some French letters from the barber?" Maisie would see this as the first step to a marriage proposal, and she isn't the one for him. He'd wanted

---

[1] coitus interruptus

to place his head in his hands, but he summoned enough chivalry to say he must get dressed and get back to the base. Maisie looked at him with a mixture of thoughts racing across her face. She wanted him to appreciate her, to love her, to show that he is grateful, to acknowledge the new phase their relationship had entered, but he couldn't, he just couldn't. Then, they heard the sound of the key in the lock as the harridan returned home early.

Maisie grabbed her kimono and ran down the stairs to intercept her landlady. Edward quickly dressed and hovered at the top of the stairs with his boots in his hands, listening for an opportunity to escape from both Maisie and her colleague. He was out into the alley in no time and pressed his back against the wall in relief. He wouldn't need to look at the hurt in Maisie's eyes. His guilt had come flooding up and he'd thumped the gate causing a loud bang, before ramming his boots on and cycling back to the dockyard, without saying goodbye.

And now he couldn't think how he could get out of the mess he had created.

Sometime later, Hattie returns alone to the hotel lounge with a serious look on her face. She speaks in a low tone. "Maisie is waiting on her monthly indisposition and is rather more anxious about it than usual," - the word "indisposition" is mouthed rather than spoken.

Miss Garrett and Ena listen to this with a sharp intake of breath. It is over two weeks since they departed, and they calculate what the possible implications of the delay to Maisie's monthly indisposition might be. Hattie explains, "Maisie believes Lieutenant Prescott will do the right thing when he knows her predicament."

Miss Garrett and Ena exchange more glances. Ena responds, "That can't be relied upon, given the circumstances of the war. Even if it can, the lieutenant might be posted before any action can be taken."

Secretly, Ena thinks that Maisie must have overplayed her hand. If Lieutenant Prescott has not proposed to her before her departure, knowing that the war clouds are gathering, and a possible posting is on the horizon, he is unlikely to do so unless forced into it. If they were at home, Mrs Bennington might be enlisted to help, but they are far away and need to act. The lieutenant won't want his superior officer to know that he has left Maisie in a delicate situation, but if he has already been posted, it might be months before he is able to do the right thing, which will be too late to save Maisie's reputation.

Out loud, she says, "It will be better for Maisie to bring her indisposition on whilst we are away from home, so no gossip can escape. It will also give her a bit of time to recuperate, should she need to."

"We can't help her if she has been foolish enough to give herself to that man," Miss Garrett says, self-righteously. "She must pay for her sins!" She stands up indignantly and folds her arms in a decisive way.

"I think Lieutenant Prescott may have forced himself on her, but she is protecting him," Hattie responds, wanting the other women to appreciate the full extent of Maisie's predicament. "When we went swimming, I saw bruises on her wrists, and I think I saw some on her thighs, but I can't be sure."

Miss Garrett shifts uncomfortably as she wrestles with her conscience. Part of her feels if Maisie has been foolish enough to give in to Prescott, then she is no better than she should be and deserves to pay the price. This is her usual reaction to finding out some woman has fallen and been shown to have loose morals. However, if he had forced himself on her, that is a different matter. She remembers that Maisie had been out of sorts those last few days before their holiday; how she had seemed to withdraw into herself, and how she has spent an inordinate amount of time in the bathroom sobbing. Whenever Miss Garrett has asked her if anything is the matter, she has responded that she is fine.

The older teacher is fond of Maisie because she really cares for her students. Miss Garrett realises the girl is probably a victim of her own innocence; she has warned her not to be familiar with the military men as they will take liberties. This is not the first time she has heard about decent girls being ruined by unscrupulous officers. But, most of all, she just doesn't want to see Maisie come to a bad end, not if she can help it. She doesn't want to see Maisie lose her post at school and all that will entail, especially if Prescott walks away scot free. So, she makes her decision to do all that she can to help the girl out.

Meanwhile, Ena, more practically, considers what can be done and enquires, "Has Maisie thought of taking any remedies to hasten her indisposition's arrival?"

Hattie responds that she thinks not, so Ena offers to walk into town to find a chemist shop that might help. "Will you come with me please, Miss Garrett? Your French is so much better than mine," Ena asks, using flattery to persuade her friend to help Maisie.

Miss Garrett's command of French is generally good. However, she doesn't know the words necessary for such a purchase, but she formulates sentences in her mind that might do the trick. "I'll get my bag," she responds, by way of acquiescence.

Miss Garrett and Ena set off into the town centre to find a chemist shop to buy some female remedy pills. Ena seems more aware of these cures than Miss Garrett would have given her credit for. Ena says, "We need to ensure they contain pennyroyal or rue, for the tablets to achieve the result we are looking for. Pennyroyal is best." Ena seems to speak with some authority and Miss Garrett ponders on why that should be; she doesn't think that Cambridge University taught that kind of chemistry.

At home, there is a society for "befriending" women and girls who help women in need. Its membership is secret to protect the reputation of those it aids. Miss Garrett doesn't see Ena as being one of the befrienders, as they tend to be married women intent on spiriting the unfortunate women away to have their babies in secret. However, she knows Ena has taught girls for twenty years and is keen to get them into grammar schools. She wants them to live independent lives away from the need to be supported by men. Ena keeps in touch with her former pupils when they go on to college or University, and although she only teaches home economics and the younger girls in school, she does private coaching for the older girls in science and mathematics, often without payment. She will do everything she can to get those girls into higher education. It is for that reason that Miss Garrett thinks a spinster like Ena might have knowledge of birth control methods.

What Miss Garrett doesn't know is Ena is a disciple of Alice Vickery, the first woman to qualify as a chemist and druggist in England. Alice gave frequent lectures promoting birth control as an essential element for the emancipation of women. Ena attended one of her lectures when she was a student. She knows that as long ago as ancient Greece the female physician, Metrodora, recommended the use of pennyroyal with wine to bring on menstruation, and this is why so many female remedies include it as an ingredient.

The transaction is less troublesome than Miss Garrett thinks it might be. On entering the chemist, a young girl comes to help them, and they ask if they can be served by a mature woman. She summons a matron from the back of the shop and Miss Garrett constructs a sentence using the French words for "monthly," "friend" and "missed." The matron seems to understand their meaning and produces a couple of packets, one of which has the word "pennyroyal" listed as one of the ingredients. Miss Garrett is pleased to see the word is the same in both French and English. The pills are purchased, and the matron wraps them discreetly in brown paper. She then produces a pack of Southall's sanitary towels from under the counter and enigmatically says, "She will need these."

The towels are also duly wrapped and tied with string. Next, the matron produces some Laudanum; "For afterwards," she explains, tapping her nose as she did so.

Finally, she almost inaudibly says, "If your friend needs any further assistance, I may be able to make a recommendation."

Miss Garrett quickly translates that to Ena, who has assumed charge and nods her assent. Miss Garrett doesn't enquire what form "further assistance" might take, and the two women pay for their purchases and leave the shop cautiously, so as not to attract attention from any other hotel residents who might be passing.

Ena then says, "We ought to have clean towels available for when the pills take effect. We can buy some in the haberdashery shop, along with a bed sheet. We can't use the hotel's as we will need to dispose of them afterwards as they will be blood-stained. We won't be able to wash them. They will need boiling. So, we had best get some we can discreetly throw into the furnace in the boiler room at the back of the hotel."

Their purchases complete, the two teachers return to the hotel for a counsel of war. However, Hattie says, "Maisie has cried herself to sleep and cannot be disturbed," so Ena and Miss Garrett set out their plans to Hattie in Maisie's absence.

Ena opens with, "It will be for the best if Maisie's indisposition is encouraged to appear whilst we are away from home." This is said with much checking for eavesdroppers and a lot of mouthing of indelicate words.

"No one else will need to know," joins in Miss Garrett, now a convert to the cause and, like all converts, all the more zealous for it.

"If Maisie doesn't receive a proposal, it will be unthinkable that she should have a child alone; her reputation will be ruined," Ena continues. Nobody mentions the sad alternative that many women in such a predicament take - suicide. Or the possibility that Maisie's family might seek to get her sent to an asylum for bringing shame on the family.

"She will be unable to teach, and if she can't teach, how will she be able to support herself and the child?" adds Miss Garrett, to bring the point home. "I don't think Mrs Kendall is the sort of woman who will stand by her daughter and find a suitable foster parent for the babe," she concludes. She ignores the fact that usually she is just the sort of woman who will blame an unmarried woman for falling pregnant as being a person of low morals.

Hattie can see the logic. However, she responds, "It is very early days, and the indisposition may arrive naturally. Maisie wants to write to Lieutenant Prescott when she is sure, and there will still be time for her to look for a remedy if necessary."

Ena is almost animated. "There is no sense in waiting; it's too risky! The remedies work best if taken as soon as possible. Leave it too late and the chances of it not working rise dramatically. Increasing the dosage is not an option, as that will be dangerous for Maisie. Too much can lead to complications. We only have a small window of time to use the pills and bring on her indisposition." Ena doesn't elaborate that complications include death.

Miss Garrett nods her support, whilst Hattie maintains Maisie's position, "Surely, we can wait a few days for either nature or the post to produce a result?" With Maisie in bed, there seems no point in discussing the matter further. However, Ena and Miss Garrett impress upon Hattie the need to establish the facts. Ena asks, "Has he actually made any promises? If not, then we shouldn't wait! She should take the remedy straight away!" but Hattie holds her counsel on the matter.

The following day, after the four women have breakfasted together, it is suggested that a walk by the lake shore might be in order. Maisie has a headache from crying, which they think some fresh air might clear as the lavender oil rubbed on her temples has not. After a little while of walking along the promenade, Hattie moves away from Maisie and links arms with Ena, whom she speaks to in hushed tones. Miss Garrett tries to crane her neck to listen, but can't hear anything, much to her annoyance. Maisie walks slightly ahead of the group in the knowledge that she is being discussed.

After a while, Hattie breaks away from Ena and links arms with Maisie again. She starts a bright audible conversation about the weather and how the war will interrupt the test matches across the Empire. Miss Garrett quickens her pace to walk alongside Ena, who repeats what Hattie has told her. "Maisie says she has only been intimate with Lieutenant Prescott once, just before they departed. The silly girl thought if she submitted to his advances, he would ask her to marry him. Hattie has asked her again about the bruises, but she just blushes and tries to move the conversation on. So, it looks very likely Prescott forced her to let him have his way with her."

Miss Garrett knows that the last time Maisie saw Lieutenant Prescott must have been Tuesday, the day she helps out with the Girl Guides after school. She recalls that on her return, Maisie seemed flustered and slightly in disarray. Miss Garrett had noticed how her hair had come loose from its pins leaving Maisie looking like a Pre-Raphaelite painting and had drawn attention to it. Maisie had said, "I'm letting it down to plait it so I can check I have enough hairpins for the journey." This didn't make any sense to Miss Garrett, as hairpins are easy to obtain and are not expensive.

Maisie was wearing her green silk kimono which Miss Garrett was sure had already been packed for their trip to Lake Geneva. It seemed odd that Maisie would have gone into her trunk to get it out, just to wear whilst doing her hair. The kimono is one of Maisie's prize possessions. Her aunt told her she had been given it by an arty friend who claimed to have been to soirees at William Morris' home. It wasn't actually made in Japan, but it certainly has the look, and when Maisie wore it, she tried to cultivate the languid air of being in that kind of Bohemian circle.

The backdoor had also been open and although the July evening was warm, Maisie did not generally wander about in the garden with her hair down whilst dressed in her kimono. Miss Garrett realised the lieutenant had probably sneaked out that way upon her return. Indeed, Maisie had kept her talking in the hallway, then called her attention to some lilacs she had placed on the parlour table, which she said she picked from the garden, but Miss Garrett had not recognised the variety as it was a much darker purple. Maisie had claimed that was exactly the reason why she had picked them, as the blooms were exceptional. Miss Garrett had been almost sure that the lilacs had finished flowering in her garden, so none of the story added up.

She tries hard to remember if she had noticed any marks on Maisie at the time, which might have indicated that Prescott had forced her, but she cannot be sure. However, she did think she had noticed a mark on her wrist on the Friday before they came on holiday, when Maisie rolled up her sleeves to help with the washing-up.

Miss Garrett also remembered that on the Wednesday, Mrs Bills had grumbled that Maisie's bed had needed changing as her monthly had come early and there was blood on the sheets. Miss Garrett now realised it was from Maisie's virginity and not her period.

It all makes sense now. Some form of intimacy occurred in Maisie's room between her and the lieutenant either, with or without her full consent, whilst Miss Garrett was with the Girl Guides. Miss Garrett is annoyed that it happened. She has never forbidden gentlemen callers to her lodgers, Maisie, or her predecessors, but it is generally understood it should not take place. Single women must always be mindful of their reputation. If Maisie had not invited him in, any misunderstandings of that kind could not have transpired, and she would not be in this mess now.

It is different for Hattie, Miss Garrett thinks. She is forever out with different men. However, the whole town knows that Hattie is off to play cricket or tennis or something else, and no one ever seems to question the morality of it. Only a few weeks ago, Hattie competed in a mixed doubles tennis tournament between civilians and the services, and won the cup with her male partner. Four young men brought her home, cheering her all the way for beating the military wives. No one thinks anything of it. But none of the other women teachers in school can behave in that way and their reputations remain intact.

Miss Garrett decides to say nothing about her suspicions and listens to Ena's account of Maisie's intimacy with Prescott in silence, before asking, "Did Hattie discuss using the female remedy pills with Miss Kendall?"

"Maisie wants to wait a few more days, but promises if she hears nothing, she will take the pills. Maisie says she will write a carefully worded letter to Prescott upon their return to the hotel, explaining her situation and requesting he send her a telegram as soon as he receives the letter," Ena responds.

It is also suggested that they should send a letter to another lady teacher in their circle to ask for any intelligence on Lieutenant Prescott's demeanour and, more usefully, any information about naval postings.

Back in the hotel, Maisie and Hattie retire to their room to compose the letter to the lieutenant, whilst Ena and Miss Garrett devise the second letter.

"I think we should write to Miss Fitch. She sometimes joins Hattie and Maisie on their walks," suggests Ena.

"I'm not convinced that she can keep a secret. Remember how she told everyone that Miss Clark had to get married. I think we should ask Miss Bostock. She is discreet," says Miss Garrett.

"She's discreet because she is lazy. She won't bother asking anyone else for any news. You know she always says it takes a lot to get her off her sofa from reading her romances."

"How about Miss Allison? She won't think it odd that we are asking for intelligence on our naval acquaintances like some might, and she is discreet too."

So, it is agreed that Miss Allison will be the recipient of the other letter.

Hattie decides she will also write to Rosie. It is unlikely she will have gathered any news, as Rosie is now heavily pregnant and is on bed rest as recommended by the naval doctor; a man of little experience in obstetrics who recommends bed rest for any woman who is referred to him for whatever reason. But her husband, Lieutenant Harris, might have some information.

Miss Garrett and Ena set to work writing their letter to Miss Allison asking for news of home and their circle of friends, including the lieutenant amongst them. They ask for word on any postings and send their best regards to be passed to their various colleagues and to Mrs Bennington. They include the latter; in case they need to call on her support to get the Rear Admiral to intervene.

A little later, both Maisie and Hattie reappear with Maisie's letter to Edward. This has been tricky to write as Maisie needs to tell him of her situation, but in a way that can be told in a letter that might be seen by others in the officers' mess. She reads it aloud to her companions for their comment and input, and after much to-ing and fro-ing, they agree the following –

*My Darling Edward,*
*I am missing you very much here in beautiful Lake Geneva. I'm always thinking of the time we*

*spent together before we departed. I may be reminded of it always. I hope you don't get posted before I return as I can't wait to share my thoughts with you on some important news I have. Please telegraph me as soon as you know anything.*

*Yours Maisie*

The words *I may be reminded* are changed for *shall be reminded,* then back again. Ena argues that if Maisie's indisposition arrives late, then to say *shall be reminded* might overplay her hand.

Eventually, the three letters are sealed and addressed, and passed to reception to catch the next post. Maisie decides to also send a postcard to Mrs Bennington at Admiralty House in the dockyard. She selects one that shows the Russian Church in Vevey, and adds a seemingly cheerful and friendly greeting –

*We are enjoying the sights. Your husband must be working Lieutenant Prescott very hard as he hasn't had time to write to me, and I so want to hear from him before he might be posted! I also have some news for him that cannot wait.*

That should do the trick, she thinks, as she pops the stamp on and places it with the other letters.

The four schoolteachers pass an anxious few days. They enjoy a trip on the lake to Montreux and catch the train into Lausanne to visit the cathedral. They attend the English church in Vevey to participate in a service. But, in between, the time drags. One afternoon, whilst taking tea on the terrace, Ena suddenly says, "I was once in a similar predicament."

The other three women turn to look at her wide eyed at this unprompted confession. Ena continues. "It is during the second Boer War. I was teaching science at a girls' grammar school in Portsmouth, near where I lived with my family. I met a young officer in the navy from *HMS Barracouta*. His name was John, John Piper. We fell in love; I was twenty-nine and thought it would be my last chance of happiness. As the day got nearer for his ship to sail for the Cape, I thought if I gave into his advances, he would marry me. I had attended some lectures on birth control at university and put into practice what I learnt, so I was confident I would be safe. I'd hoped that we could get a special licence and be married before he sailed. So, I submitted to his advances. The date of his departure was postponed, whilst work continued to ready the ship. We were intimate on more than one occasion in a discreet hotel on the sea front in Southsea.

Suddenly, he announced they were sailing the following day. I had my monthly indisposition a few days earlier, so believed that I was safe. John took me to a jeweller in town and bought me a ring. It wasn't strictly an engagement ring; he placed it on my right hand. And then, he was gone. I swapped the ring to my left hand because I wanted to believe that he meant to marry me on his return once he had told his parents. We wrote to each other for weeks and he said he loved me and missed me as much as I did him. The letters arrived in batches as they were passed to other ships sailing towards England, or were posted when his ship was in port on the way to the Cape.

"My indisposition came and went; it was never regular. But, after three months it stopped. I went to see a midwife who told me the unwanted news. The birth control we used must have failed. I wrote to John to tell him and waited weeks for the response to come back. But when I did receive his reply, he said he had always used a sheath, so the child can't possibly be his and anyway he'd been away too long. He called me some unpleasant names and said he no longer wished to see me or write to me. I was devastated.

"I had made up schemes in my head of how I could conceal my pregnancy until he returned. I could move to a different naval town and have the child whilst I awaited his return. I would call myself Mrs Piper. I looked for positions in schools elsewhere in readiness and applied to the new Broadway School in Sheerness, where I was unknown and could conceal my identity. No one need know that the baby was born ahead of our wedding, and all those dreams came tumbling down with that letter.

"I told my mother I was in trouble and asked for her help. But she told my father who called me a whore and threw me out of our family home." Ena takes a deep swallow after she says this, before carrying on.

"I cried bitter tears and returned to the midwife. She said that the remedy pills might work, but it wasn't certain as I was too far gone as I was nearly five months by that time. She said the amount of pills I would need might kill me. However, she said if I paid her, she could ensure the baby didn't come.

"I sold John's ring, and some other jewellery, and paid the midwife. She made me drink a pint of gin to numb the pain and I laid down on a bed of rags she made to soak up the blood. She told me to bite on a leather strap. I couldn't look at what she was doing, but I still felt the pain in a faraway sort of way through the gin. Then, there was such a rushing of blood, and she cleared up everything.

"She told me the baby was a girl; another poor soul saved from suffering, she said. I sat up in a dizzy haze and was sick. She said the bleeding would continue for a few days, but, if it was heavy, I would need to seek help, but I was not to tell anyone that it was she whom I had visited. She gave me more clean rags to wear and, once it was dark, I made my way to my lodgings. It took weeks until I felt well enough to go out and months before I was back to full strength.

"I felt empty inside and have felt empty every day since. In my mind, I called my baby Susannah, and every student I teach, I aim to give the start in life that my scrap of a daughter never had. And when I buy jewellery, I'm trying to buy myself back in time to the moment before I sold my ring to pay the midwife. That's why I have so much jewellery because I can't buy that moment back, and I keep trying," she ended, with a sob.

There is a moments silence whilst the three other women take this in. Ena removes her spectacles and looks down into her lap. Tears slowly trickle down her stricken face onto her hands. Hattie reaches out to comfort her, realising that this may be one of the few times Ena has ever told the story. "I'm so sorry," she whispers.

Ena gives a large sniff, balls her fists into her eyes, and shakes her head. "She would be fourteen

233

now," she says. "My Susannah. But I had no choice. Had I not seen the midwife, I would not be here today. I took up the appointment at the Broadway School and moved away from Portsmouth to start a new life. I haven't seen my family since that day. I told Miss Morrison I had been jilted and that's why I'd called myself Price when my name is Briggs. I'm not sure she was convinced. But she gave me the benefit of the doubt. I'm glad she did. I don't know what I would have done otherwise."

The women all nod. Maisie excuses herself and goes to her room. Ena stands up, smoothes her hair, and says she needs some time to think, and disappears into the garden.

Miss Garrett sits quietly and turns over what Ena has said in her mind. She has always judged other women as no better than they ought to be, if they became pregnant out of wedlock. She has always believed they are at fault. She saw them as women of low morals and lacking restraint. But Ena and Maisie have made her realise that things are not always that cut and dry. In future, she will not be so hard on others.

Sometime later, when the group reassemble in the hotel lounge before dinner, Maisie says, "I have something I want to say." They all look at her expectantly. "I was very moved by Ena sharing her confidence with us today. Whilst I don't think that

Edward is like that," (Miss Garrett sniffs loudly) "I can see that there is a risk the war will intervene. If I don't get a telegram by Friday, I promise I will take the pennyroyal pills on Saturday."

A sigh of relief goes around the table. Hattie gives Maisie a little hug. "It will be for the best," she whispers.

Friday comes and goes, without the hoped-for telegram from Edward. A letter comes by return of post from Miss Allison, but she has no news from the dockyard. Lieutenant Barnes has not attended the reading group since war was declared, so there is no intelligence to be had about Lieutenant Prescott. Rosie has yet to reply to Hattie's letter, but it doesn't look like she will have anything more to say than Miss Allison.

Maisie becomes more and more like a crushed flower as the day progresses. At half past seven, she wishes them all a good night and takes herself off to bed. Hattie exchanges glances with Miss Garrett and Ena, who almost imperceptibly shakes her head. Hattie curls back into her chair and watches her friend climb the stairs. "She will want some time on her own," Ena says.

The following morning, nobody can eat any breakfast, and they gather in Maisie and Hattie's room. Ena carries the brown paper parcels which they have purchased from the chemist in town, and

Miss Garrett orders a tray of English tea, which she carries. Hattie lets them into the room, where Maisie is seated on the bed with her feet up. Her hair is loose, and she is dressed in the green silk kimono and her night gown.

Ena unwraps the small parcel and examines the blood red tin. She opens it and takes out the paper instructions. There are twelve small green dragon's eye pills inside, and there is a distinct smell of peppermint. She unfolds the paper and asks Miss Garrett to translate it into English.

Maisie and the other women listen carefully as Miss Garrett goes through the instructions and dosage. Maisie takes a deep breath and says, "What do I say if Edward telegraphs me?"

Ena responds, "Your letter was ambiguous enough that you can steer away from your late monthly indisposition. We are only hurrying it along, so you are not inconvenienced by it, if it comes whilst we are travelling home. Men don't understand these things; their knowledge is limited to only how it affects them. If you say it was late, he will accept that, and it is the truth."

Maisie takes another deep breath and says, "Will it hurt?"

Ena is quick to reassure her. "Not too much at this early stage. You may have a reaction to the pills that make you unwell for a couple of days, but you should be fine by the time we need to travel home."

Miss Garrett joins in with, "We will need to let the French authorities and the British Consul know we are planning to travel, so if you are slightly unwell, we can blame any delay in returning home on the war."

Maisie looks at Ena and says, "Have you helped other girls in this situation?"

Ena knows only the truth will work here and says, "Yes, a couple of times with my former pupils. But, only at this early preventive stage. Not if she has left it too late. I'm not a midwife, but I do know how the tablets work. Women have been using pennyroyal since ancient times to regulate their monthlies. But, of course, these pills may be slightly different as they are not English."

She reaches out and squeezes Maisie's hand. "You will be fine. There will be some discomfort, but that part is quick. It may just be like a bad monthly, but no worse than that. Afterwards, there will be some bleeding, and you may have more cramps than usual. But it will all pass. Now, I suggest you take the pills and Hattie will run you a bath, so you can sit in that. It will help ease the discomfort." She doesn't say and will make it easier to clear up after.

Maisie nods and asks for the tea and accepts the pills that Ena hands to her. Miss Garrett produces a "medicinal" bottle of brandy from nowhere and pours a generous measure into the teacup. Maisie swallows the pills and brandy laced tea in one, and Hattie goes to run the bath. Miss Garrett tops up the cup with more brandy for her to drink.

After a little while, Maisie says she thinks she is ready for her bath. Miss Garrett and Ena say they will wait in the bedroom, whilst Hattie assists in the bathroom. Hattie promises to come and get Ena should she need her. Miss Garrett says, "Take the brandy with you. Miss Kendall will need more of it." Hattie takes the bottle and closes the bathroom door with finality.

Ena and Miss Garrett stay in Maisie and Hattie's bedroom. They make Maisie's bed with the sheet they have bought, and a rubber mattress cover they have requested from the housekeeper. They place one of the towels on top of the sheet, Hattie has taken the other with her. They leave the door ajar so they can listen out for any cries for help. They hear the murmured tones of Hattie helping Maisie undress and her getting into the water. They hear the gentle splashes. They hear Maisie's breathing become deeper and her stifled groans. They hear Hattie's soothing words as she rubs Maisie's back.

Then they hear Maisie softly sobbing as her hopes for getting Lieutenant Prescott to marry her seep away.

After about an hour, the bathroom door is opened. Maisie walks back slowly to her room wrapped in a towel with her kimono draped from her shoulders whilst Hattie supports her. Miss Garrett immediately goes into the bathroom to clear up, and Ena produces the Southall's sanitary towels and the Laudanum, and helps Hattie put Maisie to bed. They leave her to sleep and take turns to sit by her.

Tummon, one of the ratings who distributes the post to the officers at the dockyard naval base, brings Edward's mail to the small office he shares with another lieutenant before beginning work in the anteroom outside. Edward sorts through the letters and stops. One envelope causes his stomach to knot. The writing is Maisie's, and it bears a Swiss postage stamp. He is just about to put it into his pocket unopened when Mrs Bennington comes into the office without knocking. With the eyesight of a sniper she says," Is that a letter from Miss Kendall? That looks like a foreign stamp."

Edward concedes that it is. She follows up with, "Aren't you going to read it?" and stands over him whilst he reluctantly opens the letter.

"What does she say?" Mrs Bennington asks, "I hear she has sent postcards to you in the officers' mess every day."

Edward again tries to make light of it, "She has, I've have more than twenty." He waves the letter and says, "She is just saying what a lovely time we had before she left for Switzerland."

"If that is all she has to say, you can read it to me. I am very fond of Miss Kendall and would love to hear from her." The tall, elegant woman sits herself down on a spare chair and looks at Edward expectantly.

He tries his wide boyish grin on her in an attempt to put her off, "It's very brief, she hardly says more than that." But Mrs Bennington remains unmoved, he is not the first officer with a winning smile whom she has had dealings with, and she continues to look at him, till he capitulates and reads the letter aloud.

"What a happy coincidence that I dropped by," she says, "as I too had a postcard from Miss Kendall today, expressing much the same that she would like to hear from you before you might be posted. She tells me she has some important news for you. I am going to the post office and can post a reply to the hotel for you. Do you know when she is due back?"

Edward tries to reassure her by saying, "I will write to her as soon as I get back to the officers' mess." But Mrs Bennington settles herself deeper into the chair. "I'm in no hurry," she says, "And the Rear Admiral is awfully fond of Miss Kendall too. He will never forgive me, or you," she adds pointedly, "if the poor girl doesn't get a reply before she sets off for home. She must be very worried about the war. I can even take a telegraph message for you if that will help."

Mrs Bennington smiles at Edward, but he notes it doesn't reach her eyes which remain keenly hawk like, ready to strike. "I can't think what to say," Edward ventures.

"I'm sure you can, lieutenant. Miss Kendall will obviously look for reassurance that you remain constant and are anxious for her return. I take it you do still remain constant. If not, you need to tell her. A month away is a long time. But the Rear Admiral is always saying what a lovely couple you make, and what a fine naval wife Miss Kendall will be. And we both know how much the right wife can further a man's career. The Rear Admiral will take a very dim view if Miss Kendall is disappointed because your future plans are already made, especially if she has cause to be *reminded of your time together always*," says Mrs Bennington in a way that brooks no disagreement. She stands up and says, "I take it we understand one another lieutenant. I trust I will soon hear good reports." And with that, she leaves the office.

Edward crumples Maisie's letter and throws it in the wastepaper basket. He hasn't banked on her out-manoeuvring him by writing to the Old Man's wife. Mrs Bennington has made it clear; he has to make an honest woman of Maisie if he wants to progress. He considers what life with Maisie will be like. Whilst she isn't all he wants; she ticks a lot of his boxes. He can make it work. But she has no money and no family. Being a favourite with the Rear Admiral's wife will only take him so far.

But a war has just started and that always provides opportunities to gain promotion, he thinks. You can't rise high in the navy without seeing some real action. He can ask to transfer to a ship. Shore base is fine and working direct to the Rear Admiral puts you in the spotlight, but it won't help you progress as far as active service will.

Edward makes up his mind there and then, he will request a transfer to a ship straight away.

Mrs Bennington wastes no time briefing the Rear Admiral about the potential situation between Lieutenant Prescott and Miss Kendall. An essentially moral man, the Rear Admiral feels duty bound to ensure his immediate staff are beyond reproach, even if he can't ensure all his men are. He would not have seen any wrong in Prescott visiting a woman on a commercial footing. A man has his needs after all, and a dockyard town offers such women for every taste, pocket, and class. But a young lady should be treated as such, and mistakes paid for. He therefore makes it his business to send for the lieutenant at the earliest opportunity to see what the young man has to say for himself.

Edward knows when the summons comes the Rear Admiral will be displeased with him for not doing the right thing by Maisie and it will make his position untenable. But he prepares his speech in his head and is ready. He knocks on the door of the Old Man's office with a sure hand. "Come in," calls the senior officer.

Bennington sits behind an enormous mahogany desk covered in papers and nautical charts in the centre of the large wood panelled room. The gold braid on his sleeves reaches almost to his elbow. He looks up as the door opens.

"You want to see me Sir?" asks Edward.

"Ah yes Prescott. I understand from Mrs Bennington there is potentially a tricky situation involving Miss Kendall. What can you tell me about it?" asks the Rear Admiral, removing his glasses to get a better look at Prescott.

"I believe Miss Kendall is mistaken. Being a sweet innocent girl, I suspect she has mistaken our embraces for more than they were."

"Are you sure of that Prescott?" Bennington asks not quite believing him.

"Yes, I am," lies Edward. "I would never take liberties with a young lady of Miss Kendell's standing. You know how women are. I'm sure her postcard to Mrs Bennington is more innocent in content than it seems."

"I see," says the Rear Admiral, stroking his silver beard thoughtfully, "I understand she will be home shortly. Can I ask Mrs Bennington to let the young lady know you have been busy, and will be able to sort out this misunderstanding as soon as possible?"

"Certainly, Sir. However, I had intended to ask for an interview with you myself and would like to take this opportunity, if I may, to talk about my next posting."

This wrong footed the senior officer and before he can answer, Edward carries on, "I will very much like to be involved in the war on active duty. I wanted to ask, if I may, for a transfer to a ship as soon as possible. I don't want to miss the opportunity to give the Hun a bloody nose."

"I see," responds Bennington again. "Well, I'll see what we can do. I understand Commodore

Tyrwhitt and Commodore Keyes are planning an operation out of Harwich. It's early days yet, but there's a possibility of bearding the Hun in his lair. I will contact Tyrwhitt and see if he can use a good lieutenant. I'll let you know how I get on and will trust you will lay Miss Kendall's mind at rest."

"Certainly, Sir and thank you."

"Okay, dismissed," says the Rear Admiral putting his reading glasses back on and returning to his papers once again.

Edward marches out with his head high, confident in the knowledge he will be on his way soon with no intention of writing to Maisie first as the Old Man has requested.


Over the next few days, Maisie keeps to her room. She is suffering from stomach cramps and a raging headache, and she has been sick a few times, but the Laudanum is helping. Ena is worried that the pills haven't worked. But Miss Garrett assures her that from what she saw in the bathroom the sickness is probably just a reaction to the pills.

They are due to depart on Thursday, but on the Wednesday, Ena calls a meeting after breakfast and begins, "I think we need to delay our departure for a couple more days. I don't think Maisie is well enough to travel."

"Yes," says Miss Garrett, "She is still looking very pale. We can set off next Saturday. That way Maisie can fully recover and still be back in time for school to start again on Tuesday."

"I think that is right," Hattie agrees, "Maisie is able to sit up in bed and she tells me that the bleeding is lessening, but it will still be too much for her to risk a long journey."

Miss Garrett says, "I will secure our rooms until then. Hattie, can you write to Miss Morrison to say we will be delayed due to the war but hope to be back in time for the new school term, please? Ena and I will go to the British Consul in Geneva to discuss the travel arrangements for our return journey."

When they return in the late afternoon, Maisie has got up and is sitting quietly in the garden with Hattie who is stroking one of the hotel's resident cats. Miss Garrett and Ena are looking tired and drawn. "Is everything arranged?" Hattie asks as she scratches the tabby's ear.

Miss Garrett takes a deep breath and responds, "Unfortunately, the Germans are moving more quickly than the French have anticipated and its thought they may be in Paris in a matter of days. Which is bad news for us, as well as the Parisians. The French believed they could hold them, but the Germans have used their railway networks to mobilise their troops and are poised ready to strike. The British Consul says the French were not expecting them to move so fast and have been using their calvary to try to outrun the German trains, which of course, cannot be done. It is only because the Belgians have been ripping up their own railways that the Germans aren't in Northern France already. Calais is just thirty miles from the Belgium border, and the Belgians only abandoned Brussels on Monday. The situation is not looking good.

"We have two choices. The first is to travel to Paris then Calais or Boulogne and hope for the best. The second is to travel to the coast without going through Paris, but that seems impossible unless we spend days crossing France on rural railway lines.

"But one thing is certain, we can't wait till Saturday. We must go tomorrow as originally planned. Otherwise, we risk not getting home at all. The Consul has written us a letter of safe passage to go with our new passports. It should get us through any check points."

"Do you think you will be okay Maisie?" asks Hattie, full of concern for her friend.

Maisie gradually drains of colour whilst Miss Garrett sets out their position. She is still too unwell to respond with, "*I told you so, we should have left earlier*," and besides the immediacy of their situation takes priority. Instead, Maisie responds, "Yes of course."

"Right," replies Miss Garrett, "Ena, can you tell Monsieur Eggenberger our plans have changed and ask him to give us our final bill for tomorrow morning and ask him to arrange a porter to transport our trunks to the station, please. Also ask him for packed lunches and suppers. Normally it would take us about eight hours to do the journey, so if we have two meals each, we should have enough food if we are delayed. I will go to the chemist and buy more Southall's towels for Miss Kendall to make her more comfortable. I will also get any other supplies for our journey that we might need, so let me have a list of anything you want me to get. Miss Roberts, if you can help Miss Kendall with her packing that will be very useful. She can't risk lifting anything heavy. Miss Kendall, can you write letters home to Miss Morrison and to Mrs Bills to tell them we are departing here as originally planned, and say we should arrive home on Saturday at the latest?" Miss Garrett continues making travel plans and has got her *Bradshaw's* out to assist. "When we arrive in Paris at *Gare de Lyon*, we will need to cross to *Gare De Nord*, so we should find a hotel as near to there as possible for an overnight stay. We can get a motor taxi there."

"Are we going to have enough money for these extras?" Hattie asks with some concern.

Ena responds quickly, "I always have a reserve. Also, I always sew some small items of jewellery into the hem of my skirt to sell if needed for emergencies."

Maisie and Hattie are wide eyed at her foresight. Ena's jewellery collection is extensive, and they are overwhelmed she would consider selling any of it. It makes them realise how serious their situation is.

Miss Garrett says, "We won't need to pay extra for our railway tickets, as Thomas Cook guarantees our passage home via any route."

"What about the steamer?" asks Hattie.

"Well, we will have to see when we get there, but we think the tickets will still cover our passage," says Ena. "We've no time to waste, we have to be at Vevey Station as early as possible tomorrow morning to give us the best chance of getting to Paris before nightfall."

By seven o'clock on Thursday 20 August, Miss Garrett, Ena, Hattie, and Maisie are up and dressed in their travelling costumes, which given the summer weather, are likely to be uncomfortably hot later in the day. Their trunks are ready, their hotel bill paid, their packed meals stowed and their *true grit* ready. They breakfast together in the empty dining room in near silence, each swallowing down her apprehension with every mouthful.

Maisie's bleeding is almost ended, but she is worn out and feels drained emotionally as well as physically. She tells the others she is fine to travel, although another couple of days rest would see her back to full health. She has also enjoyed the attention from her friends. Her father didn't believe in coddling, as he saw it as a form of idleness and therein lay the Devil's opportunity to make work for idle hands. Whenever Maisie had been unwell as a girl, her father would berate her mother for fussing over the child. Being spoiled by her friends and colleagues is a salve to her broken heart. It gives her an excuse to lie around on the *chaise longue* or retreat to her room and be melancholy without having to try to join in. Now she realises self-pity is a luxury she can't afford if they are to beat the Germans to the English Channel.

They collect their travel essentials and walk to the station where their trunks are already waiting, having been transported by the hotel porters earlier. The sun is blazing down already, and it will be hot in the railway carriage. The sunlight flashes brightly across the lake as though sending urgent messages by Morse code as they prepare to wait for the train to Geneva.

Maisie gathers herself together and says, "I haven't really said thank you to you all. You have been so supportive. You have been true friends to me. I don't know where I would have been without you. I think it is quite apparent that Edward is not going to step in and do the right thing by me." This last statement is said with a little gulp.

Miss Garrett tries to resist but an indignant sniff escapes her, "You can never rely on a man unless they put a ring on your finger," she says.

"Not even then," says Ena from bitter experience.

Just then the train to Geneva arrives right on time and gives them hope for the rest of the return trip. The porter stows their trunks in the baggage van and the women settle in their carriage for the journey home.

Things also run relatively smoothly when they first arrive at *Genève-Cornavin* Station; the porters unload their trunks and convey them to the platform for the next Paris bound train advertised for half past eleven.

The women take it in turns to visit the newly built ladies rest room and buy refreshments from the station café, both rebuilt after the fire of 1909 and the most modern of conveniences. Maisie is able to change her Southall's towel with ease, followed by a restorative cup of tea amongst the smoke, steam, and coal dust of the station.

And they wait.

Half past eleven comes and goes with no sign of their train. Miss Garrett goes to seek information and rehearses her French as she searches for the station master. Although Maisie's French is excellent, the party decide they will call on her as little as possible to help with the journey, so she isn't overtaxed.

When Miss Garrett returns, her face is tight with worry which she tries hard to hide. "What did the station master say?" asks Ena anxiously.

"The news isn't good. Apparently, the French are engaged in a battle with the Germans in Lorraine. He says services are disrupted as several trains have been taken out of service by the French to take troop reinforcements to the front. Both the half past eleven and the half past twelve to Paris are amongst the diversions. He is confident though that the half past one will be running as it is the train that usually carries the post from this part of Switzerland to Paris. Let's hope he is right."

The women sit on their trunks and camp out on the platform amongst the forest of cast iron pillars. They unbutton their blouses at the neck and cuff and discard their jackets. They agree to eat their lunch where they sit so they can board as quickly as possible when the train appears. Monsieur Eggenberger has packed a small feast of soft white bread rolls, tender smoky ham, creamy yellow cheese, hard boiled eggs with shells as brown as their suntans, some moist almond cake, ruby red apples, and cooked spicy Italian sausage wrapped in brown greaseproof paper. (Nothing is mentioned about how the sausage reputedly made Maisie sick in the morning now that the real cause is known.) Without saying it aloud, each woman only eats part of her share, knowing that they might need to make their supplies last longer.

As each successive service is cancelled, more and more people are left stranded waiting for the next available train to Paris. The tension is palpable, and tempers fray. Small disputes break out between the passengers over nothing much at all. The four teachers become progressively more anxious as the day wears on until their nerves are so taut that it would have been possible to play some dissonant chords on them.

At around quarter to two, a train is seen approaching the platforms used for departures and arrivals from France. The four teachers don't leap up immediately as they' been disappointed before when a local train was diverted to platform seven when no other platform was available. However, this train bears the distinctive assorted coloured livery of the

*Compagnie des chemins de fer de Paris à Lyon et à la Méditerranée,* rather than that of the Swiss railway companies' operating regional services. Black and red for first class; black and yellow for second class; and green and gold lined for third class.

The station staff start boarding procedures, corralling the passengers, and checking tickets. Everyone is trying to get the attention of the flood of porters that suddenly appear. Hattie's athletic prowess comes into its own as she almost rugby tackles one into assisting them with their trunks. Miss Garrett counts out some Swiss coins in a showy way and passes them to Hattie to ensure the man knows it is in his best interests to assist them. He then uses his trolley full of their luggage as a battering ram to force a path through to the second-class carriages. Miss Garrett and Ena help Maisie board, and they secure four seats together and hold Hattie's temporarily empty space against all comers whilst she supervises the loading of the trunks into the baggage car.

The train is soon full, and yet more people crowd on. The station master belatedly starts shouting the train is for Paris only, and there will be no stops at any intermediate stations. This causes consternation whilst some people extract themselves and their luggage. This allows others that aren't able to board to squeeze into their places.

At around ten past two, the train departs for the French capital. "The Express takes around five hours, so provided there are no hold ups we should reach Paris by half past seven this evening," Miss Garrett calculates.

"That means we will be crossing to *Gare De Nord* at about eight o'clock. We should still be able to get a hotel at that time in the evening. It won't be too late," responds Ena.

The women are flushed from the heat and fan themselves to keep cool. Every window in the carriage is open. Each seat is taken, and even quite large children are sat on their parent's laps to leave seats free for others. The close proximity of so many bodies adds to the temperature and the smell of humanity is sharp in the nostrils.

For the first hour the train passes slowly through the Jura Mountains of the Haut-Bugey route, with its steep gradients and tight curves before reaching the long poorly ventilated Mornay tunnel. Regular travellers reach up to close the windows and keep the noxious smoke out, which seems an odd thing to do in the summer heat to those not in the know. But soon after entering the tunnel all the windows are quickly shut adding to the temperature of the carriage.

Maisie begins to feel a little faint but fights against it. The others eye her with concern as the colour drains from her face and she fans herself more furiously, her hand beating back and forth as fast as a hoverfly's wings. It is with relief that they burst back into the sunshine again. The windows are quickly re-opened, and everyone takes in grateful gasps of smut filled mountain air.

Lieutenant Peter Barnes bursts into the officers' mess and confronts his friend Lieutenant Prescott, as he is packing his belongings into his kit bag. "Is it true?" he demands.

"Is what true?" responds Edward guardedly.

"That you've got your orders and you are off to Harwich tomorrow."

"Ah that," laughs Edward, "Yes, I want to give the Hun a bloody nose. I've been assigned to *HMS Arethusa* under Commodore Tyrwhitt. There is a big show being planned for next week, so I'm to join them as soon as I can. Tyrwhitt is the main man on this exercise; I'm hoping that a bit of active service will do my career no harm at all."

"You lucky devil!" exclaims Barnes. "What about Maisie? She isn't back yet, is she? School restarts next week, she must be due home soon. Will you get the chance to let her know?"

"You seem to know a lot about her timetable!" Edward laughs trying to play things down. "People think we were closer than we are. I said good-bye to

256

her when she took herself off for a month. No one has cared that she has left me all these weeks! Now everyone thinks I'm giving her the elbow when she already gave it to me weeks ago!"

"Oh, I didn't realise. You didn't say," responds Barnes contritely. "I thought it was all tickety-boo."

"People assume when you see a girl a few times that matrimony is on the cards. But we were never that close. I give you my blessing if you are interested, I've seen how you are always mooning after her like a lovesick boy. Here have this," he says and from his locker he produces the photo of Maisie with lilac in her hair and a bundle of postcards and other correspondence including the Christmas card. He tosses them onto his bed in front of Peter.

"Steady on old chap. She's a decent girl. Not someone to be passed around," Peter admonishes him.

"Anyway, I can't wait to get to Harwich now. New start and all that," Prescott responds busying himself with his kit, so he doesn't have to look his friend in the eye.

Lieutenant Barnes hovers a while longer as he processes all this information. Prescott is his friend, but he has seen how Maisie has hung on his every word and follows him everywhere with her eyes. He'd also seen the numerous postcards she has sent from her holiday to Edward while she hasn't sent himself a single one, and he thought the two of them were at least friends. But he concedes the postcards she sent Prescott don't say anything of a romantic nature. He could have sworn she was in love with his friend. But what did he know? After a moment he decides to give Prescott the benefit of the doubt and says, "Drink before you go?"

"Sure thing, in the mess tonight?"

"Great, I'll let the others know. I'll return the photograph and postcards to Maisie when she gets back," says Barnes picking up the small pile of correspondence and placing them in his pocket before he returns to his duties.

After the mountains, the long haul up through the centre of France to Paris begins. Other passengers are discussing the German advance. France and Germany have disputed the territories of Alsace and Lorraine over many centuries. France takes the opportunity of the newly declared war to try to reclaim the province of Lorraine to the east, but the Germans are pushing them back. Had the English women decided to take the train line that passes through Basel, they almost certainly would have been caught up in the combat. As it is, their route is west of the fighting, but they need to get to Paris as quickly as possible in case the Germans break through.

As the train approaches Dijon station, it starts to slow. It is not meant to stop, but the hissing of the breaks and the slow whistle indicate they are coming to a halt. People start opening the carriage doors and windows to shout for information.

The station staff do their best to explain how things are going. The French have advanced towards Lorraine, but the Germans have counter-attacked and forced two separate battles on the French armies, splitting their forces. The French are defeated and retreat in disorder. However, the latest news coming through is the German pursuit is slow allowing the French commander to occupy a new position east of Nancy. From there, he has extended the right wing of his army towards the south and regained contact with the First Army enabling the French to regroup and to again face the slow advancing Germans.

The train is being held at Dijon whilst a troop train is diverted along the track to cross towards the front line at Nancy. The station master says it will be around three quarters of an hour, so advises people to stretch their legs but not to go far in case they get the go ahead to depart quickly.

The passengers spill out like peas from a split sack. It is now nearly five o'clock; the heat is less intense. The women teachers once more take turns to use the facilities and get tea. They are beginning to look like wilted flowers as the strain of the journey starts to tell on them. Their skirts are creased and there are wet patches under Ena's arms that are less than pleasant smelling. Maisie's hair is doing its best to escape its pins whilst a thin trickle of sweat runs down Hattie's back. Even Miss Garrett has high colour in her cheeks and her blouse is sticking to her, she seems very uncomfortable.

Suddenly she bursts into tears as they stand grouped together on the platform, "It's all my fault. I was stubborn. I'd arranged this holiday last year and I wasn't going to let the silly war games that men play spoil it. Now we are miles from home and those silly men are stopping us, I should have been more responsible."

Ena fusses around her, "Don't be hard on yourself, Elsie," she says. Maisie thinks this is serious as Ena uses Miss Garrett's first name. "We didn't know it was going to stop us getting home. The British Consul thought the French would be overrunning the Germans across the province of Lorraine all the way to the Rhine."

"Poor Miss Kendall," says Miss Garrett, dabbing her eyes. "She must be in so much discomfort. If we had left on 4 August, she would be safe at home."

"And pregnant and abandoned," says Hattie. "And she probably wouldn't have had the courage to tell us about it."

"Hattie is right," Maisie agrees. "I wouldn't have known what to do and I would have ended up disgraced. My own mother would have disowned me. And my father would have been spinning in his grave like a top!"

They all smile at this image, laughter being a step too far, and again they settle down to wait for the train to depart. Miss Garrett swallows her tears and once more takes control.

After about half an hour the troop train pulls in on an adjacent platform heading towards the battle front. The soldiers wear the French army uniform of ultra-marine blue jackets and scarlet trousers. They are as brilliantly attired as peacocks, and it seems small wonder that the Germans are able to pick them off at will in their dozens like so many grouse in the hunting season.

The French passengers wave to the soldiers and let out a rousing cheer of, "*Vive la France!*" Many of the fighting men return this greeting with a salute and smile, undeterred by the grave news from the front. The passengers start throwing little gifts of cigarettes and chocolate through the open carriage windows. Babies are held up for good luck kisses and pretty girls smile and give the soldiers the glad eye.

The station master blows his whistle, and the troop train pulls away. The passengers descend on him like a flock of angry birds asking when their train will depart. He shoos them away with a gallic shrug and disappears into his control box where he can be seen on the telephone gesticulating. After ten minutes he re-emerges and says they are expecting another two trains to be diverted through to Nancy.

One after the other, the troop trains duly arrive but are greeted with less and less patriotic enthusiasm from the tired, waiting French passengers and certainly fewer small presents of cigarettes and chocolate than the soldiers in the first train had been given. By now a further two hours have passed, and the time is approaching half past seven, the time they expected to arrive in Paris for the night.

Without warning, the station master suddenly starts instructing the throng to re-board the Paris train before again blowing his whistle. The passengers are thrown into confusion having been out of the train for so long. Travelling companions are shouted at to come out of the lavatories or the cafés to avoid being left behind. One or two have wandered as far as the outside of the station and are in danger of not hearing the call. But the uproar caused by the station master blasting his whistle again soon brings them running to the platform. The four teachers settle back into their seats and eat a little more of their rations as the train pulls away.

Peter Barnes sets about rounding up his colleagues to give Edward the send-off he feels his pal deserved. Especially as Prescott is going to give the Hun what for. He feels bad that he hasn't realised Maisie had given Edward the elbow so she can enjoy herself on holiday. He didn't think she could be so shallow. It didn't really seem like her. But it just goes to show, you never really know what is going on in other people's heads.

At eight o'clock, the usual crowd of Lieutenant Dollan and Lieutenant Jones meet up in the mess with Prescott and Barnes. Greenleaf, the steward, has got two bottles of superior whisky to send Prescott off with and someone produces some fine cigars. The *bonhomie* is soon in full swing. Glasses are kept topped up and the cigars are passed around filling the air with blue smoke. Back slapping and good luck calls come from all quarters. Prescott begins to believe his own publicity, congratulating himself on his presence of mind to extricate himself from a tricky situation. He thinks he will come out of it smelling of roses as both the potential hero of the hour going to face the Hun and jilted lover of a feckless woman, when Lieutenant Baker comes in the mess and joins their group. Baker is a long-standing adversary of Prescott's dating back to their days at Osborne. "I hear you're off to Harwich to join *HMS Arethusa* under Commodore Tyrwhitt," the bull-necked Baker opens with.

"Yes, I'm really looking forward to it," responds Prescott, "Chance to progress my career rather than be stuck here in a shore posting. Time for some real action and give the Hun a bloody nose."

"Have you said goodbye to that young lady of yours? Is she back from conquering the Swiss Alps yet?" Baker asks, obviously leading up to something.

"Haven't you heard?" interjects Barnes trying to deflect Baker, "she dumped him before leaving."

"Poor Prescott," replies Baker, warming to his subject, and signalling to the steward to bring him a drink. "I didn't realise you were nursing a broken heart."

There is some general manly murmuring from the other officers of "bad show" and "rotten luck" as Baker continues, "Funny that, I had it on good authority from Tummon that he heard you talking to Mrs Bennington about all the postcards you are receiving. He says that your girl has also sent one to the Old Man's wife too."

Prescott shifts uncomfortably, turning away from Baker in the hope that by not looking at him he will go away. But Baker isn't finished, "There's speculation you have got her up the duff and are not doing the decent thing by her. That's why you have asked for a transfer to get away from your dirty little mess."

"Take that back!" demands Barnes in his friend's defence, the whisky having its effect.

"Tummon retrieved this *billet-doux* from her from your wastepaper basket. He was happy to share it with me after you refused his chit for leave last week. I obliged him by signing it for him today so he can go home and see his family," says Baker producing Maisie's crumpled letter with all the flourish of a stage magician. He theatrically smoothes it out and starts to read it aloud to the assembled crowd. "*My Darling Edward,* - Doesn't sound like she knows she dumped you. *I am missing you very much here in beautiful Lake Geneva.* -Ah, how sweet. *I'm always thinking of the time we spent together before we departed.*"

Prescott makes a grab for the letter, but Baker ducks away with all the nimbleness of a fly weight prize fighter and continues to read aloud, "*I may be reminded of it always.* – Now this is the main point – what can she mean by '*Always*'?" He looks at Prescott over the top of the letter with a malicious glint in his eye, "*I hope you don't get posted before I return as I can't wait to share my thoughts with you on some important news I have.* -Important news! What can it be? - *Please telegraph me as soon as you know anything.* – Did you telegraph her Prescott? Tummon says he heard the Rear Admiral's wife advising you to as Bennington is fond of the girl. I hear that Mrs B was straight in to see the Old Man and you were summoned to his presence."

Prescott produces a fake smile to hide behind and tries to play it down, "You know what women are like, trying to trap a fellow into matrimony. It's all in her pretty little head."

Barnes has been drinking steadily. He just can't believe that Maisie can be so heartless. He knocks back more whisky as he watches Baker reading Maisie's letter and he knows instinctively what the truth is. Without any further thought he punches Prescott square in the face saying, "You bastard," and storms out of the officers' mess, leaving his former friend to dab his bloody nose on his handkerchief as the other officers silently agree Edward deserved it.

It is now almost quarter to eight with at least another three hours to Paris. A few passengers haven't re-joins the train at Dijon, some decide to return to the safety of Switzerland whilst others head towards Nancy. Some take advantage of the interruption to the journey to catch trains stopping at intermediate stations enroute to Paris. This thins the carriage out and together with the cool of the evening, it makes the travel conditions more bearable.

This part of the journey passes without much incident. There are no more major rail junctions heading towards the battle front, so they travel to Paris unhindered, pulling into the beautiful *Gare De Lyon* at about half past eleven. The station was built for the World Exposition of 1900 and boasts modern facilities and cafés. The luggage is offloaded from the baggage car by a large gang of porters, as they struggle to turn the train around as quickly as possible for its return to Switzerland. Hattie and Ena run around identifying their trunks and dragging them to one side whilst Miss Garrett fusses over Maisie as she is clearly flagging.

What the teachers haven't taken into consideration are refugees from the front are already seeking safety in Paris, as well as other movements of people generated by the war as they try to return home or get further away from the fighting. The concourse is covered with small parties of people camped out on their individual islands of belongings. Sleeping children are wrapped in blankets as though they are small parcels awaiting delivery. Dogs are

267

barking and guarding their temporary homes. Cats in baskets yowl and spit at the dogs. Caged birds in turn squawk at the cats.

The women hold a quick counsel to decide what to do next. "It's too late to travel across Paris to *Gare de Nord*," Miss Garrett says.

"I will  go and see if there is a reasonably priced hotel nearby," Hattie offers, and she ducks out the main entrance.

Ena shouts, "Not on your own," and quickly runs after her like a beetle scurrying across the concourse, her spectacles glinting in the electric lights. Maisie and Miss Garrett remain behind and guard the trunks.

Whilst they wait, they hear English being spoken by one top hatted gentleman to another. Miss Garrett very uncharacteristically adopts a man friendly persona and calls across to them, "Excuse me sir, can you tell us what is happening. We've just arrived from Switzerland and are trying to get home to England."

The gentleman raises his hat and comes over with his companion. "I'm afraid Paris is overflowing," he responds. "The Germans have reached Brussels today. The rest of Belgium will fall soon and there are already reports of thousands of refugees on the road heading for the Channel ports."

His companion adds, "They are not closing the station overnight as they usually do, so you can stay here. Not much sleep to be had, but at least you will be safe. Then first thing tomorrow, you should be able to travel across Paris to *Gare de Nord*."

Miss Garrett and Maisie thank them, and the gentlemen tip their hats again and move away. As soon as they are out of earshot, Miss Garrett dives into her bag and produces her well-thumbed copy of *Bradshaw's Continental Railway Guide* and begins checking departure times whilst cursing the men simply for being men. Just then Ena and Hattie return, "There are half a dozen hotels just outside the station, but they are all full," reports Hattie. "we went in a couple, and they said everywhere is overflowing."

"We will have to stay the night here," counsels Ena, "And wait till morning."

"Let's go to the ladies' waiting room and stay there. We should be safe enough," Miss Garrett suggests. "We can take a motor taxi first thing to *Gare de Nord*. I have looked in *Bradshaw's* and there is a Calais bound train at quarter past seven, then again at quarter past eight. We should be able to board one of those with a bit of luck."

Hattie goes on a reconnaissance mission to the facilities but returns with the news it is already full. They make themselves as comfortable as

269

possible by wrapping themselves in shawls and coats from their trunks to stay warm overnight and try to snatch a little sleep whilst awaiting the dawn.

At five o'clock in the morning, the station begins to spring back to life and Hattie flags down a porter to take their trunks to the taxi rank. A quick transfer across to *Gare de Nord* will put them in the best position to catch an early train to Calais.

Miss Garrett spots the station master as they are following their baggage out of the concourse. She makes a beeline for him, and asks, "Do you know if the trains are running to Calais or Boulogne?"

"Ah, madame," he responds, "There are troop movements and refugees bound for the Channel. All the trains will be full. May I suggest the Dieppe via *Gare de Saint-Lazare* might be a more viable option for you?"

She thanks him and catches up with the others. Without consulting anyone, she decides they should press on to *Gare de Nord* as the situation seems to be changing by the minute.

They don't need to wait long before one of the thousands of Parisian black Renault Type AG motor taxis arrives to take up position outside the station. These taxis will play a key role in transporting troops to the First Battle of Marne in just a few days' time. One thousand three hundred Parisian taxis will be requisitioned to carry six thousand soldiers to win the battle. Thereafter, the Type AG will be known as the "*Taxi de la Marne*."

The taxi is not big enough to take four women and four trunks, but within seconds several more cabs are pulling into the rank and so two are engaged for the short journey to *Gare de Nord*.

Maisie hopes they will get to see some of Paris on this trip. They did not have time to stop on their outward journey to Switzerland, so she has been looking forward to seeing more on their return. But they only pass *Notre Dame* cathedral, and she can see nothing else of note from the window of the motor car. The city is already awake and bustling, and even this small glimpse is exciting with its *Belle Epoch* and *Baroque* architecture. There is so much traffic even at that early hour, horse drawn carts, motor cars, new electric trams, hand carts and bicycles vie for space whilst pedestrians risk life and limb as they dart between.

As they reach *Gare de Nord,* they can already see groups of people outside even though it is not yet six o'clock. The beginning of the Belgian refugee tragedy is being played out before them. It is difficult to know if people are arriving or attempting to depart, or simply staying still in a bid to avoid the Germans.

The motor taxis have to battle through the growing crowd to eventually pull up outside the station. The women get out and pay the drivers. There are no porters available, and all the luggage trolleys are already full of other people's belongings, so they manhandle their trunks out of the taxis and onto the concourse themselves. Hattie insists on helping Maisie with hers. Inside the station is a sea of humanity stretching as far as the eye can see. The scene is the same as at *Gare de Lyon*, only the nationality of the people has changed from French to Belgian refugees.

These people have fewer belongings than those from Lorraine as the Belgians had less time to pack, only bringing with them what they can carry. Rumours of German atrocities in central and eastern Belgium are already circulating. It is said that German troops, afraid of Belgian *francs-tireurs* ("free shooters"), are burning homes and executing men, women, and even children, and the women are raped repeatedly. Almost one and a half million people will flee from the tiny country of Belgium in those early weeks of the war.

The French are beginning to respond to the unfolding crisis. Nurses attend the sick, whilst officials attempt to deal with the situation by finding temporary shelters for those people before them, knowing that this will be just the vanguard of what is to come over the next few days. There are already several make-shift soup kitchens distributing food and other essentials to the refugees. Soldiers vie for space on the already overcrowded concourse. Their bright blue jackets and red trousers making a stark contrast with the travel-stained dusty clothes of the refugees. The Belgians sit huddled together defeated whilst the soldiers stand proud ready to face the German aggressors. There is little room for four English women with large travelling trunks amongst them.

"I'll have a look on the main concourse to see if I can track down our train," offers Hattie.

"No, you can't go on your own, your French isn't good enough. I will accompany you," Miss Garrett insists. Ena and Maisie guard the luggage and pool the remaining food to see what they can rustle up for breakfast. They divide the bread and cheese between four along with some cake. The meat is starting to sweat a little in the August heat and Maisie is about to throw it away when she notices that the small group of Belgians nearest to them are watching their every move. She exchanges a look with Ena and without a word, they further divide the food to share with their neighbours adding the ham and sausage to the refugees' portion, rather than waste it.

Hattie and Miss Garrett return bringing bottles of Lipton's iced tea from the café and report the unwanted news that there are no trains departing for the Channel ports for civilian passengers. The French Army has commandeered all available rolling stock to transport soldiers to the Belgium border and many of these are departing from *Gare de Nord*. Added to that, the British Expeditionary Force is being transported from Southampton to Le Havre and from there to Maubeuge on the Belgian frontier by train, leaving few services running for non-combatants.

Miss Garrett finds out from another English passenger that trains are still running from *Gare de Saint-Lazare* to Dieppe, but it is uncertain if steamers are still departing for Newhaven. *Bradshaw's* promises that Thomas Cook has "interpreters in uniform" at *Gare de Nord*, so directly after they have eaten, Miss Garrett (supported by Hattie) armed with all the tickets, seeks out the uniformed official.

The flustered interpreter is easily found as he is at the centre of a small crowd of British tourists all asking the same question, how can we get home?

"Please, calm yourselves *Mesdames et monsieurs*. Your tickets are valid on the Dieppe route. However, the steamers are no longer going to Newhaven," he warns in his accented English. "The port has been requisitioned under the *Defence of the Realm Regulations* by the British Government and a reduced service is now running to Folkestone. You should all be able to get home safely."

The advertising slogan which promises, *"A Cook's Ticket Will Take You Anywhere,"* at the cost of six pounds, twelve shillings and eight pence each, is about to be tested. Miss Garrett again silently congratulates herself on her foresight. It means a further motor taxi ride to *Gare de Saint-Lazare* but fortified with the confidence they will be able to travel home from there, the women happily pay the additional fare. They have to wait at the taxi rank with dozens of other British passengers, but the queue moves quickly, and they are soon on their way.

By the time they arrive at *Gare de Saint-Lazare,* it is nearly eleven o'clock. The Parisian sun heats the streets and cooks the drains giving off a nameless, acrid stench. This mingles with the prevailing smell of rotting vegetables emanating from the rear of the cafés and restaurants. The women discard their jackets and unbutton their collars and cuffs. Hattie and Maisie remove their hats, but Ena and Miss Garrett have larger hats, which double as sunshades.

Miss Garrett's *Bradshaw's* says the train is 10:18, so they know they have missed the service that will deliver then to England today. The next train is 21:20, which means waiting until nine o'clock in the evening, but they can ensure they are booked onto the service and possibly register their luggage so that they can have a wander round Paris for the day. It will mean a second night without proper sleep, but at least the train will be in London by half past seven the following morning, according to the timetable.

There are less people at *Gare de Saint-Lazare* than at *Gare de Nord* or *Gare de Lyon.* It is possible to find a porter to take their luggage to the registration desk and book their places on the evening train and the night ferry from Dieppe. Business here is brisk, but they are very early booking onto that service, so are guaranteed seats throughout the journey.

Miss Garrett presents their tickets to the desk concierge, who registers their places and accepts their luggage. There is a little to-ing and fro-ing as the women decide what items they want to keep with them to use on the journey, as this will entail carrying it around with them until they are able to board. The official explains they can board one hour before departure and directs them to the platform where the train will leave from.

Maisie and Hattie are keen to explore Paris, all Maisie's tiredness has gone instantly at the prospect of some free time in the French capital. Ena and Miss Garrett decide they will get lunch and buy provisions for the journey. They agree to meet back at the station at six o'clock for a meal in the café, before getting ready to board the train as soon as it is possible.

Maisie and Hattie almost run down the road heading towards the *Place De La Concorde, Notre Dame,* and the Seine. Maisie feels free for the first time since their holiday began. She can't believe she is in Paris; it is so cosmopolitan.

When they reach the *Place De La Concorde,* they stop to catch their breath. Hattie visited Paris the previous summer and wants to show her friend the sights. Maisie looks around in awe. It seems so vast and busy. The obelisk at the centre, with its Egyptian hieroglyphs, is like something from another world. The grand fountains splash cooling water around to the delight of small children; the spectre of war driven temporarily away by their tumult.

"I feel so much better," Maisie says. "When I was living with my parents in our small village, I never dreamed I would ever get to travel, and especially to Paris. Despite all that has happened, I'm glad I came on this holiday."

Hattie gives her a hug,. "You can start afresh when we get back. No one need know. Edward is likely to move on, so you won't need to see him anymore. If you meet someone new, you can take precautions. The *Malthusian League* publish literature on how to prevent pregnancy, I have a copy I will lend you. You can buy something called a

277

diaphragm which you insert inside yourself, and it can be used more than once. We can buy one at a chemist here in Paris, so no one need know."

Maisie blushes, but keeps listening and determines that she will do so.

"Do you use one?" she asks Hattie, immediately regretting it as it is probably prying.

"Yes, I have done," Hattie responds. "We all do," meaning her circle of friends. "If I had known you were planning on sleeping with Edward, I would have made sure you had one."

"Didn't Rosie have one?" Maisie enquires.

"Yes, but she didn't know that Lieutenant Harris was going to surprise her with a hotel room in London. She wasn't carrying it with her on our trip to meet Lieutenant Barnes' sisters. It wasn't something she thought she would need at the pickle factory!" The two young women laugh and continue their exploration.

Miss Garrett and Ena find a nice café where they eat the *prix fixe* luncheon at one of the pavement tables and feel much better for a proper meal, if you can call wild boar sausages served with just green beans a proper meal, although Miss Garrett has to admit to herself that she enjoyed the fruit tarte for dessert. They both indulge in a glass of red wine and finish with a French coffee, tee-total ideals left in England for the duration of the holiday. They sit back and watch busy Parisians go about their daily lives.

They enjoy being part of the street café scene as other customers drink pastis or black coffee from tiny cups whilst smoking strong French cigarettes. Even some women smoke cigarettes in little holders, which makes the two older women feel life here is so sophisticated or maybe even decadent.

They notice again how there is a mix of Africans from places like Senegal, Arabs from Algeria, and even some Chinese from French Indochina, passing amongst the crowd. There are soldiers everywhere as all French reservists have been called up, their ultramarine blue jackets visible through the crowds of dark clothed workers thronging the lunchtime streets.

There is a strange atmosphere in the city. There is a certain jubilation that greeted the war, as the French see it as an opportunity to right the wrongs of the Franco-Prussian War of 1870. They cannot forget their defeat lost them both Alsace-Lorraine and their imperial influence on the world stage. But already, after not quite three weeks, the Germans have the upper hand, and fear and dread are beginning to be felt. Rumours of heavy casualties have reached the city and people are beginning to worry about loved ones. It means there is a brittle gaiety to the other diners and the street scene in general.

The Parisians still go about their everyday activities, selling flowers, cleaning windows, mending shoes, laughing, and singing, but underneath they are watchful, reading the news reports from the front and speculating about the size of French losses already thought to be in the thousands. They have not expected this, believing themselves to be the superior force, and the strain of the uncertainty is beginning to show in the corners of their mouths and the downward cast of their eyes.

Ena and Miss Garrett feel unable to relax completely as everybody tries to act as though things are normal. A group of ragged children come along the pavement, holding out their hands and begging. Some people give them small coins, some give them food from their plates, others shoo them away. Ena looks in her purse, many of the small silver coins she has are Swiss, but it is possible to use the loose change in France or Belgium as they are all part of the 1865 *Latin Monetary Union*, so she digs out a few cents each and hands them over.

Miss Garrett ignores the children and picks up the menu, as though reading it. Just then, one of the beggars grabs her tapestry travel bag from beneath her chair and runs off with it. The others scatter like leaves in the wind, and Miss Garrett gives chase encumbered by her long skirts. Ena also jumps up, knocking off her spectacles, and overturning her coffee cup as she does so, adding to the hullabaloo. One of the waiters joins Miss Garrett in running down the street in pursuit, his long white apron flapping before him as though shooing people out of his path.

The street urchin flashes a look back over his shoulder to size up his chances of escape and decides to relinquish his spoils, which is much heavier than he expected when he snatched it. He throws the bag down and increases his pace, weaving in and out of the lunchtime shoppers. The waiter retrieves the bag and returns it to Miss Garrett who is forced to stop as she is out of breath. "*Merci! Merci!*" she gasps. "Our tickets and passports are all in this bag," she says, clutching it to her chest. They are tucked in her copy of *Bradshaw's*, the weight of which has caused the boy to drop his booty.

Ena gathers together some francs to reward the man and presses it on him despite his protestations. They ask for their bill and retreat to the relative safety of the station to await the return of the younger women.

Hattie and Maisie walk on to *Notre Dame*, watching the Seine glitter and sparkle in the late August sunshine. The heat rises up from the pavement, which feels like passing a blacksmith's workshop. They buy Italian ice creams in the new American waffle cones from a street vendor and savour the sweet coolness whilst watching life on the river go by. Surprisingly, there are many activities going on under the bridges: men are being shaved, others are bathing, life carries on.

Hattie and Maisie notice how some women are dressed in what must be the latest fashions. The designer, Paul Poiret, has introduced softer, more feminine lines, doing away with the need for corsets. The Parisian women move more freely than in the more formal clothes still worn in England. The two women make mental notes to see what they can emulate. In the Paris heat, few women wear jackets and most sport smaller hats. They ooze confidence and self-assurance that make the two English women feel gawky and provincial.

On reaching the cathedral, they stop to buy more iced tea and crepes from street vendors and sit on a low wall by the river to eat them. It seems odd to eat pancakes when it isn't Shrove Tuesday, but it marks the beginning of a Lenten period as the war begins.

Hattie says, "It will be strange to go back to England with a war going on. It will be like we've missed the beginning. I read in the paper that the *Women's Social and Political Union* are calling a truce on militant activities and saying we should all pull together for the duration of the war."

Maisie thinks about this, "Yes, it's strange, isn't it. This war is already changing peoples' lives. We will be straight back to work when we get home. I wonder what will happen to Edward. Where do you think he might be posted next?"

"Don't worry about him, he's probably going to land on his feet where-ever he goes," Hattie responds dismissively. "I never felt he cared for you enough. It's easy to say that now, but I never believed you were the centre of his world as he is yours. And you deserve better. There are plenty of men who will treat you as you should be treated, like our friend, Peter Barnes. He's half in love with you already! You ought to wear that lovely brooch he bought you."

"Do you think so?" Maisie asks. "He is a little gawky looking! But I do enjoy his company. And when we went to London, I felt safe having him with us when we were in those rough streets behind the pickle factory." She pauses for a moment as she remembers that day before continuing. "But maybe we've been wrong about Edward. There may be valid reasons why I haven't heard from him."

Hattie hmphed. "Don't start going soft on him. He isn't worthy of you, and he could have telegraphed you from anywhere. He will start treating you like a mistress if you show him any forgiveness, and you are better than that! Are you sure he didn't force you to submit to him and bruise your wrists?"

Maisie takes a deep breath and says, "I kept something back from you. I am so ashamed."

"What?" enquires Hattie, concerned at this sudden change in her friend's demeanour.

"When we went to the circus, a man raped me behind the wagons. I couldn't tell anyone as I didn't know why I'd agreed to walk with him, but I was lost, and he said he would take me to my friends. He was one of the cowboys. He had been so heroic in the show; I was taken in by him. I know if anyone finds out, they will think it is my own fault, that I must have encouraged him. But I didn't. I really didn't! It was horrible. It was him that gave me the bruises you saw. I was bruised all over. You only saw my wrists, but my breasts and thighs were just as bad. It is a wonder my face wasn't bruised as well, where he had silenced me with his hand. And to top it all, I missed my monthly. I didn't know if I might be pregnant with the cowboy's or Edward's baby." She suppresses a little sob that tries to escape. "I kept thinking what if Edward marries me and it isn't his baby, how can I deceive him? I thought what if Edward knows I'd been raped and won't marry me because he thinks it is my own fault? But I also thought I needed Edward to marry me whoever the

284

father is, or I would be disgraced. And then I realised that although Edward wasn't brutal with me, he has discarded me in the same way as the cowboy. He has used my body and walked away, and I felt even worse. It is such a mess."

Hattie gives her a fierce hug. "You could have told me," she says, comfortingly.

"I know now I should have, but I felt so sullied and scared. Please, don't tell anyone." Maisie gives into the tears that have been building within her. It is such a relief to tell the whole story to Hattie.

"Of course, I won't tell anyone, silly!" says Hattie. "We will keep it a secret. It isn't your fault. Don't blame yourself. The world isn't fair to us women, and men take advantage. No one else need ever know."

Hattie doesn't confess to Maisie that she has already told Miss Garrett and Ena that she thought Edward had raped her because of the bruises. To her mind, he had treated her friend just as badly as the cowboy did, and if others now think less of him, it is no more than he deserves.

At six o'clock, as arranged, the women meet up on the concourse of *Gare de Saint-Lazare.* They eat their supper together in the station café and drink a glass of wine each before finishing their meal with a coffee. They pass the evening without incident, and board the train as soon as they are permitted. They know they will only be able to cat nap home as the train journey is just three hours, arriving at Dieppe at half past midnight. Then, on to the steamer to arrive at Folkestone, before boarding the train to Charing Cross on Saturday 22 August.

They settle into their seats and are relieved when the service departs more or less on time. As the train pulls away from the platform, they feel reassured they are heading home with each turn of the wheels.

When eventually they arrive in Dieppe, they disembark, half asleep. The train terminated on the quayside adjacent to the steamer and there is an immediate flurry of activity as the porters begins unloading the baggage onto the quay and the stevedores in turn load it on the waiting ship.

"What time will we get to Folkestone?" Ena asks.

"I don't really know," Miss Garrett responds hazily. "The Thomas Cook official wasn't able to tell us that as the service has changed from that advertised in *Bradshaw's*."

He had also explained that it is possible that services may be withdrawn at short notice. The British and the French military are requisitioning ships for use in the war, and this is bound to reduce the timetable. At the moment, there are still two

286

crossings a day, but the official had been unsure how they might be affected. Miss Garrett hasn't shared this information with the others, as it would be bound to cause them further distress, so she bears the worry alone. She is much relieved to see the steamer waiting for them.

The women troop up the gangplank and head for the second-class ladies' salon and the temporary comfort of the red plush seats. Hattie once again checks their baggage is being safely transferred from the train to the steamer. By now, she sees it as her duty as the fittest member of the group to oversee this task.

Maisie goes to change her Southall towel in the lavatories; she has almost run out of them, but fortunately doesn't really need them anymore as the bleeding has all but stopped. She returns with cups of tea and scones for everyone to bolster them up through the crossing. On her blouse, she wears the brooch that Lieutenant Barnes bought for her birthday. Ena's jackdaw eye spots the addition of the jewellery, but says nothing about it to the others.

They make themselves as comfortable as possible, when a steward comes into the salon and speaks to the various groups of ladies as he passes through, setting each group atwitter, like little birds spying a cat.

"I don't want to alarm you," he starts, "but there are reports of German U boats in the Channel. We are waiting for the 'all clear' before departing. We won't be able to leave at the advertised time, but we hope we won't be delayed too long."

"Surely, they won't attack a civilian steamer?" Miss Garrett asks.

"We just don't know," the steward responds. "This is going to be the last night-time crossing, just in case."

The women settle back in their seats and wait. This will be their second night without proper sleep, following over a day and a half travelling. They are feeling very jaded. As the salon is half empty, they spread out and try to sleep as best they can on the sofas, covering themselves in shawls and jackets, following the example of the other women passengers. Except for Miss Garrett, who remains upright, ramrod straight and unable to decide if she is shocked at the behaviour of her companions or not. But even she nods off, her head thrown back, and her mouth open wide, unable to fight the sleep deprivation for long.

At around two o'clock in the morning, the steward returns and whispers to any ladies he finds awake that the ship will not leave port until first light, to be safe. This means they won't depart until around six o'clock.

When dawn finally arrives, those that have managed to sleep are disconcerted to find themselves still at Dieppe, but most of the passengers have awoken at one point or another and accept the delay with stoicism. It is with great relief they hear the engines being stoked up in anticipation of their departure.

Hattie and Maisie track down the steward and order coffee and rolls for everyone, before joining the queue for the washrooms to freshen up as best they can. Ena goes up on deck to find out what is happening and purchases more rolls from a harbourside vendor, prior to the gangplank being raised in preparation for the voyage home.

At about half past six, they finally cast off for Folkestone. The women eat their breakfast in the salon, then go up on deck to watch the French coast receding in the early morning August sun.

Suddenly, after about an hour and a half sailing, there is a lot of activity from the crew. One of them is gesticulating in an animated fashion towards the horizon. The word quickly goes round the passengers that an enemy vessel is sighted ahead.

The U boat is cruising at its top speed of around fifteen knots, whilst the steamer has been making seventeen and is in danger of catching the other craft up. The German vessel looks like it is heading towards the North Sea and its home port of

289

Heligoland, rather than towards the steamer. The U boat has to surface so the crew can look out through the portholes in the conning tower to navigate. The periscope only provides a limited view and suffers from vibration when travelling at speed. This deprives it of one of its greatest advantages – stealth. When it is submerged, it is undetectable by the technology available of the day. But its ability to plot a course is limited whilst underwater, and it is this flaw that enables the passenger ship to spot it.

The steamer's captain and his officers are seen discussing what to do, and the vessel slows. The officers pass messages to the telegraph operator to contact the Coastguards of both France and Britain. The stewards start passing among the passengers, telling them not to worry; that they are going to let the U boat go ahead and wait till they are sure it has gone. They are currently mid channel, but will hug the coast as much as is possible and if necessary, seek shelter in the nearest allied port.

All passengers are asked to assemble on deck until the danger is past, and they huddle together and whisper their concerns to one another. Children are crying, and their mothers try to calm them, whilst the crew pass around the deck handing out cork life jackets, should they be needed.

Eventually, it is decided that the danger is over as the U boat sails into the distance without turning back to intercept the passenger vessel. The steamer continues its journey to Folkestone, in sight of land for the rest of the trip. The passengers return to the salons or enjoy the sunshine on deck. Once they approach Romney Marsh, the Channel narrows into the Straits of Dover and the South Downs turn into the White Cliffs. The stewards announce that they will be docking in around half an hour and the passengers should get ready to disembark.

Miss Garrett reaches for her trusty *Bradshaw's* to work out their train times home. They decide to catch the train along the coast to Dover, then go from there to Sittingbourne and home. This diversion will only take a little while longer, but will save them having to get across London from Charing Cross to Victoria with all their luggage.

As the port of Folkestone comes into view, the stress of the journey falls away, and everyone chatters like machine guns rattling. The passengers are waiting for the gang plank to be lowered, and the stewards have to usher people to stand around the deck to distribute the weight evenly, otherwise they will be in danger of capsizing the vessel. As soon as the crew stands back from securing the steamer to the quay and getting the gang plank in place, there is a surge to get off as quickly as possible. Miss Garrett is nearly knocked over by a substantial businessman who is keen to get safely ashore and doesn't care who is in his way. His behaviour just confirms her opinion of men, and she finds herself cursing him quite loudly in a mixture of French and English, quite unlike her usual restrained self.

Already the first Belgian refugees are arriving in Folkestone, fleeing from the advancing Germans. The town will eventually welcome over sixty-five thousand. Many stay with residents and others are helped to find safety across the Kingdom. The town is on high alert and the various ships are being turned around quickly so that they can help evacuate people from the danger; consequently, there are chaotic scenes as everything is done at breakneck speed.

The four teachers are swept along like so much jetsam onto the quay side. Hattie races ahead to intercept their trunks from being loaded onto the waiting boat train, and persuades the porter to place them ready for the train to Dover, by the means of a threepenny bit. They will need to clear customs there and then, but fortunately the diversion that the war has made necessary, results in the officials being willing to be flexible for once as other passengers are negotiating different routes away from Folkestone back towards Newhaven.

It is now almost two o'clock in the afternoon, with a two-hour journey ahead of them, before reaching Sheerness. Trains to Dover run every half hour, giving them twenty minutes to snatch some refreshments and survey Folkestone Harbour. Miss Garrett and Ena spend the time browsing at the WH Smith book stall, whilst Hattie buys the latest newspaper and a copy of *Woman's Own* for Maisie.

All of a sudden, a scuffle breaks out between two groups of men waiting to board the return steamer to France. It is just as rapidly broken up by the crew and the parties separated and made to wait in different areas. The porter explains that large numbers of German men work in the town's many hotels, and they are being sent home. There are also many French men returning to enlist and frequently the two warring protagonists end up on the same steamer. It is the war played out in miniature on the quayside.

Soon, the guard blows his whistle to proclaim it is time for the Folkestone train to leave for the short route to Dover, and it is with relief the four women begin the last part of their epic journey home.

Miss Garrett makes Maisie a cup of beef tea when they got home, and puts her to bed. She will need to be well enough to teach on Tuesday when school starts again. She is clearly exhausted, although she insists that she is fine. But Maisie sleeps for fourteen hours, awaking on Monday morning to the sound of Mrs Bills singing tunelessly to herself. The housekeeper makes a flat drone sound, like bagpipes without a chanter pipe, and it is only the occasional word that gives any indication of what the song is supposed to be; *Abide*; *Joshua – Lemon Squash*; *Dilly Dally*. The short, sturdy woman might reach a crescendo accompanied by a flourish of polishing or mopping, *On the Way*!

Miss Garrett has gone to the school to help Miss Morrison prepare for the beginning of the new term the following day, and this enables Mrs Bills to practice her arias to her heart's content, without being asked to be quiet.

Maisie gets out of bed, puts on her green kimono, and ventures to the toilet, thanking her stars that the house is fully plumbed in. No blood, and apart from a dull ache, no other signs that she has taken the pennyroyal tablets.

Just then, there is a knock at the front door. Mrs Bills goes to answer it and Maisie stands at the top of the stairs, just out of sight, to see who it might be. As the door opens, she can see the lower part of a man wearing naval uniform and her heart skips a beat, but, as he speaks, she knows it is not Edward, but Peter Barnes.

"Is Miss Kendall in?" he asks Mrs Bills.

"She isn't up yet," she replies.

Maisie calls down, "It's okay, Mrs Bills, I'm just getting up, but I'm not dressed yet. Can you wait five minutes, Peter?"

Mrs Bills ushers Lieutenant Barnes into the hallowed front parlour reserved for special guests, and busies herself with making some tea. She leaves the door ajar so that she can hear any goings on. As Miss Garrett is out, she feels it is her responsibility to ensure that nothing untoward happens.

Maisie dresses as quickly as she can and, having got her hair into some sort of order, goes down to meet Lieutenant Barnes. She is unprepared for the sudden rush of happiness she feels when she sees him as she steps into the parlour.

Peter has folded up his long heron like legs to sit in an armchair and sits rigid, trying to avoid contact with the anti-macassar on the back of the chair. He turns his hat round between his hands repeatedly, whilst he composes his thoughts. As Maisie comes into the room, he springs up, nearly knocking over one of the lamps. "Hello, Peter," she greets him.

"Hello," Peter responds. He takes a deep breath and launches into what he has to say. "Lieutenant Prescott has transferred to active duty on *HMS Arethusa*. He left yesterday morning to join her. I'm sorry."

A small "oh" escapes Maisie, but she looks Peter in the eye and says, "Did he leave a message for me?"

"No," says Lieutenant Barnes, giving his hat a few more turns in his discomfiture. "He didn't. He just asked me to return these." Peter produces Maisie's photograph, postcards, cards, and letters from his pocket, and lays them on a side table. "I can't apologise enough for his treatment of you," he finishes lamely.

Maisie looks down at the returned correspondence and knows Hattie and the others have been right about Edward. She wonders what she should say to Peter, but he takes another breath and continues.

"There is a rumour in the mess that he may have left you in some difficulty."

Maisie looks up horrified that others know of her secret and opens her mouth to speak, but Peter holds up his hand and pours out his heart.

"Hear me out. I have loved you since the moment I met you Maisie, and whilst I realise that I am not Prescott, I would be honoured if you will consider becoming my wife."

Maisie tries to respond, but Peter again signals to her to let him continue.

"I will treasure you above all things. I am able to keep you as you should be kept, as I have my share in the family business, as well as my officer's salary. You don't have to say yes right now, but with the war, and other factors," he says, whilst blushing, "we can get married under licence within days." At this, he drops to his knee and finishes with, "Maisie, will you marry me?"

Maisie is taken aback by this declaration, and tries to order her thoughts. Her heart wants to tell Peter it is all a mistake, there is no 'difficulty' any longer, and there may never have been, but at the same time her head says Peter is still a good prospect, and she isn't getting any younger. But she knows she will need to be honest about the possible pregnancy, otherwise, how will she explain the lack of it in a few months. She takes Peter's hand.

"Your proposal has come as a bit of a shock, on top of the news that Edward has left for active service."

Lieutenant Barnes rises to his feet and says, "Of course, yes, of course. I don't mean to hurry you, but we can all be sent on active service, so I want to ensure you are provided for."

"You are too kind, Peter," Maisie responds. Just then Mrs Bills clatters in with the tea tray and Maisie releases Peter's hand.

"Has Miss Kendall been telling you their adventures getting back from Swizzerland?" she asks, barely noticing that she has interrupted something important as she puts down the tea tray on the table and busies herself setting out the cups and saucers. "Right palaver! Lucky to be home. They met one of them ewe boats. Let me know if you need anything else," she says over her shoulder, as she bustles back out again.

Maisie wonders how much she has heard and shuts the door after her. She pours the tea, indicating to Peter that he should sit down, and uses the moment to decide where to begin as she sits opposite him.

"Peter, I must tell you now, that I am not in any difficulty. If Edward told you I was, then, I must have given him the wrong impression when I wrote to him. I was just being a silly girl."

"Oh dear, I seem to have blundered in as usual," is Peter's dejected reply.

"No, please let me finish," Maisie says, reaching across the table for his hand once more to give it a quick squeeze, before sitting back to look Peter square in the face. "I am very flattered that you have asked me to marry you. Any woman would be. But if there are rumours in the mess, that I am a fallen woman, then marrying me can only bring you shame and derision.

"You are a lovely man, and I very much enjoy your company. In fact, I realise now how much I missed you when I was walking out with Edward. He rather swept me off my feet on his return in May. But, if your offer of marriage is sincere, I would very much like to think about it and give you an answer by the end of the week."

Peter brightens visibly and is by now almost wringing his cap like the neck of a rat in his agitation, as he agrees to give Maisie some time to consider his offer.

She sees him to the door, and, once he has gone, she leans against it and considers what she needs to do next. There is only one thing to do, consult with Hattie. She grabs her jacket and hat, then she calls out to Mrs Bills that she is going out. She opens the door cautiously to ensure she is not going to bump into Lieutenant Barnes and rushes to Hattie's house.

Hattie unpacks her travelling trunk and sorts out her laundry. But she is dawdling over the task as she keeps stopping to reminisce over her souvenirs and making a fuss of Tibby. The cat has stopped sulking at her mistress' neglect of her by going away and is making herself comfy in Hattie's dirty washing. So much has happened in such a short time that it is hard to take it all in, so she is caught off guard when their housekeeper, Mrs Hancock, lets Maisie into her room as she hasn't heard the door.

"Maisie, my dear," she greets her, "I wasn't expecting you."

Maisie almost slams the bedroom door shut and stands with her back to it to repel any unwanted boarders. Without stopping for breath, she launches straight away into what she has come to tell Hattie.

"Peter has asked me to marry him. The rumour in the mess is that Edward has left me pregnant and deserted me, and Peter wants to do the decent thing by me," she gasps. "I've told him it's a misunderstanding, but said I would still like to consider his offer if it stands. What do you think I should do?" she finishes, and moves to the bed where she collapses from the exertion.

"My goodness," Hattie responds, having closed her mouth which had dropped open in surprise.

Maisie starts talking again. "I'm twenty-seven, I have no family to keep me, should I need it, and I have no other income than my teaching. Peter has prospects, has a share in the family business, and I will never want for pickles again," she jokes.

"But how do you feel about Peter? A month ago, you were in love with Edward," asks Hattie.

"Peter is a lovely man. He is funny and caring. And if I say no, will I get another offer?"

"We are not living in a Jane Austen novel. If you say no, you can earn a living like the rest of us, and be independent. Is the fear of being an old maid a good enough reason to marry Peter?"

"Frankly, if it's a choice of ending up like Miss Garrett, then YES!!!" she laughs. "He told me Edward has transferred to active service and has gone already, without saying goodbye. He gave Peter all my correspondence, and my photograph to return to me, no message or anything. I don't think he really cared for me at all. I'm so glad I listened to all of you and took the pennyroyal tablets, otherwise I would have been in a right mess." Suddenly, the reality of what might have been hits her and she bursts into tears. "I'm sorry," she says. "I did love Edward, but he is not who I thought he was, and he certainly doesn't love me."

Hattie sits down beside her and puts her arm around her. "Marriage isn't the only option for young women like us today. We have our careers; we can make our own choices. You can choose companionship instead of matrimony. We can always rent a home together. Lots of the older teachers live that way."

Maisie looks up at her and brushing her tears away, says, "I know. But I want my own home and children. Peter is a good catch and I know he will do everything to make me happy. And I am genuinely fond of him. I think I will write to my mother and ask her opinion, but I know what she will say. And my aunt will be right behind her."

"The only thing I will add is that if you do decide to accept him, you had better tell him soon, before he is posted away!" Hattie responds, hugging her friend.

Lieutenant Prescott longs to see action, but now the day is here, the butterflies in his stomach are doing a war dance. Outwardly, he remains calm, as the *Arethusa* steams south towards the enemy fleet's position, north-west off the German coast at Heligoland Bight. It is just seven o'clock and the North Sea is like a mill pond. It promises to be a fine day. Visibility is good.

Accompanying *Arethusa* are the sixteen destroyers of the third flotilla. Further back, *HMS Fearless* waits with the first flotilla of sixteen destroyers and behind them is Commodore Goodenough, with the six cruisers. Commodore Keyes commands a squadron of submarines.

Suddenly, a shout goes up that German torpedo boat *G194* has been spotted. On the bridge, Commodore Tyrwhitt raises his binoculars and consults with his officers. Satisfied that it is indeed the enemy, the Commodore gives the command for four destroyers to engage.

The *Arethusa's* crew springs into action; this is what they have been waiting for, what all their training has been leading up to. The order is given, and the ship's guns begin to fire a volley at the enemy craft ahead of them. The sound of shelling alerts other ships in the German fleet to the hostile action, and they turn back to join the fray.

Edward's adrenalin races as the British flotilla attacks in earnest, hitting four of the enemy's ships. The earlier clear visibility disappears as an unexpected light mist begins to gather, obscuring the vision of the German coastal artillery, and preventing them engaging. This change in the weather is a bonus for the British, cloaking their fleet from the enemy's view.

Within an hour, a full-scale battle is in progress. The Royal Navy has taken the war to the Germans and bearded the lion in his lair. *HMS Arethusa* engages with the *Stettin* and the *Frauenlob,* and is badly damaged by gunfire. All but one of her guns are knocked out. The ship slows as the crew tries to repair the damage. Lieutenant Prescott has never felt more alive as he oversees the work on the guns. He spurs the men on and mucks in where help is needed. His men respond to his hands-on approach and most of the guns are swiftly brought back into action.

But then, the German cruiser, *Stralsund* attacks the *Arethusa*. Edward heads to the bridge to report the damage to the Commodore. He races up the stairs two at a time and salutes Tyrwhitt. Just then the *Stralsund* fires again, hitting the *Arethusa*, and some flying shrapnel catches Prescott in the temple.

He falls to the deck in front of the senior officer. He is killed instantly.

The battle rages on; the mist causes confusion as two British ships are mistaken for Germans. Ships appear and disappear out of the gloom. Several Royal Navy vessels are damaged by the enemy's artillery, but none are lost. Three German ships sink, which means that later it will be claimed as a British victory.

When writing his report of the battle, Commodore Tyrwhitt says –

*Lieutenant Edward Prescott[2] was killed at my side during this action. I cannot refrain from adding that he carried out his duties calmly and collectedly and was of the greatest assistance to me.*

Edward had always wanted to be mentioned in despatches, but now he won't be around to revel in the glory, nor will it advance his career.

---

[2] **LONDON GAZETTE NAVAL DESPATCH - Gazette No. 28948 - 20 OCTOBER 1914** *Admiralty, 21st October 1914.*
Commodore Reginald Y. Tyrwhitt, Commodore (T.), H. M. S. "Arethusa," "Lieutenant Eric W. P. Westmacott (Signal Officer) is killed at my side during this action. I cannot refrain from adding that he carried out his duties calmly and collectedly, and is of the greatest assistance to me."

There is much confusion following the battle, so it takes several days for Lieutenant Edward Prescott's friends to learn what has happened to him. Little by little, the story comes back of how brave Edward was, how calm he had been looking after his wounded men, how heroic he was in the face of the enemy.

Amongst Edward's belongings is a brown paper parcel containing the photograph of his mother, her Bible, her wedding and engagement rings, and her gold cross, together with the photograph of Edward in his uniform that was taken at Whitehead's studio in Sheerness with Maisie. The package is addressed to Mary Andrews, C/O Gieves Naval Outfitters, Portsmouth. Inside, he had written a short letter requesting all his worldly goods be passed to his long-standing girlfriend.

In Portsmouth, Mary's heart is broken when she discovers her handsome naval officer, whom she has loved since she was fourteen, has died a hero in battle. His fellow officer, who has been asked to pass on the lieutenant's belongings, tells Mary how much Edward loved her. He had a photograph of her in his jacket pocket when he died.

---

When the news comes through that Lieutenant Edward Prescott has lost his life at the

Battle of Heligoland, Peter knows he has to be the one to tell Maisie, before she hears it elsewhere.

As soon as he can get away, he goes into the Broadway School and searches for her in her classroom. She catches sight of the tall officer through the glass door panel and asks the girls to excuse her for a moment. He takes her hands and opens with, "There is something I must tell you. Edward has been killed in action. I am so sorry."

Maisie's eyes fill with tears, and she bites her lip. Peter continues. "I know that deep in your heart you still care for him. My offer of marriage still stands. I promise you that I will look after you as no other man will. I know you will never love me as you loved him, but I will do everything in my power to make you the happiest woman alive."

Maisie knows then that all hope of ever being reunited with Edward is dead. She makes up her mind and decides to make the best of it. She looks into Peter's eyes and says, "I realise now it was not a deep love I felt for Edward, more a schoolgirl crush, as no one had ever shown an interest in me as a woman before. I know you will be a better husband than he ever would have. I am just sorry that the bright career he wanted for himself has ended so abruptly in this way."

Peter holds his breath as she continues. "I wish I had spoken to you sooner, as it will look to some like I have treated Edward's memory shamefully. I have been thinking about your offer all week, and I realise it's you that I have looked to all these months past. It is your good opinion I sought, it is your smile and your laughter that gladdened my heart. I only wish I had come to my senses sooner – so yes, I will marry you. I am only sorry I may have caused you pain over these months."

It is then Peter notices she is wearing the suffragette brooch that he bought for her birthday, and knows it is true. He clasps her tight and kisses her. "You won't ever regret it," he says. "We must make arrangements as soon as we can, in case I am posted."

"Yes, let's talk properly about this later, but now I must return to the girls," she says, as she opens the door to the classroom. The air fills with the sound of the girls scrambling back to their seats from where they have been watching Miss Kendell through the glass of the door.

## September 1914

Rosie goes into labour early on a wet September morning. It was decided, when war was declared, that she should remain near her mother. Plans to move to Plymouth were put on hold. Lieutenant Harris has taken a house for them in the same street as her family, so that they can help when the baby comes.

As the rain pours down, Rosie hammers on her mother's door in just her night gown. She shouts up at the window, "The baby is coming!" until a light comes on, and her sister opens the door to her. Rosie is brought in, and Mrs Dale and Betty set about drying her off and calming her down. Between them, they determine that there is some time to go, and tell Maisie to rest until the contractions are more frequent.

Betty sets off in the downpour to notify the "kitten-drowning" midwife that Rosie is in early labour. On the way, she stops at Hattie and Ena's to keep them posted and to ask them to let Miss Morrison know she won't be in school today, as she is assisting with the birth. She returns home with some newly baked bread rolls to keep everyone's strength up from one of the first batches from the baker that morning.

Little Alberta is sent next door to keep her out of the way. Mrs Phipps promises the child some cake and says she can look at the pictures of Peter Pan in her daughter's book. This is enough to appease the child and she happily goes into the neighbour's house to enjoy these delights.

Mrs Embleton, the midwife, arrives shortly after with her old black leather Gladstone bag to examine the patient, whilst Mrs Dale draws water to boil, and her elderly mother gets the towels ready. The grandmother clucks around, getting in the way whilst saying how things were different in her day. Lieutenant Harris wanted the naval doctor to deliver their baby, but Rosie and the women who surround her, feel childbirth is no place for a man, especially a naval one.

Some days earlier, the midwife felt Rosie's bump and expressed her concern the baby might be breach. She could feel the head was not engaged and recommended Rosie begin some exercises to turn the baby. This involved getting down on her hands and knees and, for about ten minutes a day, rocking back and forth on all fours. The midwife said it will give the infant space to turn around. Rosie follows this advice religiously and is anxious as her contractions start in case it hasn't worked. If it hasn't, there is a possibility of complications as the umbilical cord might be caught around the baby's leg, or worse around the neck.

Rosie walks about in her mother's bedroom riding the contractions, wearing a clean but old nightgown that has been put aside ready for this day. Betty helps her braid her hair in readiness for the impending birth.

Mrs Embleton asks Rosie to expose her belly so that she can check if the exercises have worked. She has a jolly good feel, but is non-committal.

"We will have to see which way it pops out," she says, busying herself getting things ready and rolling up her sleeves to reveal meaty forearms, ready to wrestle new life into the world.

Whilst Betty stays by her sister's side, the midwife manoeuvres Mrs Dale out of the bedroom and onto the landing by asking if she has any strong spirits she can use to clean her instruments, just in case. Rosie's mother sees the tools of the midwife's trade when she unrolls her chamois leather case from her bag. It contains three sets of forceps, two perforators, various sized wicked looking hooks, and most ominously, one pair of bone cutters. Mrs Dale is only vaguely aware of what all the items are for. She isn't keen to ask, knowing that the hooks are not there to make crocheted woollen bootees for a new-born babe. Instead, she asks, "Do you think you will need those?"

310

"Hopefully not, and if we do, let's trust it's just the forceps," Mrs Embleton replies briskly, emitting a slight whiff of strong spirits herself as she does so.

The midwife checks the progress of Rosie's cervix and times the frequency of her contractions. She encourages everyone, especially Rosie, to eat and Mrs Dale makes up the bread rolls with cheese and some pink brawn. It seems like a very odd tea party.

"I will come back later. Rosie has some way to go yet," Mrs Embleton says. "Come and get me again when the contractions are more frequent, or when her waters break." She starts packing up her bag as she speaks. "I'm going back home to bed for a few hours. I got very little sleep last night," she explains. "I had to deliver a baby to the McDonald girl. Only fifteen. Father away in the army. He's only a kid himself. Family says he is due home by Christmas, then he will marry their Cathy; she'll be sixteen by then. She'll be lucky with the war on. But her dad and uncle will give the soldier boy a pasting if he thinks he will desert her. They are determined those interfering, befriending women won't take the baby for adoption. They will keep it in the family. The mother will bring it up as her own, if necessary. Good on them, I say," she finishes, without stopping for breath. Mrs Dale agrees, thinking of how she loves Alberta as her own.

When the midwife returns later in the afternoon, Rosie is nearing her time and the kettles and saucepans boil ready for the birth. More strong spirits are requested, and again Mrs Dale can't decide if it is the instruments or Mrs Embleton who smells of brandy. A further examination reveals the head is now engaged, but the midwife remains concerned that all doesn't seem well.

Hattie stops by. "Can I be of any assistance? Shall I get fish and chips for everyone?" she offers. But nobody feels like eating by then.

"Mrs Phipps has promised me she will give Alberta her dinner and tea, so we don't need to worry about her," Mrs Dale explains. So, the women continue to wait on Rosie. It is now around fourteen or fifteen hours since Rosie's labour started, and the midwife is getting concerned as Rosie is clearly beginning to tire. Mrs Embleton decides that it is time to intervene and break Rosie's waters with one of her smaller hooked tools, in the hope of speeding things up.

The midwife examines Rosie again and breaks the membrane to release her waters, and explains that the contractions will be stronger now. Betty, Hattie, and Mrs Dale hold their breath, knowing that if this doesn't move the baby on, Rosie will soon be too tired to push. But it does the trick, and, in the end, the baby arrives safely by late evening, and without further need of Mrs Embleton's instruments of torture. It is only now that Mrs Dale notices the most evil looking hook is cleaned and laid out in readiness.

Baby Samuel is very robust, and as red and beefy as his father. His lusty cries can probably be heard in Plymouth, where Lieutenant Harris is currently stationed. He is soon cleaned and swaddled, and placed in Rosie's exhausted arms, much to the joy of her sister and mother.

"First thing in the morning, I will go to the post office and send a telegram to the new daddy to tell him the news, but I think we all need a rest first," says Betty, collapsing in a chair.

"Do you have anything to wet the baby's head with?" asks Mrs Embleton, holding up the mysteriously empty brandy bottle. Mrs Dale says she will see what she can find.

Hattie starts walking out with Bill West from the cricket team. This is no surprise to anyone, apart from Hattie. She has never noticed how he hangs on her every word and is first to open the door for her or fetch her some tea. He always champions her right to participate in sport and is the man who adds her name to the cricket eleven. But the coming of the war emboldens him to speak candidly to her about his feelings, without mentioning cricket once. He

313

decides to volunteer and wants to let her know how he feels before he joins up. It slowly dawns on her how often he is around, and how much she enjoys his company. When he leaves to join the navy, it is with a very large lump in her throat that she waves him off.

Miss Garrett and Ena continue to teach the dockyard girls in the hope of them becoming independent women. Following the *Representation of the People Act* in February 1918, the two teachers are first in line to register to vote at the autumn elections, both qualifying as householders and being over thirty.

Betty also marries one of the men teachers, Alf Streeter, after the war. She has carried a torch for him for some time, but the war makes him grow up and see her worth. Alf returns minus his right arm, but is still able to accurately hit a boy in the back row with the blackboard chalk, having been a first class shot in the Rifle Brigade.

Maisie and Peter marry by special licence as quickly as they can. Usually, this leads to speculation about the prospect of an unplanned pregnancy, but lots of people are getting married before the men are posted overseas, so it doesn't cause any undue comment.

The couple take a house facing the promenade; the grandest house Maisie has ever lived in, with six bedrooms and three reception rooms. A general maid and cook are engaged, along with a man to do the heavy work.

The house is furnished, which is a relief, as there are many rooms to fill, and Maisie's small trousseau from the rectory hardly dents what is needed. One or two pieces are sent from the Dowager House by her mother and aunt as a wedding present, the transportation paid for by her aunt's stepson. He doesn't do it out of generosity, but as a way of not having to buy a separate present for his stepcousin.

All Maisie's friends attend, and the school children again form a Guard of Honour. Nobody mentions the sad loss of fellow officers at the Battle of Heligoland. Nobody toasts absent friends.

With the shrewd use of the contraceptive diaphragm Maisie purchased in Paris, she is able to delay starting a family. A new baby boy arrives more than a year later, silencing the tongues of the town gossips. However, there are still colleagues of Lieutenant Barnes who believe the baby is Lieutenant Prescott's, despite the mathematical improbability of it.

Lieutenant Barnes gets his wish and transfers to the Flying Corp, later to become the infant Royal

Air Force at Eastchurch. But his height makes him too tall to fit in the cockpits of the Short Brothers' aeroplanes, but there are other land-based roles to fill, enabling him to get in on the ground floor of the new service and progress up the promotion ladder.

As the war drags on and the town is bombarded by German air raids, Lieutenant Barnes temporarily moves his family to Southwark, to be near the family business where it seems safer for civilians from the enemy attacks. His two sisters are more than ready to help with their little nephew's upbringing and teach him how to run a pickle factory.

Edna and Margaret are extremely disappointed to find that they are not entitled to vote in the 1918 election. This is because they do not meet the property qualification in their own right, as they neither own or directly rent any property, nor are married to a man who does. But upon the death of their father in 1920, Peter makes them joint owners of the pickle factory, making them financially independent and enfranchising them in one act.

Maisie grows to love Peter, and they have many happy years together. But she always dreams of Edward when she sleeps alone.

**Afterword**

As part of the WWI commemorations, I was involved in researching the role of women on the Isle of Sheppey. I read every copy of our local newspaper from 1 January 1914 to 31 July 1919, when Peace was officially declared, to see what work women were involved in.

I came across the story of how four "lady" teachers had gone on holiday to Switzerland and had declined to return when war was declared. There were several updates as their friends awaited their return, until they came home, explaining how they were caught the wrong side of enemy lines.

The names of the teachers appear in other news stories, including how their pupils obtained the best exam results in the competition for scholarship places at the local grammar school, as well as organising extracurricular activities to help the war effort. They must have been truly remarkable women. However, being women, their opportunities were limited, and they were only able to follow their career if they were unmarried – unlike their male counterparts.

This made me wonder what might keep them in a foreign country once war is declared, when such sensible women should have headed straight home.

At the same time, there were regular reports in the newspapers on the activities of the "Society for Befriending Women and Girls." These are written in cryptic terms, but obviously about how many women and girls are assisted when an unwanted pregnancy befell them. This assistance took the form of sending them to "homes" depending on what category they fell to. These are listed as "preventative;" "doubtful;" and "rescue" cases. I suspect that some of the women are not pregnant, as the article goes on to describe how some cases are sent to maternity homes and others to the workhouse. "Motherless children (offspring of soldiers)" are found homes. Over five thousand visits are reported as being made, so either these are not isolated incidents, or they visited the women and girls many times.

The President of the society is Mrs Hyde-Smith, the wife of the Rear Admiral who is Superintendent of the Dockyard. She saw her role in the town as being one of bringing relief from the actions of the servicemen, as she was involved in a number of different causes. I would imagine that such a woman would take a very dim view if the officers set poor examples to the men.

I researched the alternatives for women, for whom the Society for Befriending Women and Girls was not an option. What did they do should an

318

unwanted pregnancy befall them? I found that there was a roaring trade in "Women's Remedies."

Historically, pennyroyal tablets were available in chemists and by mail order. They were used to regulate periods as well as to bring on miscarriages. Although there was a risk involved, women were prepared to take it to be rid of an unwanted pregnancy. A milder dose taken early on was used in a similar way to modern morning after pills. The dose at which pennyroyal could cause miscarriages in later pregnancy is also a lethal dose to the woman taking it. The herbal supplement is **not** considered safe to ingest for any use today.

My other main source for this story was the logbooks maintained by all the schools. These were transcribed by a volunteer in the Kent Archives, as part of their commemoration of WWI. They gave an insight into the working lives of the teaching staff and provided information on such diverse things as the chimney demolition, child labour, illnesses, and the weather. Mrs Hyde-Smith pops up as a visitor to the schools.

And so, the adventures of Maisie, Hattie, Rosie, Betty, Ena, and Miss Garrett were born.


*All names have been changed except where they are a matter of historical record.*

Printed in Great Britain
by Amazon